"WHAT, SIR, ARE YOU GRINNING AT?"

"Why, Miss Taylor, you *are* husband hunting. And, if I do not mistake the matter, *I* am your prey!"

"What?"

"Although you have a most unusual way of telling me, ma'am." Having finally risen, he tucked her arm in his and proceeded toward the house. "Come, Miss Taylor, we shall be the last pair up the gangplank."

She pulled away from him and scowled, trying to maintain some dignity. "Take your hands off me, sir." The action caused her to slip on the grass, however, and he took back her arm to steady her. This time, she did not reclaim it.

"Allow me to explain my deduction, ma'am." He pointed at the bottom of her gown. "You are wearing my petticoat, Miss Taylor. Well, of course, it is not precisely *mine*, is it? Not any longer. Not since I gave it to *you*, that is. But, the point is, why else should you wear it? Hmm?"

Lavinia looked down and gasped. When the light fabric of her gown became wet, the violets on the hem of the petticoat showed through, quite clearly betraying her secret.

"Oh, no! You do not understand, Lord Templeton. It was never my intention to wear this! And as for wishing to marry you, why I am happy to say that I have never entertained such an addle-pated thought. . . ."

He leaned closer and whispered in her ear. "Never?"

BOOK YOUR PLACE ON OUR WEBSITE
AND MAKE THE
READING CONNECTION!

We've created a customized website just for our very special readers, where you can get the inside scoop on everything that's going on with Zebra, Pinnacle and Kensington books.

When you come online, you'll have the exciting opportunity to:

- View covers of upcoming books
- Read sample chapters
- Learn about our future publishing schedule (listed by publication month *and author*)
- Find out when your favorite authors will be visiting a city near you
- Search for and order backlist books from our online catalog
- Check out author bios and background information
- Send e-mail to your favorite authors
- Meet the Kensington staff online
- Join us in weekly chats with authors, readers and other guests
- Get writing guidelines
- AND MUCH MORE!

Visit our website at
http://www.zebrabooks.com

THE COUNTRY MOUSE

Jessie Watson

ZEBRA BOOKS
Kensington Publishing Corp.
http://www.zebrabooks.com

For my parents

ZEBRA BOOKS are published by

Kensington Publishing Corp.
850 Third Avenue
New York, NY 10022

All Kensington titles, imprints and distributed lines are available at special quantity discounts for bulk purchases for sales promotion, premiums, fund raising, educational or institutional use.

Special book excerpts or customized printings can also be created to fit specific needs. For details, write or phone the office of the Kensington Special Sales Manager: Kensington Publishing Corp., 850 Third Avenue, New York, NY, 10022. Attn. Special Sales Department. Phone: 1-800-221-2647.

Zebra and the Z logo Reg. U.S. Pat. & TM Off.

First Printing: December, 2000
10 9 8 7 6 5 4 3 2 1

Printed in the United States of America

One

The slightly damp air was a brownish yellow color that smelled as bad and unhealthy as it looked. The odor emanated from a dozen sources: unwashed bodies, sausage, fish, eel, even flowers and herbs peddled by street vendors, clogged drains, the milk cows grazing in Hyde Park, the refuse and waste that filled the gutters, the fetid stench of the river at low tide, and the slaughterhouses of Newport Market in nearby Leicester Square. And there were noises peculiar to London that could be every bit as unpleasant and relentless as the stink of humans and garbage. They arose from the never-ending rattle of iron carriage wheels on stone and packed dirt, the ringing of harnesses and the clomping of horses' hooves, from people talking, laughing, and arguing, from the peal of church bells, the cries of the watch, and the sounds of vendors advertising everything from potatoes to cockles to lavender to ink to pamphlets, in baritones, bassos, and sopranos that might not have been out of place in the opera at the King's Theatre (at least at the beginning of the day, before the hoarseness set in), and in thin, reedy, pathetic children's voices that could never be heard above the din. Not infrequently, for poverty was more the rule than the exception in London, a gentleman might be heard to reprimand the person who jostled his arm as he passed, to cry out to the thief to stop, or to call to the assemblage to find a constable. In such a place, then, it was not in the least fantastic to see an indignant man and an equally angry woman arguing in the street, a then-nameless dog providing the chorus to their antics.

The tightly furled umbrella came down with a most satisfying thump on the man's head, knocking the silk top hat from his none-too-clean curls into the filthy gutter and eliciting an oath of surprise and outrage. The voices of the woman and the dog were raised in disagreement.

"Wha . . . What the devil? My hat! You've hit me! How dare you strike me, madam? And what are you going to do about my hat, I want to know!"

"Woof! Woof, woof!" The scrawny, bedraggled cur danced around the man, barking. *"Woof!"*

"How dare *I*? How dare *you* kick a poor, hungry dog who only begged for a bit of your pie? You ought to be ashamed, you vile creature," the woman shouted back. *"And* I do not care a *fig* for your hat!"

"My hat! I say . . ." he began just as the dog started to growl at him. "Filthy beast! Why should I care if he's hungry?" He licked the juice that had dripped onto his fingers and brushed ineffectually at the crumbs littering his hideous red waistcoat. His foot lashed out again, but this time failed to connect with its intended canine target, thus failing to reproduce the yelp of pain that had, a few moments earlier, originally claimed the woman's attention. The dog darted behind her skirt, barking, as she brought the umbrella down once more onto the man's head. The remains of the pie tumbled from his hand and landed in his upturned hat, greasy juices leaking from inside the pastry and staining the already questionable lining. The street peddler who had sold the pasty now saw an opportunity to earn another penny.

" 'ere, guv!" He held out his tray still filled, even this late in the day, with too many pies; how he would pay the rent he owed his landlord he did not know. "Care to buy another? You already know how good my pasties are!" He grinned in encouragement.

The man growled in response and swung his arm in fury in the pieman's direction, very nearly knocking the tray of food out of his arms.

" 'old on now. No need for that kind of behavior now, is there? I'm just tryin' to make a livin', and you got no call to strike me! I'll call a constable!" He nodded vigorously, pointing his finger in the bully's direction. "You're a *menace*, you are!"

A small crowd had begun to assemble, and many of its members were loudly expressing their support for one side or the other. Some shouted for the vendor, for too many of them were in the same poor financial straits, the current state of the economy not yet having recovered from the end of the war with the Corsican devil. Some spoke for the man— no one would have described him as a gentleman even if his language had been better. Some sided with the lady, whose station was clear to all, even had she been without her private conveyance. A servant now loomed at her side and delivered a quietly threatening look calculated to intimidate the screaming man.

"Come, Miss Taylor, you should not waste your time with the likes of *him*." His pointed look in the man's direction promised more than a thwack from an umbrella, and the man stepped back a pace, his howling now reduced to a more circumspect sputtering.

"I take it that the dog will be coming with us, ma'am?" The coachman's eyes twinkled, something they had never done much before he had come into Lavinia Taylor's service a year ago, but which they seemed to have done quite frequently since then.

"Yes, thank you, Peach." She nodded and smiled. Had there ever been a more ludicrous mismatch between a man and his name? Peach was an imposing figure—tall and bulky, with an unusually large head topped with a great deal of prematurely gray hair, a booming voice, and hands that, although they were the size of dinner platters, were nothing but gentle when tending her horses. She smiled at his immediate grasp of what, to many, would have been a trivial situation, and certainly not one that would have resulted in a four-footed passenger in her best carriage.

The butler peeped discreetly around the deep fringe of the silk drapery and looked out at the carriage that clattered to a halt before the spacious house in Hamilton Place. The door of the vehicle was opened by a grinning Peach, and its passengers, the well-dressed lady who owned the house and the filthy dog who, if history were anything at all to go by, soon would behave as if he did, emerged and dashed through the raindrops toward the house.

"Ellice!" The drapery was allowed to slip silently back into place, and the butler called over his shoulder as he went to open the front door, "Better get that old tub up from the storage and set some water to heating. Here comes another one." There was not the slightest hint of surprise or dismay in his voice, nor did the maid thus addressed feel the need to beg her superior for particulars.

"The estate agent called, ma'am, while you were out," the butler announced a short time later.

"Good!" Lavinia and Ellice were bathing the recent arrival. "Did Mr. Penn say he would call again, Sims? Oh, heavens! Did he get you? The dog, that is, not Mr. Penn. Dear me, do not even bother to answer, for I can see that he did! Oh, no, dog, *no!* Do sit still!" Lavinia tried, with little success, not to laugh.

To the butler's credit, he managed to dodge much of the soapy water sloshing in grimy waves from the tub where the dog wriggled and rolled with exuberance, clearly perceiving the entire exercise as a great game. Sims applied a towel to the water dripping from his chin and raised a brow. "He is the first one who seems to like his bath, ma'am, wouldn't you say?"

She laughed and nodded in agreement, pushing some wet strands of hair from her face. "I think we should call him Neptune, since he seems to like the water so much."

"Ready for the rinse, now, Miss Taylor?" Ellice sat next to her on the floor and both had fared far worse than had Sims, for their aprons and sleeves were sopping wet.

"For him, Ellice, or us?"

They both laughed and, in time, all were properly rinsed, dried, and brushed, and the new boarder was in the kitchen tucking into his second meal since arriving at the Mayfair house. Lavinia, now attired in a blush-colored afternoon dress, sipped her tea and adjusted the spectacles that rested on her nose. Finding her from home, the estate agent had written a note and left it for her with Sims. She read eagerly for several moments, then walked to the bow window that faced Hamilton Place and looked out into the quiet, well-groomed street as if it were a prison. "At last!" Her grin could not have been wider. "Mr. Penn has found it at last. We can finally be quit of this place!" She gathered up the nearest slumbering cat who, roused unsuspecting from his nap, first panicked at the wholly unexpected expedition, then glared at her with resentment as she waltzed him about the room. "Kitty, we are going to have a new home in the country!"

His expression seemed to ask if he might expect to have any peace in whatever this thing called "the country" might be. Lavinia was recently out of mourning for her widowed uncle with whom she and her brother, Samuel, had gone to live following the deaths of their parents. It had galled her that Society would not countenance her setting up her own establishment, as she had wanted to do when she and Sam were left alone. But the intervening years had taught Lavinia that a girl only a few years out of the schoolroom, which she had been at the time, was hardly capable of looking after herself and a younger brother, not to mention a household. She had been content keeping house for her uncle, for they had been close even before her parents' demise, and since Lavinia was a responsible young woman, she had always enjoyed considerable freedom under his roof. There was only one part of her life with which she was dissatisfied—living in London. She hated the noise, the smells, and the dirt, and longed for the fresh air and the open spaces of the country.

Absently, she reached out and rubbed the soft

ears of the nearly blind greyhound who sat beside her waiting to be noticed. Phidippides knew the geography of the London house, and she realized it would take him some time to adjust to his new surroundings in Painswick, the location mentioned in Mr. Penn's note. Still, moving to the country was largely to benefit him—and Orpheus, of course, the canary who tilted his head at her now and began to sing off-key. Poor bird, he had not sung any sweeter since the day she moved him here after Lady Dunwich died. And Kitty, too, would be better off in their new home. So would Lucky and Pumpkin, the two other cats. *No, three other cats,* she remembered, since she hoped to be successful any day now in luring the latest stray into her care. Feathers, Lavinia knew, would thrive in his new environment. The old carriage horse was too tired to pull any longer and too beloved to send to the knackers. She smiled as a vision came to her of Feathers peacefully chewing clover in an idyllic meadow in Painswick, and she sighed with pleasure.

Lavinia had made only a few visits to the country—once to Cornwall to visit a cousin and another time to Somerset to stay with her friends, Edwina and Jerrold Somerville—but her experiences had been sufficient to show her how different life could be outside of London. A house in the country would have given her and Uncle Amory more and better room for the animals they took in whenever they came upon one in need, and it would be more peaceful for the people in the household, as well. In the beginning of her campaign to leave the city, she had hoped that the welfare of the animals would help to bring him around to her way of thinking. After all, it was he who had instilled in her the love and devotion she had for animals. Uncle

Amory had shown her how to care for the sparrow that had limped into the bedroom window of her childhood, and it was he who had taught her, through all his acts and deeds, of her responsibility to care for any creature that needed her help. Their house had always been full of barks, meows, and chirps, and any human who ventured past the dark blue door of Number Seven Hamilton Place could soon expect to find a cat in his or her lap or a dog offering a toy in the hope of a game of fetch. They also could expect to find the odd cat or dog hair floating in their teacup, but few of them minded since neither Lavinia nor her uncle would have given a straw for anyone who turned up their nose at such a development.

She had tried time and again to talk Amory into moving, but despite all her pleas and reasoning that it would benefit all of them to be free of the city, nothing could ever convince him to live anywhere else. He would stubbornly remind her that they had always managed with the house they had, and nothing would convince him to change his mind. Her brother, Sam, was at Oxford, so after Amory's passing there was nothing to keep Lavinia in London. As soon as it was seemly to do so, she had been in touch with Mr. Penn. She had told him only the sum she could pay and that she wished a house of goodly size with plenty of surrounding land, and had determined to keep her mind open with regard to its location. The situation he had found for them in the Cotswolds sounded perfect, and she sat at her desk to write a note of acceptance to the agent.

"You may let me out here."

The jarvey looked at the gold coins pressed into

his hand and whistled. "Thank you, sir. Thank you very much, indeed!" He tipped his hat. *Wait till Peg sees this!*

His passenger, a gentleman in evening dress, had chosen to alight a full two blocks away from his club because he had no longer been able to tolerate the confines of the carriage. He wanted to shout with joy, but could hardly do so in the cab and terrify the poor driver and his horses, nor within the precincts of White's, the oldest and most exclusive gentlemen's club in London, and his intended destination. The man rounded the corner into St. James's Street, his step decidedly jaunty. Such energetic perambulation was hardly the languid pace normally adopted by a marquess or a Corinthian, both of which he was, but he could not help himself. His stick, the silver-headed one given him by his late father, made a rapid, satisfying *clomp, clomp, clomp* as he ran it along the wrought-iron fencing that surrounded the buildings to his left.

A few minutes later, inside White's, he leaned casually against a wall not far from a fire that took the chill from the fresh, early spring air. The clock had just struck eleven, a bit early for him to arrive at his club, but this night was rather different than the usual. Charles Templeton had just departed the house of his mistress, Althea Hubbard, something he did not ordinarily do until the small hours of the morning. Still, even at that time a gentleman, were he so inclined, could find a game of cards at White's, or at any of a dozen such establishments in the metropolis. He sipped a glass of Madeira and watched four silent gentlemen intent on a game of whist at one of several tables arranged for this purpose. One of them wore his coat inside out for good luck. It was evident that they had been thus engaged for some time and, judging by the whispers of other onlookers, that a great deal of money had been changing hands.

Not that the transfer of huge sums of cash, as well as other possessions, within White's and other clubs—the play was even deeper at nearby Brooks's, for example—was anything in the way of wonderful, for it was not. Members found themselves done up all the time. Young men lost inheritances, some while their fathers still breathed. Older gentlemen lost entire estates, and more than one man had put a period to his own existence because of the disgrace. Some years back, Lord Foley's sons had borrowed sums so large to repay their ruinous gambling debts that the annual interest alone came to an astonishing £18,000. Women were excluded from the clubs, but this discrimination did not prevent them from gambling, for card games, among other amusements, could be found easily at any number of fashionable, and not so fashionable, houses. Nor were ladies either too careful or too lucky to amass massive debts. The Duke of Devonshire was the unhappy inheritor of more than £100,000 of his late mother's gambling vowels.

Presently, a splendidly dressed older man strolled between Templeton's line of sight and the players, quickly assessing their hands with eyes that betrayed naught of what he saw.

" 'Gad," the man whispered in Templeton's ear, "Baskins is a fool, ain't he?" He nodded in the direction of a man whose face was hidden by the wide brim of a hat pulled low on his forehead, whether to eclipse his expression from his companions' gaze or to shield his eyes from the light of the candles above the table, one could not have said. "They're playing diamonds, which he is holding, and trumps is hearts, which he is also holding, and there he sits, baffled. Purcell will shoot him for his stupidity if he isn't careful," the man predicted in reference to Baskins's unfortunate partner.

Templeton grunted in agreement. They watched a few moments more and Baskins, apparently as big a fool as the man had suggested, smiled triumphantly and played a spade. "Good God. Let's get out of here. I can't bear to watch any more of this," the older man remarked, and they moved farther down the room where things were a bit more lively. Here, gentlemen played at faro and hazard, and at a table by the window two members were quietly concentrating on the mother-of-pearl inlaid backgammon board that separated them. The more raucous rattle and roll of the dice at the hazard tables accompanied by the calling of numbers thrown, created an excitement absent from the hushed atmosphere surrounding the whist tables.

"Care for a game, Grover?" Templeton asked his companion.

He shook his head. "No thanks, not really in the mood. Anyway, I've had a bit too much port and I like to keep a clear head when I throw the dice. You younger men"—he grinned at Templeton—"play much too close to the edge for my liking."

Templeton smiled and raised his brows to signal his acceptance of this remark; then he asked, "Hear Scranton got pilled?"

"What? When?"

"Last week."

"Ah. I've been from town. Only just returned yesterday. Damn, I'd loved to have seen that arrogant young pup's face when he heard he'd been denied at White's. Ha!"

Before Templeton could respond, Grover continued. "Have you seen the Betting Book lately?"

Templeton's shrug might have indicated denial or indifference, but his friend—really a mentor, who had taken the green, young Templeton under his wing when the latter had joined White's years ago—clearly was not waiting for his answer. He gripped the younger man's arm with, it seemed to the one who owned it, unnecessary vigor, and led him discreetly toward a highly polished table in a momentarily deserted corner of the room.

"As I mentioned, I have been away these past few weeks and just had occasion this evening to stop in here and take a glance at the book."

Lawrence Grover referred to the large, leather-bound book, commonly known as the Betting Book, that was, and had been for more years than any member cared to count, a fixture within the elegant walls of White's. It was used to record bets between and among club members. Such speculations were not limited to wagers on whether the Duke of Everby's horse might prevail over one raced by the Prince Regent; rather, the pages were peppered with inane bets that only the bored, the foolish, or the callous could concoct, much less care about.

5th April 1813, Ferdinand Welles bets Herbert Henslow 50 guineas to 10 guineas that Gerald Dawson wears his bottle-green waistcoat again on Saturday, the 10th.

2nd May 1816, Mr. Percy Sackville promises to give his snuffbox enameled with stars to Ernest Crane if The Hon. Theodore Prynne is not adjudged bankrupt by quarter's end. If Mr. Crane loses the wager, he agrees to give his snuffbox enameled with moons to Mr. Sackville.

28th April 1817, Mr. Thaddeus Overby claims that he can survive for two weeks eating only raisins soaked in brandy. Mr. Robert Hatfield predicts that Mr. Overby will fail and promises to pay the sum of £200 if he should be wrong. Sebastian Fox stands with Mr. Hatfield and wagers an additional £25, while Mr. Thomas Dobbyns pledges the same amount for Mr. Overby's side.

The book contained many sillier bets and more serious ones and for several minutes Templeton and Grover perused the entries.

"Damme, Grover, do you recall that one?" Templeton pointed to an entry dated more than two years earlier. Grover nodded.

"I do. How could I forget the sight of Peter Braithwaite and Alvin Roxton competing in the coffee room to see who could balance a spoon on his nose for the longest time?"

"Ha! Yes, and then Dutton decided to 'make it interesting' by suggesting that they balance a wineglass on the back of each hand at the same time! Do you recall how Roxton backed up into the common table and sent all the crockery flying everywhere?"

They chuckled over this incident and that while Grover fanned through the pages, until they came to those of more recent vintage.

"I wonder, Charles, if you've seen this?" Grover asked quietly, pointing at the flowery black letters under a date of some ten days previous.

Templeton's eyes skimmed the words. Grover looked at the thick wreathes of lashes that dusted

his friend's cheeks and saw his entire face turn
scarlet.

> *Freddie Widdoes, James Bishop, William Astley, Ian
> Spinner, and Maynard Richards wager that Charles
> Templeton will, by October of this year, be made a father
> by one Mrs. A— H—. If they are wrong, which they
> deem unlikely in the extreme, the five gentlemen prom-
> ise to give 100 guineas to the poor.*

The entry did not indicate what the men would
gain if, indeed, they were correct; doubtless it was
something as frivolous as the wager itself. For a few
moments, Templeton could not meet Grover's eyes.
These men, Bishop, Widdoes, Spinner, and the rest,
were—he had *thought*—friends of his. Yet, they had
made a May game of him, for the Betting Book was
open to any member who chose to examine it, and
most did in order to keep up on club happenings
and to be certain they were in on the latest jokes.
This one had been at Templeton's expense.

Finally, he glanced at Grover, who led him wordlessly to a secluded corner and ordered fresh bran-
dies for both of them. They settled into comfortable
chairs by the window. Grover sat without speaking
and looked at his companion. Presently, Templeton
cleared his throat.

"Well, don't I look the fool, eh, Laurie?" He took
a swallow of his brandy.

His old friend did not attempt to disabuse him
of this notion, for there could be little doubt that
it was true. He waited for Templeton to continue.

"I, ah . . ." He shut his eyes for a moment and
shook his head. "How do you imagine they found
out?"

"Most likely the servants, Charles. You know how

they talk. And God knows we all give them enough to talk about."

So, it was true, Grover thought. *Well of course it would be, the network for gossip in London was seldom wrong.* He looked at his companion. *Good God, if Althea is pregnant, the scandalmongers might turn on him.* Templeton was well-liked, but one could not expect affability and good-standing with the ton to carry one unscathed through a tantalizing tale like this. Once it got beyond the doors of White's—which, evidently, had not yet happened, a circumstance that surprised and pleased him simultaneously—it would be in every drawing room in town and that would make it only steps away from the cartoonists and the bookshops. Grover pursed his lips in disdain. How Polite Society had ever got its name was beyond his comprehension.

Grover wondered if his friend would marry that Circe, if it came to it. Yes, he supposed that he would. Templeton would never abandon the creature if her husband divorced her, no matter that Grover had hinted—and such hints had become broader and more frequent as time passed—that his friend put such a lovely and potentially dangerous bauble back on the shelf where she belonged. He had counseled him to let some fool like Davison, who anyway had a reputation he did not care about and a fortune he could easily afford to lose, dally with Althea.

Of course the ton, capricious in its choice of whom to torment and whose transgressions to overlook, could choose to ignore the whole thing; it would depend to some extent on what else—and *who* else—was in the gossips' stewpot when the news got out. The ton might overlook an affaire d'amour between a marquess and a married woman, in fact, they did so every day; such liaisons were hardly out of the common way, after all. Some men and women were together so frequently that, despite one or both individuals having exchanged marriage vows with entirely different persons, they might be invited into society as a couple. To consign them to the outer limits of Polite Society would have meant eliminating a not insignificant number of its members.

When Caroline Lamb, wife to William Lamb, consorted quite openly with the "mad, bad, and dangerous to know" Lord Byron, she might only have been emulating her mother-in-law, Lady Melbourne, who had been publicly disporting with a succession of lovers, the Regent among them, for years. But Caro Lamb refused to go quietly when Byron grew bored, while Lady Melbourne had the good manners—and cunning—to step aside while making a profit on her congé; when Lord Coleraine reportedly sold her services to Lord Egremont for £13,000 she took a share of the payment for herself.

If example did indeed influence behavior, one could hardly have expected better, or at least more circumspect, conduct from anyone with pretensions to the upper reaches of society—certainly not while the Regent or his wife were at the pinnacle. The prince was, apparently, a bigamist, having wed his first cousin, Caroline, to secure the succession several years after taking to wife Mrs. Maria Fitzherbert, a Catholic of all things, in what was intended to be a secret ceremony. He was reliably rumored to have fathered at least two children by Mrs. Fitzherbert, and there were stories of other bastards elsewhere, including one by Lady Melbourne, as he cavorted with numerous women from all stations in life. Princess Caroline provided no better model for the la-

dies of the day. She amused herself with a number
of lovers, and was accused of giving birth to a son
whose father was definitely not the Regent, since
that gentleman had long before publicly cast off his
wife after a disastrous wedding night and only a few
subsequent days of less than blissful wedlock.

Templeton leaned back in his chair, all of his earlier effervescence vanished, and laughed at the
irony of the situation. When he had left Althea earlier, he had been happier and more relaxed than
he had felt in a fortnight.

"Charles, my darling, do sit down," she had patted the silk-covered sofa cushion and smiled when
he arrived. "I have something of great importance
to tell you."

Oh, God, he had thought, *this is it. She's going to
tell me that she is certain she is pregnant.* After nearly
two weeks of uncertainty following her disclosure
that she might be with child, he still had not come
to stomach the thought of spending the rest of his
days with Althea, as of course he might have to do
if her suspicion was correct; what else could they
do but marry if her husband turned her out? Surprisingly, more than a few husbands kept wives who
gave birth to another man's child, just as many a
wife overlooked the bastards fathered by their husbands. Silvester Hubbard knew of Templeton and
Althea's affaire but had been, so far, too enamored
of his current mistress to care. Still even his toler-
ance must have its limits. Some lovers might pack
their pregnant mistresses off to France with enough
blunt to raise the brat and keep herself in high
style, but Templeton was not such a one. If she were
with child and he was the child's father, and this
he had no cause to doubt, they would marry and
that would be the end of it—that is, it would end

eventually, once the ton had finished picking their bones.

Unfortunately, he did not wish to marry Althea, a realization that had not come to him until it was too late, apparently, to do anything else, not unless he wished to part permanently with his conscience. Grover and one or two others had told him that she was a schemer who would only use him but, blinded by her considerable beauty, not to mention other charms, he had refused to listen. Now it was too late.

She took his hand and held it to her breast. Templeton held his breath.

"My dearest, I am relieved to tell you that I am not enceinte, after all." Althea patted his cheek and gave a little, light laugh. "Or, perhaps, you wanted to be a father, sweetheart?" she teased him.

He had assured her that he was just as pleased as she at the turn of events and, with a clarity of thought that he had not experienced in some time, knew that he must leave immediately, otherwise he risked finding himself in the same straits all over again. It was not until he had stepped from his cab and walked toward White's that he became aware of a total lack of desire to ever see her again, much less keep her as his mistress. He had told her in the sweetest possible terms that he could not stay and she grudgingly accepted; that it would be the last time but one that they would ever be alone together he would tell her in a day or so.

And now, here he sat in White's beside the man who was his closest friend in all the world, a man to whom he might confess any crime but this unutterable stupidity. He looked, shamefaced, at Grover, feeling that somehow he had disappointed him, and said that he must think him the greatest idiot ever born.

"Oh, I doubt it, Charles. Not the greatest idiot ever *born;* that would be doing it up much too brown." He toyed with a beautiful enameled snuff-box, a gift from the Regent who did not know that Grover detested snuff—and him—and glanced around with a dry look. "Probably not even the greatest fool in this room, old boy. Although you just might be the greatest fool of the past fort-night." Templeton's lips twisted in a wry smile. "Well, but you knew that, didn't you? Not to worry too much, Charles, you'll come about. This will be a nine days' wonder and then all the old White's tabbies will be on to someone else."

Templeton sighed. "I know you're right, Laurie. But I am furious with myself for not listening to you in the first place. . . ."

"And well you should be," his friend interjected with a chuckle.

He nodded his acknowledgment. "And for putting myself in a position to be ridiculed in this way." He thought he could detect a few mocking glances from various points in the room. Well, he would simply have to ride out the storm. "The awful thing is that I cannot even say I haven't done my share of betting and sniggering. My name is in there"— he inclined his head in the direction of the Betting Book—"more than once. Arrogant dolt, wasn't I?"

"Oh God, Charles, don't be quite so hard on yourself, I beg of you, or you will become quite tire-some." Grover spoke these words mocking the bored drawl of a pretentious dandy. "Most of us can be found in there, you know."

Templeton returned his friend's steady blue-eyed

gaze. "I'll *wager,*"—he gave a little grin—"that your name is not among them."

Grover pulled a face to make little of his discretion. "Gambling is not my cup of tea. You know that."

Templeton was falling into the dismals again, convinced that the laughter he heard from across the room must be directed at him. "Laurie, I have learned just this evening that my . . . friends . . . are wrong. Althea is not pregnant, thank heaven, so this will come to nothing. Still"—he moved his brandy glass in a small arc—"of a sudden, all of this nonsense palls. What do you think I should do?"

His friend pondered a few moments. "Well, you might consider taking a repairing lease at your house in—the Cotswolds, isn't it? You've told me more than once that you haven't been there in donkey's years. . . ."

"Not since I was a boy, actually."

Grover laughed. "Well, there you are. That's what comes of having such a large inheritance, Charles. You've so many estates, you haven't even got to that one yet!"

Lavinia slowed the ponycart almost to a walk as they came into the turn. The curve was most deceptive, and she approached it with practiced care, just like a lifelong resident of Painswick, never mind that she had arrived here only a few months ago. After bending to the right, the narrow rutted lane twisted sharply to the left. As tall hedgerows obscured the view, more than one driver unfamiliar with the neighborhood had come to grief in this treacherous spot.

"Good boy, Puck," she praised her pony as they

hugged the side of the road. Rounding the corner, Puck suddenly pulled in even closer to the hedges and uncharacteristically dug in his heels, halting the progress of the carriage. The tips of the shrubbery that brushed her arm were just beginning to soften with new pale green growth in the warm spring sun. In front of them, on the other side of the road, lay a carriage tipped unceremoniously into the bushes. Only one of the carriage's two required horses was in evidence. He had been released from his traces and tethered to a tree where he stood contentedly munching grass, his nonchalant air seeming to disavow any involvement in the accident that had provided him with this impromptu meal.

No one else was in sight. Lavinia glanced at the elegant device picked out in black paint on the carriage door. *Probably some stranger driving neck-or-nothing when he took the corner,* she decided with a disdainful shake of her head, once again feeling pleased at having left behind the noise and pretensions of the metropolis.

"Well, Puck, get along. We cannot stop here, or we shall just cause another mishap. Apparently, no one was badly hurt, for I do not see anyone about. Along with you, now."

The little horse began to move forward, but then tried to nose toward the rear of the broken-down vehicle. Lavinia leaned forward in the seat, the better to see. Lying on the grass, propped against an ash tree, was a very disheveled and very handsome stranger. She coaxed Puck onto a small patch of grass to the side of the lane and, once certain he and the cart would present no obstacle to other drivers, hopped down and walked briskly to the figure on the ground.

She stood, hands on hips, and surveyed him criti-

cally for a few moments. The man appeared to be
several years older than she. One glance at his tai-
loring, now much the worse for wear, told her
clearly that he was a gentleman, and a rich one at
that. A cut on his brow, surrounded by a large,
mean-looking spot fast turning a hideous blue, had
trickled blood into his nearly black hair and partly
down one clean-shaven cheek. His white shirt was
open and his left arm lay limply across his lap, while
his right hand clutched some red-stained linen, in
its previous life, his cravat, and a bottle of port. It
was the bottle that led her feminine logic to conclude that he was not in imminent danger of expir-
ing.

As she examined him, he raised the bottle and
took a large swallow, his heavily lashed brown eyes
performing their own languid inspection of her. He
took in her plain but pleasing features and the thick
wavy, blond hair grown out of its fashionable London coiffure and now pulled back simply with a yellow ribbon that had once matched the shade of her
faded dress. His gaze wandered slowly down a tall
body to a pair of very scuffed half-boots, then ran
with the same bold assurance back up to her now-
blushing cheeks. *Not much there,* he sized her up
quickly. *Still, for a country mouse she does have potential,*
he considered. Had she heard his judgment, Lavinia
might have had to fight an urge to clout him. As it
was, she opened her mouth to deliver him a sharp
set-down for his leisurely examination, one hand betraying her as it reached up to feel just *how* wind-
blown her hair had become, but she was forestalled
by his speaking first in a scathing drawl.

"Well, madam, do you intend to stand there all
day gawking, or will you be good enough to extend
me some assistance?"

" 'Gawking'? I assure you, sir, I was not. I was merely observing how well you seem to have survived your own stupidity."

"Survived? Stupidity? What would a female know about it?"

Lavinia smiled sweetly and dropped a mocking minuscule curtsy. "Indeed, sir, I believe you have the right of it. Stupidity does so often seem to be the sole province of the male of the species. And, as for surviving, why you have me at a disadvantage there as well." Here, both pique and triumph nudged her voice up an octave, something she detested but, so far, had never been able to curb. "For, why else would you be lying there and I be standing here?" She sighed, fluttered her lashes, and laid a hand daintily across her heart. "Gentlemen do have such a way with the ribbons. And I see you are even toasting your own skill!"

"Hellcat!"

"Bedlamite!"

"Bedlamite?"

"Only such a one would drive so dangerously in an unknown neighborhood. And, clearly, you are foreign to this area, else I would remember you," she countered, not realizing until much later how ridiculous this sounded. "You must be either a lunatic or a fool."

"A fool!" He tried to rise, doubtless to strangle her, she concluded from the look in his eyes. She stepped back a pace. "Oh!" He groaned loudly and fell back against the tree trunk, causing his shoulder and head further grievance and producing a furious oath.

Remorseful at his evident distress, Lavinia knelt at his side. "Oh, are you indeed hurt, then?"

The man's eyes opened wide in disbelief and in-

dignation. "Am I hurt? *Am I hurt?* By God, and you
with the cheek to call *me* a fool. Of course I am
hurt, woman!" he fairly bellowed. "Why the devil
do you think I am lying here in this state?" The
effort to scream at her was far too much for his
pounding head, and he put his hand to his temple,
groaning again.

"Well, of course I can see that you are hurt," she
retorted frigidly, rather miffed with herself for having made such a dull-witted remark. "I only meant
that I had not realized your injuries might be quite
so . . . bad."

" 'Quite so bad,' she says. Madam, a child can see
that I am, at present, far from healthy."

"So I see, sir, although I am not a child."

"So I see, madam," he rejoined in a much different tone of voice, a cracked head and much-
abused shoulder not being quite sufficient to make
him impervious to charms of the opposite sex.

She had bent to examine his head, but now
glared at him. "Why don't you have another drink?
Or, perhaps there is none left?" She could not resist
adding that last barb, although she immediately regretted it. *The man is in pain,* she chided herself,
and the liquor might lessen his discomfort. Besides, she
was not one of those top-lofty people who preached
against the evils of spirits. Before she could beg his
pardon, however, he snapped at her again.

"I have barely touched the port, madam. I drink
it, first, to relieve my discomfort, which I believe we
have just agreed is considerable, and second, because, since it's been shaken-up in this spill"—he
gestured toward his disabled vehicle—"it is ruined,
anyway."

His being so quick to catch her up had raised her
hackles. "Ah. Of course. But tell me, sir, if it is ru-

ined, how can you drink it?" she inquired with very deliberate and infuriating logic.

"Sheer willpower," he ground out in a low, threatening voice. "On the other hand, I suppose I could dispose of it by pouring it over someone's head."

She had no doubt that the "someone" he referred to was she. "I daresay," she remarked blandly, and stifled a smile that she knew would only aggravate his clearly overwrought state. Her examination progressed to his shoulder, which she probed gently. Though he made no sound, she could see from the whiteness around his tightly shut lips that he was in much distress. The head wound caused her the most concern however, for while the cut looked superficial, she feared he might be concussed.

"Do you feel sick at your stomach?" Her extensive readings had informed her that nausea was one sign of this injury.

"My stomach is fine. It is my head and shoulder that ail me."

That was reassuring. Still, one should not take chances and she believed it efficacious to keep him awake. She daren't slap his cheek to prevent his nodding off, as his drooping eyelids showed he might do, for his poor head already was much abused. For that matter, she considered, this boorish man probably would slap her back. *Well,* she decided, *I shall just have to keep talking.* This was no mean feat for Lavinia, normally a quiet woman with no use for idle conversation. She sighed. Best to start right in.

"Well, it is fortunate for you that I came along, is it not?" she asked cheerfully.

"Good manners preclude my answering that," he drawled.

"Are you always so ill-tempered?"

"Only when my carriage is wrecked, my head broken, and my shoulder wrenched apart. At all other times, I assure you, I am judged to be the sunshine in everyone's day."

"I daresay. Well, I do not think any of it is as bad as that. As I was saying, it is lucky that I came by, for this road is not all that frequently traveled."

"Yes, well, my valet should be back soon. We both jumped free of the vehicle when it began to tip and, thankfully, he and the horses were unhurt. He has ridden one of them to go for help."

"Ah, so you were not alone. How long ago did he leave?"

"About thirty minutes ago, I should think."

"Then he should reach the Swan's Nest soon. That is the first place he would come upon, you see. Well, I cannot leave you lying here." *Much as I might wish to.* "If you have the strength, I shall take you there now in my carriage and send for Dr. Whitney. He will take good care of you." She gave him no opportunity to respond and, under more usual circumstances, he might have bristled at her presumption.

"Before we go, I think you will be more comfortable if you have a sling for your arm. Perhaps your neck cloth?" She took the stained linen from him and held it at arm's length. "No, not large enough."

"Are you wearing a petticoat?"

Taken aback by his effrontery, she blinked at him. Lavinia was not a milk-and-water miss, but this man seemed to possess an unhappy talent for putting her out of countenance. "I *beg* your pardon?"

"I asked if you are wearing a petticoat, for if you are . . ."

"Well of course I am," she snapped. "Do you suppose I go about without one?"

He managed a rakish smile. "There's a good girl. You might, you know, tear off the flounce—I presume it has one—and use that for a sling."

She wanted to bash him for his patronizing tone and his leer, but she did not. "I—oh. Yes, certainly. I suppose that I could. . . ." She rose and saw him grin as he watched. "If you would be so good as to turn your head?" She spoke in what she hoped was a quelling voice.

Still smiling, he turned. Lavinia raised the hem of her frock. The lace that edged her petticoat had a few small tears and the linen was no longer as white as it had been when she had worn it only for daily calls and shopping trips in London. She had not been terribly concerned about this until now that a strange gentleman was about to see the condition of her undergarment. Lavinia was embarrassed. She gave the lace-trimmed flounce a tug, but, despite its weakened condition, there was no answering rending of stitches. Again she pulled. Nothing. "Blast," she muttered, her head bent to her task. "The stupid things tear easily enough when one least wants them to." She heard a snicker and looked into a pair of teasing eyes. Her skirt fell back about her ankles. "You were supposed to be looking the other way!"

"That position was very uncomfortable."

"If I can ruin a perfectly good petticoat, sir, you can suffer some discomfort." She marveled at her boldness in thus describing the garment, but managed to contain a blush.

"Very well." He sighed, unable to dispute the fairness of this. "But use this, or you'll be forever about it." He handed her a pocketknife and turned resignedly, the vision of a pretty pair of ankles still in his mind.

She had the flounce off in another moment and fashioned it about his neck in a large bow, then stood back to survey her work and went into gales of laughter.

"What the devil is so funny?"

"You! You should see yourself with a lady's petticoat ruffle tied round your neck!"

It was his turn to redden. *Damn the woman, she could have folded the thing to disguise its origins.* Instead, the ruffle made him look like a chicken ready for the dinner table, and he was unable to adjust it. "Well, can't you fix it?" Templeton demanded.

"I could. But I shall not."

"You . . ."

"I should not like to jostle your shoulder further, you see."

"Wretch!"

She smiled sweetly. Slowly and with no little difficulty, Lavinia helped him to stand, then advised him to lean on her as they proceeded to her carriage. She saw that he favored his left leg; apparently, it too had been bruised in the accident. He looked down his aristocratic nose at her neat little ponycart.

"Good God! What is that? You said you had a carriage! To call that *monstrosity* a carriage is blasphemous." Reluctantly, he allowed her to help him climb in, then leaned back in the seat, the exertion dampening his brow with perspiration.

"Well"—the effort and the insult put a decided huff in her voice—"I am sure it is nothing so fancy as you are used to, sir, but dear little Puck here serves me quite nicely. He could not possibly pull anything bigger." She patted the pony's neck.

" 'Little' Puck, did you call him?"

"Yes."

"Madam, I put it to you that this overfed creature is anything but little. Now that"—he gestured to the handsome beast still stuffing himself with grass within the shade of the tree—"is a horse to be proud of. *This*"—he looked back at the white pony, then at her squinting at him. He could not help himself. "Good God," he said, and burst into laughter.

Lavinia glared. "Perhaps you would like me to hitch *him* to the cart?" She thrust her thumb toward the trees.

The man sobered instantly. "You are joking. Aristotle? Pulling this thing? Good God, madam, he would never forgive me! Still, we had better bring him along. Would you . . ."

"Oh, very well." She hopped out and hitched the horse to the back of the cart. "But you must stop insulting Puck or you will hurt his feelings. Now, you can cease your bleating and be grateful for the transportation, sir, or you and His Majesty may wait there under the tree until your valet comes for you."

"Ahem. You are correct, of course, madam. I have been, ah, insufferably rude and ungracious. Your . . . horse . . . is a marvel of equine . . . um . . ."

"Thank you," she said airily and, grinning, gave Puck leave to clop happily down the lane.

Puck drew the vehicle back into the lane more smoothly than the man might have expected. "You call him Puck after Shakespeare's sprite, I collect?"

"Yes. A little fairy. A little horse." She nodded her head in the animal's direction, then looked at her passenger from the corner of her eye and they both laughed.

He gave a thought to his appearance. His head was bloody, his arm draped in a lady's undergarment, and he was being carried to God knew where in this ridiculous cart by a female rescuer and, apparently, a bumpkin at that. What a fate for one of London's most sought-after bachelors and elegant men about town. He laughed to himself, thinking that if any of his cronies saw him they would never let him forget it. While he had never exactly been a slave to appearances (to his valet's distress) and never given tuppence for what others said, he could not but give silent thanks for the unlikelihood of his being recognized here in what he considered the outer reaches of the kingdom and in the company of such an unpolished creature.

Templeton examined Lavinia once more. Rather nice to look upon, but unsophisticated and definitely not pretty, she was not in his usual line at all, *and* she was sharp-tongued. Probably unwed. A fellow would have a time overcoming the urge to throttle her. Well, once she deposited him with the doctor, he would never have to see her again; that at least was a blessing. Still, he considered, she was a good deal more interesting than most other females of his acquaintance. And capable. Everyone else he could think of would have been useless in this predicament.

Lavinia's attentions were fixed on the road. She guided Puck carefully, but some of the ruts could not be avoided entirely and, even though they moved fairly slowly, her passenger was a bit shaken.

"Good God, some of these ruts are the size of small rooms! I should think you would be able to avoid them! Don't you know how to drive even this poor excuse for a vehicle?" Had Templeton's friends observed his present circumstance, they would have been just as surprised by his behavior as by his appearance, for normally he was a pattern card of proper manners.

She gave a speaking look that said something about pots calling kettles black, then turned her eyes back to the lane. "Oh, do be quiet! You are quite the rudest man I have ever met. I pity Dr. Whitney, for you are sure to be the worst sort of patient, too. And as for my driving, I would remind you that it is your carriage that lies back there in the ditch"—she jerked her head behind them—"*not* mine! You must be the most ham-fisted driver ever to take the ribbons!"

Templeton was never one to boast, but this slur on his ability as a driver, a talent well-known in London, was more than he could take. He was tempted to explain that his valet had begged for the chance to take the reins and allow him a rest, and thus it had been he who had driven them off the road. *Oh, what would be the point?* he asked himself. *Doubtless she would not believe me and I would just appear even more pathetic for trying to blame a servant for this hobble.* Instead, he merely told her in even tones that he had misjudged the turn and that he was generally considered to be a fine driver by his friends in London.

"You? Ha! And I suppose all the prime whips in London drive their vehicles *off* of the road instead of *on* it?"

"You call this a road? It is, rather, an ambush, madam, lying in wait for the unsuspecting traveler, lulling him into a false sense of safety before it attempts to murder him!"

"Good heavens, it is not alive, you know." She chuckled.

"I promise you, it is." They were quiet for a moment or two, then Lavinia remembered that she wanted to keep him talking.

"What are you doing, by the way, on this road? It is not much traveled by any except the local inhabitants."

"We were headed for Painswick."

"Oh." She nodded her head in a backward direction. "But your carriage appeared to have been pointed the wrong way, sir, to get to Painswick, which is about three miles in the opposite direction. Of course, it is difficult to be sure," Lavinia added slowly as if she were judging her words with the greatest care, "since it was upside down. . . ."

He did not reply for a moment, and Lavinia feared that he had fainted. She looked at him and saw that he was wide-awake and chewing on his lip with apparent consternation. "Well?" His response was unintelligible. "What did you say?"

"I said we were lost, damn it!" He growled the words through gritted teeth.

She gave an unladylike snort. "Lost? That is famous!"

"It does sometimes happen, you know." He saw no point in mentioning that the same hapless valet had lost their map of the district as far back as Fairford.

"To be sure."

"You see, I misplaced our map and we must have missed the turn for Painswick after we came through Cirencester, so . . ."

"Mmm. Well, you are not too far off. And I know just where you went wrong," she interjected with a knowing nod.

"Yes, I am sure that you would."

Gad, the woman was infuriating. Finding himself at a disadvantage was an entirely new experience for Templeton, and he found that he detested it. As Lavinia chattered about the local geography, he lapsed gladly into silence, wishing only that their trip would be over before she wrested some other humiliating experience from him, even if she had to go back to his childhood to find it. And each word she uttered reverberated in his head until it seemed fit to blow off his shoulders. He could not abide a rattling woman—or man for that matter—at the best of times, and this morning certainly did not fit into that category. His discomfort made him more obstreperous, and his previous admiration of her capabilities now dissolved into a very decided impression of a blabbering, managing female who browbeat all those unfortunate enough to stumble unwittingly into her path. Templeton did not pause to consider how aptly this described the circumstances of their own introduction. He could just picture her reading Improving Works and telling everyone and his dog how to run his life.

He sighed and tried to block out the sound of her voice.

"Generally when I take up a man in my carriage, sir, I know his name. Would you like to tell me yours?" She smiled at him.

"Oh, yes, forgive me. Charles Templeton."

Of course. Lavinia remembered the name from her years in town, and the crest on the carriage door helped to assure her that memory had not failed. Indeed, how could it? Everyone in London with any aspirations to admittance to even the outer fringes of society, knew of Charles Templeton and his title, his elegance, and style. Thus, Lavinia, who did not mix in the same social circles as he, had never met him but knew him quite well by reputation. Some considered him nothing more than a fashionable fribble, a man of the town, others declared him top of the trees.

"Marquess Templeton?" she blurted, and mentally chided herself, for she surely sounded as if she seldom went into society, much less mixed with the peerage.

Templeton cringed and nodded. "At your service, madam." He spoke the words automatically.

Lavinia could not help but laugh outright at such a chivalrous offer given by a gentleman in his condition. "Indeed, Lord Templeton?" Her eyes sparkled with mirth and he chuckled despite himself.

"This round to you, ma'am."

The carriage rattled and shook its way to the inn. She had spoken as if they were equals, although he would swear she could be no more than a country squire's daughter and probably the runt of the litter at that. *Who the devil does she think she is? For that matter, who the devil* is *she?*

"I beg your pardon?"

Templeton had not realized that he had spoken his last thoughts aloud. She had stopped chattering while awaiting his response and for a moment he considered letting her think that he had fainted and been babbling in his sleep; anything for quiet. His pride, however, got the best of him. Ah, well, the question needed asking anyway, though perhaps in more genteel terms. She had aided him, after all.

"I asked, madam, if you would be so good as to tell me your name."

"Indeed you did not," she chided brightly. "For you have not been so polite since we met. But I shall tell you just the same."

"Too kind."

Slam!

"God save me from you and this road, whoever you are!"

"My name is Lavinia Taylor."

He cradled his arm like a baby, eyes shut tight. "Very pretty."

"Thank you." She gave the reins a gentle pull, slowed Puck to a halt, and turned to him with a wide smile. "I really cannot take you to the inn looking like this, can I?" She slowly and gently folded and tucked the sling to hide the fullness of its ruffle from view. The lumpy knot that took the place of the offensive bow made his lips twist in a smirk, but he knew better than to tease her with it. Still, he could not entirely control his tongue.

"You are all kindness, Miss Taylor. It is *Miss*, is it not?"

The last definitely was not intended as a polite question and she looked into his eyes, so near because of her ministrations, and raised a brow.

"You are rude." She gave the flounce a small tug, trying to make some sense of the knot. *Really, it is just impossible to be nice to this man.*

"Ouch! Damn it, how can you be so clumsy?"

"How can I not? You have only just finished telling me *again* what a blockheaded driver I am." She gave Puck leave to go.

"I was rude. I apologize."

Lavinia eyed him with great surprise. "Do not consider it, I pray you. I daresay folk are always thus when they wreck their carriages."

"I should think so, madam, although I cannot speak from experience."

She gave an unconvinced snort, despite the fact that he had uttered the words with a straight face. "Mmm," was all she said in reply, and urged Puck to a quicker pace.

"Tell me, sir, are you visiting in the neighborhood? Have you friends hereabout?" She dearly hoped not, for the district was fairly small and the thought that she might have to meet him again was not one she relished, for all he was the handsomest man she had met in a twelvemonth.

He gave a sigh of resignation. There was nothing for it but to tell the truth. He could only hope, although he could already see it was in vain, that the area was large enough to comfortably require of them no more than a nodding acquaintance; or perhaps he might be truly fortunate and learn that *she* was the visitor.

"I am to live in Painswick."

She gave an involuntary spasmodic tug on the reins, and Puck complained with great surprise.

"Oh, dear, I am sorry, my sweet boy."

"Here, leave the poor beast his mouth, you foolish woman!"

Lavinia bit back a hot retort and flushed. If he cared about a horse he had taken such pains to mock, then he must be fond of animals in general, she decided with pleasure. She gave her passenger an abashed smile. "Yes, that was entirely clumsy of me, wasn't it? Darling Puck. I'll have my man take a close look at his mouth and give him an extra portion of oats, when we arrive home." She paused. "Puck, I mean."

Templeton trod warily. Clearly, meekness was not in Lavinia Taylor's character. "I rather thought that you did refer to Puck. And extra portions of anything are not what the creature needs, as I believe I already explained."

She frowned and he immediately felt more at ease. "So," she picked up their previous thread of conversation, "you are to live here. . . ." It was all she could do not to pull on Puck's reins again, for she thought she knew just *where* this person was going to live, and her voice was decidedly downcast. "You own Templeton Park."

He nodded. "I do. I have not been there since I was a boy and I, um, thought it time that I returned."

She looked at him askance. "Mmm. Rusticating? How long do you mean to stay?" she asked without an ounce of shame for her bluntness.

Templeton blinked. "Why, I have not yet decided, ma'am." Clearly, she hoped he would depart as soon as possible, but he would be dashed if he would give her the satisfaction of saying he probably would not remain above a couple of months. "However, I may make a long stay. A *very* long stay." She grimaced and he could not resist adding with relish, "perhaps I shall make my home here. It will depend in part, of course, on how welcoming I find the neighborhood."

"Indeed?" Lavinia asked archly. She believed she knew when someone was tweaking her nose and she did not like it any more than she did the prospect of his presence in Painswick. "And may one ask *why* you have suddenly come to this momentous decision, sir?" she asked dryly. Later, she would blush at her temerity.

It was his turn to be discomfited. "I, er, well . . . no, Miss Taylor, you may not. That is," he amended hastily, "there is no great tale behind it." Her glance revealed her considerable doubt. "I simply decided the time was right, as it were."

"Mmm," was all she uttered in reply.

Templeton narrowed his eyes at her. What did she know that he did not? "You know the Park?" Well, of course, who would not? It was, after all, an estate of great prominence and, if memory served, beauty.

Lavinia slewed her eyes at him. "I do," she replied tersely. He waited for elaboration. "It is the property next to mine."

"Oh, no!" he said before he could think of the proper, polite response.

"Oh, yes!" she chimed with no more grace than he showed.

TWO

Greenbriar Lodge, Painswick

Dearest Edwina:

At long last I write because, finally, I have something to say! There has been an "event" here in Painswick, as your Mrs. Peterson might say. You know how much I love life here in the country, but I would be lying were I to claim that it is especially fascinating or even very eventful. First, however, I must say how glad I was to know that little Horatio has gotten over the mumps. I was sorry but not surprised, as I am certain you know, that Jerrold did not prove to be of much support to you and Nurse during the illness. Nor, do I suspect, were you much struck, given that he has been as little help with the older boys, going all weak at the knees at the sight of blood when Howard fell out of the pear tree and cut his arm or when Henry was down with measles. And such behavior from a man whom I know would defend his family to the death against all manner of footpads, murderers, and highwaymen! Had he indeed wed me, Wina, I do not think that I could have been half so tolerant as you!

Yes, my dear friend, I know that I have kept you on tenterhooks to hear my great news, have I not? When

I was out driving yesterday, I happened upon a gen-
tleman who had had a carriage accident—well, I can
say that he had the appearance *of a gentleman and*
he did claim to be one, but as for his manners . . .

Lavinia went on for another paragraph to de-
scribe her encounter with the stranger, spicing her
account with a witty retelling of Templeton's foibles
and even one or two of her own.

Well, we met his valet just coming out of the Swan's
Nest. He and Mr. Johnson, the landlord, having al-
ready sent a message to the doctor. After seeing the
marquess—she had saved this part until now and
pictured her friend's face when she read these
words—*(yes, dear, a marquess) settled, I felt my duty*
done and left. One would not care to say that we parted
the best of friends. Truly, Wina, he is the most dis-
agreeable man—no the most disagreeable person *I*
have ever met. Ungrateful and high in the instep.
* A marquess indeed! Doubtless he is the greatest dis-*
appointment to his family, for he is quite the clumsiest,
poorest-mannered specimen of a peer of the realm.

Lavinia could predict her friend's rejoinder to
this, and so she had quickly added:

I know, Wina, I know. You will say that one cannot
expect more of a gentleman who was as shaken as he
from his carriage mishap. But, I promise you that the
greatest injury he suffered was to his very considerable
pride.

As Edwina Somerville turned the pages round
and round and over to read the words that filled

every possible margin of the small squares of paper, she smiled. Lavinia had so far omitted a description of the unhappy marquess's appearance, and she envisioned a paunchy, aging dandy absurdly deflated by his precipitous landing in the dusty lane. He did sound stuffy. But Lavinia often judged people immediately upon making their acquaintance. If Edwina found fault with this, and she frequently pointed out that she did, she also had to concede that her friend's character assessments generally were accurate. This tendency to form instant opinions was not malicious. In fact, Lavinia's nature was kind. Those people whom she decided were snobs were avoided because she had a hard-to-control bent for speaking her mind. Not beautiful as Edwina was, Lavinia's looks were merely unremarkable, but her ready humor and, it must be said, large fortune—above £10,000 a year people rightly estimated—had earned her sufficient London admirers during her debut Season on the town. Still, admiration had not resulted in a vast number of proposals of marriage. The ones she did receive were from gentlemen who were utterly done up. Both young women had recognized that Lavinia's intelligence and independent, outspoken manner might have contributed to her still-unwedded state.

Of course, the major cause of Lavinia's single status, Edwina knew better than anyone, was Edwina's own fault because she had married Lavinia's beau. Lavinia had been quick to point out that she and Jerrold Somerville, who had lived nearby both young women, had never actually been betrothed and thus she could not be outraged at his transfer of feelings from her to Wina. Nevertheless, Wina had assured her over and over again that she had never consciously done anything to win Jerrold's attention and that she would not for *worlds* have done a thing to jeopardize her friends' future together. Jerrold had been an attentive, if undeclared, suitor, not to mention old friend, of Lavinia, and it had been one of Fate's jests that her two special friends had fallen in love. Lavinia, who really was not terribly overset by the turn of events, was able to perceive the irony in the situation, when she found herself soothing both Wina and Jerrold who was also repeating his own profuse apologies and practically insisting that they wed.

After many assurances that her heart was undamaged, as it truly was not—well, not much and not for long—Jerrold and Wina had married. Shortly thereafter, they had removed to Somerset where he had come into a large property, and had spent the intervening years—nearly eight now—raising their brood. All three remained as close as such a distance would allow, and the two women corresponded regularly. Lately, Edwina had begun to wonder if the sedate measure of country life and her unwed state were not beginning to tell on Lavinia. But it had been some time since she had been as animated as she seemed in her letter. She was, to Edwina's mind, too concerned about what Samuel was getting up to at Oxford, whether the man in the cottage down the lane was feeding his dog properly, or if Cook's rheumatism was any better. (It never was, but the letter also contained news of that woman's imminent departure and the cryptic mention of the local woman Lavinia had lately interviewed as her possible replacement.)

"Well, that is something, anyway," Edwina mumbled. "That woman spent more time complaining than she did cooking."

"Hmm? What's that, dear?"

Edwina looked up and blinked at her husband. "What? Oh, Jerrold, I'd forgotten you were there." She smiled across the table at him and asked if he cared for more tea.

He chuckled and shook his head. "No, Win, thank you, for I've finished two cups while you have been so engrossed in Lavinia's letter."

"Oh, dear, I am sorry."

"No, no, not a bit of it. She is keeping well I hope. Did I hear you say something about cooking? Not our cook, I hope." Jerrold Somerville appreciated a good meal, so there was genuine concern in his voice.

His wife explained. "Ah, I see. Well, no point in keeping her on if she cannot do the job, I suppose. And heaven knows Lavinia will send her off with a handsome pension! Finish your letter. I'll be off now and you can tell me all the news when I get back. I shall look forward to it."

Edwina raised her cheek for a kiss and nodded absentmindedly as she squinted to make out the puddle of ink that appeared to say something about buns and the new cook, but for the life of her she could make no sense of it. It was midafternoon before she got to finish the letter. Her attention had been claimed, indeed demanded, by both younger boys, who had cut her peace again and again as they threw balls and wooden boats at one another, then tossed them down the front staircase to land with noisy and maddening repetition on the marble floor of the entryway. For a time she wondered what there could be to so intrigue the boys in the mindless exercise of casting a thing down the stairs only to have to climb down to get it and bring it back up, then to go through the same process all over again. Edwina decided it must be a fascination inherited from her husband's side of the family, or perhaps a propensity more natural to boys than girls, for surely she could not recall having played such pointless games when she was a child.

By the time she settled on the sofa with the last pages of Lavinia's letter, her head was pounding from the racket of toys clattering down the stairs, and high-pitched young voices screeching boisterous, laughing warnings to any hapless soul who happened by below. Pandemonium frequently reigned in the Somerville home, and Edwina sighed and wished that she could be a stricter parent, for she knew that both she and Jerrold had spoiled their three boys, perhaps beyond redemption.

They were not bad children, but at ages four (Horatio), six (Henry) and seven (Howard) their undirected energy set the entire household on its ear with alarming frequency. It was bad enough that their parents seemed incapable of exerting much control over their little brood, but the nannies— they were on their second—whom they hired seemed no better equipped for the task. More than once, she had heard phrases such as, "Now, madam, the little one did not mean to pour the inkpot over the carpet; he was just curious to see what it would do." Of course, what it did was ruin a once perfectly lovely Axminster. Edwina blushed to think how they would spoil their next child if it were a girl, as she and Jerrold both hoped. Patting her still-flat middle, she recalled how pleased he had been when she'd announced the other day that she was pregnant again. *Yes, we shall just have to take especially good care that she does not become as spoiled as her brothers,* Edwina thought, hoping she could hold to her resolution. She turned back to the last of Lavinia's letter and its world without noisy, demanding children.

And so, my dear, he has already taken up residence at Templeton Park and need I tell you that the neighborhood is, heaven help us, agog at the presence of a marquess in our little province. Honestly, Wina, you might think, were you to wander our High Street, that Painswick had wanted just his presence to make our lives complete. And to think that he is injured only somehow adds to his distinction, and that he sustained his wounds—which it may not surprise you to learn grow bigger and worse by the day, or so the village gossips would have it—upon his arrival here, well, my dear, you might believe that the entire population of Painswick, down to the children and the grandmamas, all had on their hands the blood of an innocent marquess! Said blood, apparently, can be redeemed only by the abject contrition of said residents. I have it on good authority that no fewer than fifteen loaves, half a dozen haunches of beef, and countless numbers of perfectly innocent pigs have been sacrificed, and scores of fishes, cakes, and pies all have been left at the door of Lord Templeton.

The rest of her friend's letter was taken up with the usual minutiae of life in her small town, news that Edwina never failed to find of interest and amusement. But the next letter received, as usual, a couple of weeks later, devoted a mere page to the marquess, a development that disappointed its recipient, who had been anticipating the latest tale about Painswick's newest resident.

Lavinia wrote that she had thought it proper to call at the inn the day following the meeting on the road, but pelting rain had kept her indoors. Once the weather had improved to one of the bright, fresh days that too infrequently tag along behind a heavy rain, a call at the Swan's Nest informed her that the object of her visit had already departed for Templeton Park. *Oh, dear,* she thought, *he's wasting no time.* Although what else she had expected, or even wanted, him to do—other than depart immediately for the return trip to London—she could not have said.

By the time Lavinia had deposited Templeton at the Swan's Nest, he had supposed that his mood could not have become much blacker or his life much worse. Since his life, at least until the past fortnight, had been largely free of misfortune, it was not at all surprising that the recent disagreeable occurrences seemed to him nothing short of cataclysmic; at the same time, his previously unchallenged optimism told him that things surely would promptly return to their normal, unruffled pleasantness. Unhappily, Templeton was to be quickly disabused of all of these naive beliefs.

Rideout was still in the midst of arranging for his master's rescue when that gentleman suddenly appeared at the Swan's Nest Inn, a passenger in the most disreputable vehicle imaginable. The valet abruptly suspended his conversation with the landlord, who followed his gaze out into the small, crescent-shaped inn yard. Rideout stepped quickly, albeit with negligible enthusiasm, to the ponycart, his distaste no less evident than it might have been had he held his large, beaklike nose.

Beset by guilt at his having caused the carriage mishap, the valet began speaking before he had even reached Templeton. "Lord Templeton! I had not expected to see you! I have just concluded arranging with Mr. Johnson here"—he waved his arm in the direction of the man who followed in his

wake, nodding and smiling—"for a carriage to . . .
Good heavens! What is that?"

As Templeton had turned to exit the vehicle, the
much-despised petticoat sling had come into view.
His master might as well have been carrying a reticule. Templeton tossed Lavinia a look that promised
he would avenge this cruel treatment, even if he
had to wait until another life to do it. She smiled
sweetly in return and decided to let both Templeton
and his manservant stew in their own juices before
she would absolve him of complicity in the petticoat
sling.

Rideout, who clearly took his master's current appearance as a personal affront, sputtered with disdain and indignation.

"Come, sir, allow me to assist you to disembark
from this . . . this . . ." Words seemed to elude
him. *Dear me,* Lavinia thought, *the poor man looks as
if he might faint.* "This vehicle," he managed, "and
we shall get you up to your room—it is ready and
waiting for you, sir—to rest until the doctor arrives,
and to remove this—*thing.* To see a gentleman such
as yourself, my lord, a *marquess,* tricked out like
a . . . a . . ."

"Oh, very well, Rideout, leave off," Templeton
said somewhat testily. "No need to get yourself into
a pucker. It isn't anything permanent, you know.
After all, it's not as if I had my teeth filed the way
some of the younger pups do, so that I can whistle
just like a coachman on the box."

Good God, the way the man was carrying on, anyone might have thought that his looks were all
either of them cared for, and that was not quite
true. The marquess was indeed well noted for his
always elegant appearance and understated tailor-
ing: the immaculate neckcloth tied with a simple

knot, the coats so admired by his circle, the dark
hair, whose waves owed nothing to the curling
tongs, framing his rather stern-looking face. Still,
Templeton could not have said if he would have
been turned out half so well had Rideout not cared
quite so much or not worked quite so hard to make
him so. But now here was this woman who, between
his own behavior a short while ago and Rideout's
reaction now, must think Charles a veritable dandy,
a species he despised. Much later, when he lay in
his strange new bed unable to sleep, he would ask
himself why he should care what a mere country
nobody might think of him, but at the moment he
knew only that all this rattling on about appearances made him feel no better than a fop.

Poor Rideout was gasping at the mental picture
he had formed of his master whistling through his
teeth as he cracked the whip over a team of powerful horses. Templeton, endlessly grateful for his
safe deliverance from both Miss Taylor and her driving, mustered as much dignity as he could under
the circumstances and spoke rather stiffly.

"Miss Taylor, pray accept my sincere thanks for
your aid." Her face was set in stiff, unyielding lines,
for she was not yet prepared to forget the unkind
remarks of this gentleman and his valet. "You are
very good, ma'am, to have taken the trouble to assist me," Templeton continued, patting Puck's neck.
For the first time, he noticed the bright blue ribbons interwoven through the horse's jaunty fore-
lock. *How is it I didn't see them before?* he wondered,
chuckling despite himself at the little satin rosettes.

Lavinia, watching his attentions to Puck, also
grinned, her eyes sparkling. "Not at all, sir, I was
more than glad to be of, um, *service* to you."

For just a moment, he must have gaped at this

riposte. *Yes,* hc chided himself as he lay awake later, *I am certain that I* gaped *at that woman.* And he blushed to think of it, for he had not behaved in such a callow fashion since he was a youth. But this shock at her boldness was quickly replaced by his sense of the absurd, and by his ability to laugh at himself, though, admittedly, this could sometimes take a while to happen, and he chuckled.

She whistled a sharp, clear note, and Puck resumed his cheerful pace, pulling the unusual, maddening, and rather captivating creature out of the inn yard, back into the lane, and out of his sight. *Little country mouse,* he thought again and allowed a small smile that no one else could have detected.

After the doctor's very thorough examination of his injuries, Templeton was washed out and too weak to continue on to Templeton Park that day. Mr. Johnson, the proprietor, was only "too honored" to provide his "very best bedchamber" to the marquess. As he told his wife while he scurried needlessly about badgering the bootboy plying brushes and the maids sweeping the stone floors, he was "glad that Lord Templeton was too peaked to have an appetite," since the inn had recently lost the services of their exemplary cook, Mrs. Beatrice, and her replacement could not match her skill.

Templeton and Rideout stayed the night at the inn and set out the next morning. Rideout had fussed over him all evening in a manner that Templeton's mother would have described as that of a hen with only one chick. Despite his manservant's ministrations and his pleasant wood-paneled bedchamber, Templeton had passed an unpleasant night, the discomfort from his injuries keeping him from sleep until the small hours of the morning. As soon as he had finally dozed off, he was jolted

awake by hot wax dripping onto his hand, as
Rideout leaned over the bed to ascertain if his master had stuck his spoon in the wall. Templeton had
wanted to box the man's ears, but had not had the
strength. "Go away, Rideout, I am not dead," was
all he had been able to manage.

A look in the shaving mirror the next morning
confirmed his fears of the night before. The bruise
above his right eye had turned a most disagreeable
dark blue color, and the area had swelled considerably since the last time he had touched it just before
he had gone off to sleep. He assessed the ugly
bruise once more, gently, with his fingertips and
winced in pain. *It's no wonder,* he thought, *that I feel
as if Vulcan himself has been beating on my head with
his hammer.*

Rideout managed to convince his master to break
his fast before they set out. The servant, too, had
spent as restless a night as his master, but was too
highly strung to take his own advice about dining.
When he had not been hovering over the groaning
Templeton, he had been tossing in his own bed just
as he had done every night since his master had
announced their imminent removal to Painswick a
fortnight ago. While it was quite common practice
for Templeton and others of his class to spend time
in the country at the conclusion of the London Season, Rideout could not for the life of him imagine
why a gentleman should wish to go there for no
particular purpose and, worse yet, with no specific
date of departure from said backwater. Not being a
complete slow top, the valet understood that Templeton must have his reasons for leaving and certainly it was not *his* place to question them. He even
believed he had a good notion of the cause of their
leaving. Still, in Rideout's mind, the marquess could

do little that was wrong and certainly nothing that could justify their *positive exile*, as he had described it to Cook back in Templeton's stately London town house.

You mark my words, he had told Mr. Pride, as the latter had rolled out the pastry for the marquess's truffle pie, *this will come to no good. And what are we going to do there, I ask you? In the* country? *It's all right for a few weeks for shooting and fishing and visiting friends. I do know that Lord Templeton is fond of a good amateur theatrical when we go to stay at his friend, Mr. Harland's estate in Cheshire, but that's just for a* time, *isn't it? I mean to say, it's no place fit to* live. *I'm telling you, there's nothing there for Lord Templeton. You just remember that I warned you*, he had predicted, just as if the whole thing had been the cook's idea. And the presence of Lavinia, her ponycart, and that *horrid thing*, as Rideout kept muttering to himself about the makeshift sling, rolling from one side of his narrow inn bed to the other, had only served to reinforce his worst fears. How could a person have done such a thing to a gentleman of his master's stature?

Percy Rideout was proud and then some to be manservant to a marquess. It certainly set him up nicely with his friends and family—his good-for-nothing cousin, Harvey, was positively green with envy—and, while he would never have admitted it, their removal to Painswick, never mind that it was a large and impressive estate, could only serve to diminish his own standing, as well as that of his master. To him, nothing could compare to London, its clubs, its balls, its parks, its very way of doing things. Why, there was really nothing so far as he could see to dress for in Gloucestershire, and heaven knew there was no one who mattered to see how one looked or behaved. He could only hope that Templeton would tire of the place and the country as quickly as he did of most things once their shine had faded, and that they could return to civilization without undue delay.

Still fussing over his master as they departed the inn at midmorning of the day following the accident, Rideout's shoe caught the uneven threshold of the front door. As he fell headlong into the yard, the poor man let out a yelp that could be heard clear around the back of the establishment, where the maids were spreading freshly washed sheets on the shrubbery to dry in the breeze.

Templeton had been remarking to himself on the superb quality of the accommodations provided to him and his servant. The Swan's Nest Inn was a fine establishment built in the middle of the sixteenth century and was the main posting house in the area. It even claimed to have the oldest bowling green in the kingdom. Ted Johnson and his wife, Amanda, worked hard to maintain their excellent reputation; the linens and the mattresses in their rooms were always fresh and the staff accommodating. All of this was lost on Rideout, however, who had determined long before his departure from London to dislike anything and everything about his destination; it mattered not that the Swan's Nest staff and management had provided him with as fine an accommodation as even his master might wish. Rideout lay where he fell, holding his left leg and moaning a good deal more loudly than his injury demanded. Templeton limped to his side, his own handicap preventing quicker movement.

"Haven't I been telling you to fix that step, Ted?" The innkeeper's wife hissed, and sent a sharp elbow into his ribs to be sure of his attention. Ted Johnson, who had been following his guests to the door, had already begun to move to the injured man's side and thus was spared the full effect of his wife's thrust; he was not often so fortunate.

"Oh, no! Mr. Rideout! Oh, dear me, are you badly hurt? Here, Reg, Reg! Bring that chair over here, boy. Mr. Rideout, let's try to get you up on this, shall we?"

Rideout groaned ever louder as the innkeeper and his potboy raised him slowly from the floor, while Templeton could do no more than hold the chair steady and offer encouragement and direction.

"Amanda, best send for the doctor again," Ted Johnson called out and, luckily for him, managed to keep unspoken the words, *and make some proper use of yourself instead of carping at me.*

The large village of Painswick lay rather high in the steep Cotswold hills between Stroud to the south and Cheltenham to the north. The wool and cloth trades had made Painswick, as well as Stroud, prosperous for countless years, and woolen mills dotted the banks of the Wick stream that supplied the mills' power. The current beautiful and spacious residence of Templeton Park was fairly new, having been constructed around the foundation of the old one that had been pulled down more than one hundred twenty years before by the fourth marquess, then in his declining years. It was a proud and graceful old estate that, like most of the local architecture, was built of golden Cotswold limestone quarried from Painswick Beacon, the tallest point in the vicinity.

The mansion sat on a hill far from the road, surrounded by a nearly mile-wide curtain of woodland, largely beech and firs, that assured privacy, quiet, and game for the Templeton table. The old marquess had breathed his last only months after the rebuilding project had begun, his demise provoked by a furious encounter with the hapless builder who had dared question his plans for the eccentric design of the stables. Fortunately, the nephew who inherited the Park, as it was commonly known, loved the place and was well-off enough to indulge his keen, and it must be said, more tasteful, interest in architecture. Construction of the main house and outbuildings took almost two years, and decoration of the interior and laying out and planting of the new grounds to conform to the altered size and shape of the structures consumed almost as much time again.

The village proper was a small collection of streets and lanes that dispersed from New Street and old St. Mary's church. The town buildings were an amalgam of architectural styles from cottage-type shops constructed in medieval times, to Georgian mansions, merchants' houses, and shops built in the last hundred years, in grander proportions than the efforts of earlier times, but of less imaginative and provocative appearance.

The village was positively buzzing with talk of Templeton's arrival, a man whom many insisted was not a stranger in their midst, despite his never having spent above a month there, and that when he was but a boy of ten. The basis for this peculiar notion lay in the fact that, long before the marquessate was bestowed, the Templeton family had been contented landowners in Painswick for centuries, as well as kind and generous members of the community. The Templetons had always been rich; in fact, that adjective was an understatement, and they had never hesitated to spend buckets of money on the estate and its tenant farms and cottages. Generations of the family had lived quite happily in Painswick, journeying to London for the entertainments of the Season and so that the marquess could take his seat in Parliament, then gladly returning to the slower rhythm of life in Gloucestershire. Life had followed this happy pattern without much noticeable deviation until some sixty years earlier, when the then-marquess had precipitately deserted the little village, leaving nearly two dozen able-bodied folk to find other jobs, since an empty house had no use for maids, footmen, butlers, cooks, grooms, or coachmen.

"Can you imagine," some of the local inhabitants explained to those now too young to recall, "Lord Edward Templeton, he who was the present marquess's grandfather, you know, up and left! One day he was courting Miss Drabble—she lived over at Greenbriar Lodge, and a sweeter, more beautiful lady he could not have wished for, *and* rich as he was to boot—and the next he was gone. Just gone, without so much as a 'by your leave,' to anyone here, not even to Rebecca Drabble! Course, he and those who came after him always saw that the place was kept up and none of the tenants has ever wanted for anything at all."

This last was always added to be sure that the listener did not take with him the impression of an ungrateful local populace. Another native would then add that, "Yes, but Lord Templeton never did come back here. Never. Not once. Well, those who came after him did, but only for a few weeks here and there. It's almost as if the Park was forgotten." After all the intervening years, there were still sad shakes of the head at the conclusion of the history.

Seated around an old wooden table was a group of men and women of varying ages and occupations. Some were related by blood and all had lived in Painswick for generations and had ancestors who had once been in service at Templeton Park; two or three had worked at the Park as youngsters. The grandfathers and grandmothers, aunts and uncles— the number of "-greats" to be appended to these titles depended upon the age of the present-day individual—eventually found employment elsewhere, but few of them in their former occupations or mostly for employers whose station was, perforce, far below that of the long-ago Lord Templeton. Footmen and maids became shop assistants; the cook, whose gooseberry pies had been the reason, he so often complimented her, that Lord Templeton was inspired to arise every day, went to the Swan's Nest Inn, where her great-granddaughter, Irene Beatrice, had cooked until she had recently gone to work for Lavinia Taylor. One of the gardeners returned to work in his father's hardware shop that subsequently boasted the finest garden in the High Street; thanks to his nephew, now a spry eighty, it still was. It was in the back of this shop that the group sat, the proprietor, Galen Waters, having seen off the last of his customers and joined the others, who had begun to gather about thirty minutes before.

"Ah, thank you, Sarah," Waters said to his wife, and sipped at the tea she had handed to him.

"But look now, here's Lord Templeton come back just like that!" someone was pointing out brightly, as if this very fact had not given rise to the present meeting and discussion in the first place.

" 'Come back'?" rejoined Alfie Sharp, who never let anyone get away with anything. "You make it sound as if the man had only been gone long enough to take the air!"

A stocky, fair-haired man suggested the marquess might not stay long, and the elderly woman seated to his left chided him.

"Honestly, William, you're ever the gloomy one!"

A man of an age near that of the lady interjected dryly, "Irene, I won't disagree with you, for William is the most melancholy man I've ever known." William Tabbard folded his arms across his barrel chest and twisted his lips at his chuckling comrades. "But in this instance," Cornelius Pratt continued, "I feel we should follow his lead and be more cautious in our expectations. After all, we have no reason to believe that the marquess will remain at Templeton Park for anything more than a brief visit."

There were murmurs both of agreement and dismay, and Tabbard nodded. "Didn't I say?" he asked sagely. Teacups were passed up the table for refilling.

Mr. Pratt glanced around the table and smiled. "I see we still await completion of our numbers," he remarked with the touch of formality that was typical of his speech, even amongst old friends and acquaintances as he was. "Has anyone seen Mr. Wainwright?"

"Well, when I met up with him today," Jim Lewis replied, "he said as he might be a bit tardy, him having to depend on when Lord Templeton might let him go and all."

"Tell us, Jim, how he likes it up at the Park," Stephen Willard called out above the chatter bubbling around the table.

"Pity's sake, Willard, I've *told* you already, just like I did the others. Clean your grubby ears now and again, why don't you!" he shot back good-naturedly, and Stephen Willard took the jibe in good stride. "All right, all right, I'll tell you—*again.*" His listeners, all eager to hear the paltry details once more, chuckled and made encouraging sounds.

"I was just coming out of Friday Street early yesterday morning when I spies old Nev up ahead of me, and . . ."

"Was you going *up* Friday Street or coming *down?*"

Jim blinked at this pointless question. "And what possible difference would that make, Alfie?"

Alfie Sharp shrugged burly shoulders. "Just trying to set the scene in my mind's eye, Jim. No need to get your feathers all ruffled," he replied with a great air.

"Oh, you was? Is that so? And what would *you* know about setting scenes, Alfie, old man? If you don't mind me asking, that is!"

His opponent leaned muscular arms on the table and said, "I'll have you know that *I* like to keep my mind *busy* whilst I'm mendin' fences and such." This was spoken with great dignity. "Unlike *some* people, I do not get much enjoyment from conversing with horses and such."

"Now, see here . . ." began Jim Lewis, who worked in the Painswick livery stable.

"Gentlemen, gentlemen," Cornelius Pratt intoned. "Enough, I beg you." Everyone's chattering ceased and the two squabblers looked at one another doubtfully. "Thank you. Now, Jim, even though we have heard the story"—he grinned over his shoulder at Stephen Willard—"we might as well hear it again until Neville deigns to grace us with an appearance." He smiled encouragement at Jim Lewis, who dutifully took up his tale once again.

"Ho! That you, Nev? I say, Nev!"

The man up ahead stopped and turned in the narrow street and waited for Jim Lewis to catch up. "Good day to you, Jim." Neville Wainwright smiled at his friend.

"Good morning, Nev, you're looking well. You don't need to tell me—working up at the Park must agree with you."

Wainwright nodded with enthusiasm. "It does that, Jim."

"So, the marquess is a good master, then?"

"He is." They fell into step side by side.

"Well, Nev, you finally got your wish. Got out of Mr. Tembo's Gentlemen's Shop *and* found a situation as a manservant to a real gentleman. Good for you." His good wishes were sincere.

"Thank you, Jim. I have been fortunate, for I thought I was doomed to spend the rest of my days measuring and delivering for Mr. Tembo and his clients. The life of a shop assistant isn't all it's made up to be, you know," he confided in lowered, sober tones. "But, I should not complain. Mr. Tembo could have been a great deal worse, and he paid me a decent enough wage. It was just that I wanted to make more of myself, as you well know, Jim. I remember the tales my cousin used to tell about working for the marquess That Left. Oh, Jim, he told me *such* stories."

Jim Lewis had heard all this from his friend a hundred times over the years, as Nev had hoped against hope that someday he would realize his dream of being valet to a gentleman, but he let him go on, just as he always did, as if the words were fresh and new and every bit worth hanging on. He nodded his encouragement. "I am real pleased for you, Nev."

Neville slapped his friend's shoulder and smiled

his thanks. "I know you are, Jim. But listen. I was going to call on you. I think you should get the others together." The "others" to whom he referred made up the group now gathered round Mr. Waters's table. "I don't want you to say too much, because I want to tell them myself, and anyway, it is difficult to be certain yet. . . ."

"Certain about what, Nev? Get to the point, man," Jim said eagerly.

"Well, it appears that the marquess intends to remain at the Park for a few months at least."

Jim Lewis gasped. "Does he, indeed?"

Neville nodded. "He does. He told me so only this morning. . . ."

"And?" His friend could not help interrupting.

"Steady on, Jim." Neville laughed with the removal of one who has found his dream *and* the wages to go with it. "The marquess"—he already spoke the title with a great deal of pride—"told me that he shall need to take on some additional staff. . . . Here, Jim!" He laughed again as his friend hooted with delight. "If you can get everyone together, I'll tell them the news!"

"And so, Willard, there you have the tale—*again.*" Jim had, as instructed, omitted the part about the marquess planning to stay on in Painswick, but still the story was enough to give them something to think about.

As he uttered these words, the door to the little parlor opened to admit a trim, cheerful man of just below average height. He was well-dressed, immaculately turned out, with round cheeks and an enthusiasm about him that was bound to infect those he touched. The cries that went up reflected restlessness, friendship, and anxiety.

"Nev! Haven't seen you much lately."

"About time, Wainwright. Think we've got all night?"

"Come in and have a cup of tea, Neville." This from Sarah Waters as she patted his shoulder fondly.

"Think you're just the Queen's canary now, I suppose, eh, Nev?" Stephen Willard joked.

"Still late, as usual. Some things never change, do they?"

Neville accepted a cup of fragrant tea and sipped it carefully. "Sarah, you make the best cup of tea in Painswick."

"Never mind that, Nev," she rejoined promptly. "Tell us why we're all here, why don't you? Not that we don't all enjoy one another's company no end." She laughed and the others joined her.

"That's right, Neville," Mr. Pratt continued, for even he could not contain himself any longer. "Pray inform us as to why you have summoned us together this evening."

Neville looked slowly around the table, meeting the eyes of each person in turn. He smiled. "Seems he's staying."

There was a sound of cheers, huzzahs, and hoots as the assembled company expressed its pleasure with these words. Presently, Cornelius Pratt called the group back to order. "And for how long, may one inquire, Neville?" He asked carefully.

"Now, that I cannot say, Mr. Pratt, for the marquess has not confided those plans to me yet." He dearly hoped that his listeners might infer from this that the marquess had already formed the habit of disclosing his most private thoughts to his new valet. "However, I *can* tell you that the gentleman does intend to stay at least several months."

"Didn't I tell you?" Jim Lewis asked the table at large. He cast an amused glance at William Tabbard, who appeared to be grudgingly interested by this news.

"And he has asked me if I know of folks who might like to work for him whilst he is here." More glad noises. "I can tell you that he's a decent man who pays a fair wage."

Quiet had descended around the table as the friends looked at one another, and Neville let them ponder the news. Presently, Alfie Sharp broke the silence.

"So, he'll be needin' a porter, will he, Neville?"

Neville nodded. "He will, Alfie." He looked across at Will Tabbard. "Matter of fact, there's much work to be done and he needs two porters. Will, are you interested?"

"Aye, that I am."

"Well then," Alfie replied, "be nice to have regular, good-paying work for a change." He allowed a small smile.

"And a groom, Nev? He must need a groom." Jim Lewis's voice barely concealed his anxiety. He enjoyed his work at the Painswick livery stable but, like Alfie, he knew he could earn more from Templeton.

"He says as he does, Jim, although he hasn't many horses. Still, he wants them cared for properly. . . ."

"Well, I should hope so," interjected Jim, who was a great lover of animals, horses in particular.

Neville gave a laugh. "I know, Jim, I know. Well his groom will go back to London—his father is ailing—with the coachman." He turned his eyes to Stephen Willard, who sat next to him. "So he says, do I know a good driver?" Willard's eyes widened and Neville continued maddeningly, "I told him I would need to ask about and see if I could find someone who might be able to do the job."

His friend punched his shoulder and Neville feigned a groan. *"I'm* his man, Nev, and well you know it! You tell him that!" He smiled.

"I do and I will!"

"What about a cook? What's the poor man been doing all this time for his meals I should like to know." Irene Beatrice was as plump and as round as a biscuit, and it pained her to think that someone's meals might be less than they ought.

"Now a cook he has, Mrs. Beatrice, came here with him from London and would like to stay. A *man* don't you know!"

"Ooh!" cried the table at large, for male cooks were more expensive than their female counterparts and, in the country, were much less likely to be found.

"Lucky for Lord Templeton, since your services are already spoken for," Neville continued. "Getting on well at the Lodge are you?"

Irene smiled and nodded, her cheeks flushed with pleasure at the compliment. She patted beautiful waves of white hair. "Well, that's good, then," she pronounced in reference to the London servant. "My, yes, I have a very good position, and Miss Taylor is that nice to cook for. And it's a good deal better than doing for all those folks at the inn. Never knowing how many will be wanting a meal and catering to all *sorts* of tastes. Why, I could tell you stories. . . ."

"I am certain you could, Mrs. Beatrice. But to get back to Lord Templeton. The other servants who came with him don't much want to stay for one reason and another, so he's told them that as soon as they're replaced by you lot, they can go back to their jobs at his house in London."

Neville turned to the two oldest men at the table.

"Mr. Pratt, what say you? And you, Galen? He asked most particularly if he could find a good butler and an experienced gardener here in Painswick."

Cornelius Pratt was in service to a squire in the next village and was not especially happy there. He nodded. "If the marquess thinks that I might give satisfaction, then I shall be very pleased indeed to be butler at Templeton Park."

"Good!" Neville turned to Galen Waters, who had been in quiet discussion with his wife. They looked at each other now and nodded in unison. "We're thinking that Allen"—he referred to their son—"might be glad of the opportunity to manage the shop on his own, and those gardens at the Park can use all the help they can get, although I must concede that they're in better heart than you might expect with just the few men who have tended to them over the years. Nevertheless, they need a good deal of work and I must confess"—he grinned at Sarah—"that I'm itching to get my hands in that soil!"

The remaining members of the group, Alice Patch, Godfrey Brent, and Ursula Willard, sister to Stephen, had no steady work and all assured Neville of their interest in working as maids and footman at the Park.

"I assume," Cornelius Pratt put in, "that the marquess will be desirous of meeting with each of us before he makes any sort of formal commitment to extend employment to us?"

"He will," replied Neville. "I will speak with him about this meeting when I return to the Park, but I think you might come at around ten tomorrow morning to speak with him. I know that he will want you to begin as soon as you can."

"I'll go and make us some fresh tea." Sarah Waters got up from the table.

As they did sometimes when they gathered, the group began to exchange both first- and second-hand reminiscences about life at the Park.

"He is not a married gentleman, is he?" Mrs. Beatrice's assumption about the marquess was confirmed by the table at large.

"So," ventured Alfie Sharp, in a rather joking manner, "maybe while we're there, we can help the marquess find himself a wife—and *us* a permanent living. Be a far sight more than that other lot managed all those years ago!"

Several people exchanged glances. "Do you really think we might, Alfie?" Alice Patch inquired in her high-pitched, thin voice.

Alfie had spoken only half in jest. "Well," he replied thoughtfully, rubbing one eye with a large, gnarled hand, "you never know, Alice. Stranger things has happened, hasn't they? And it was their fault, them who worked at the Park for the marquess That Left I mean, that he *did* leave. And since they was our relatives, so to speak you know, who was responsible for the Park bein' closed and all, well, now that we have jobs there again . . ." He caught Cornelius's look. "All right, Cornelius, now that we *think* we have our jobs there . . ."

"Look, Alfie, those who were in service at the Park at the time can't be blamed because Lord Templeton and Rebecca Drabble didn't make a match of it." This came from Stephen Willard, well-known for his practical views of life. "I've never held with that old nonsense," he added sternly. "And neither should any of you."

"Ah, Stephen," chided Alice, ever the dreamer, "you don't have a romantic bone in your body."

"And I am that glad of it," Willard replied sharply.

"Well, but perhaps we did play a part in it, Stephen, if inadvertently. I was hardly more than a lad at the time, working as a boot boy at the Park." Cornelius Pratt's words were spoken slowly and with care. "The marquess and Miss Drabble had been smelling of April and May for some time. They were so much in love that it had become almost unusual to see one without the other. Everyone believed that the banns would be called quite soon."

Everyone in the room was familiar with this tale, some like Cornelius Pratt and Galen Waters, because they had lived it, others because they had heard it told so many times, but all listened as if the story had only just been written. Alice Patch sighed and made sheep's eyes at Godfrey, who was determined not to notice her.

Galen Waters took up the tale. "Always sending messages back and forth by the servants. *Meet me here,* she would say, or he would send her a posy or some trinket. And then one day, a message went undelivered. The two lovebirds had had a terrible argument. Afterwards, Miss Drabble had walked to the Park to see the master, but could not bring herself to go up to the house. Then, she saw little Jem Stoker, who worked in the stables, and sent him to the marquess to say she was sorry and would he come to call on her that afternoon. Only, Norman Blair, the head groom, sees little Jem heading up to the house and grabs his ear and puts him to work mucking out stalls. By the time the poor lad finished, he had forgotten his errand, so the message didn't get delivered. Of course, the marquess didn't know that a message had been sent and Miss Drabble didn't know he had not received it; she just assumed he was still angry at her.

"The next morning when Jem remembered his uncompleted task, he was too embarrassed and frightened to confess. He took his job so seriously, and he hated the thought that he had failed to carry out the lady's instructions. He told Blair . . ."

"That old rotter," William Tabbard put in.

"He told Blair what he had done—or *not* done, I suppose," Galen continued, "but the old rotter"— he gave a nod of acknowledgment in Tabbard's direction—"told him that if the master found out he had not done as he was told *when* he was told, there would be hell to pay, no matter that it had been chiefly Blair's fault that Jem had failed—I need not point out that he did not say that last part to him. And of course, Jem believed him. So he delivered the message and never said that it was the *previous* afternoon that Miss Drabble had wanted to meet the master. Poor mite, he was only eight as I recall; I was not much older than that myself, and he was not the brightest lad going. He didn't know any better."

Cornelius Pratt picked up the story again without missing a beat. "And so, Lord Templeton went to the copse—that is the spot where they often met— at the hour she had told to Jem, but he was a day late, only he didn't know it. Well, Miss Drabble was not at their spot, of course, when he arrived, just as he had not been there the day before when she went to meet him. He waited and waited, same as she had, but the lady never came. The master was a gentleman of considerable pride and he believed that she had deliberately made a fool of him. And as I already said, Miss Drabble thought he had not met her because he was still angry over their argument.

"Soon, it became apparent that matters between the pair had gotten worse, instead of better. Jem, once he realized both what had happened and the part he had played in it, went to Blair. So very upset he was. He asked Blair what he should do. Should he go to Miss Drabble or Lord Templeton? And Blair told the boy to keep his mouth shut. So did the other servants he asked. It was not long after this that Miss Drabble's cousin came for a visit and, before anyone knew it, they were betrothed and gone off to Devon to his people, where they would marry and make their home. So the two of them—the master and Miss Drabble, I mean—never did make it up, and the marquess left very soon after, as we all know."

"Aye," Alfie put in, "and shut up the big house and left all those people with no place to work. Nor those that came after them, neither. And I *still* say, and I've said as much before, that we've been paying for someone's carelessness ever since."

"You've the right of it, Alf," Tabbard interjected. "They made a mull of it and *that's* the truth. We might have had good lives at the Park all this time."

"Yes," Alfie continued, "and the Lodge fared no better. With Miss Drabble gone, her people left soon after, and ever since it's only ever been short-term tenants with their own servants and no real care for the place. No jobs for us there, neither."

"Now, Alfie, William, it isn't as if anyone's starved," Jim Lewis pointed out. "Those dismissed from the Park found work—well, I know it took some a while—and we've all been able to earn our crust since then, in one way or another."

Mrs. Beatrice agreed. "I say we've all put too

much stock in those old stories. Life at the Park sounded perfect, but it surely had its ups and downs just like everything else."

"Well, there's no arguing with that, Irene." Sarah Waters nodded her agreement and stirred more sugar into her tea.

"Still," Mrs. Beatrice went on, "it *is* nice to cook in a private house for a real lady, you know. The marquess probably is used to all sorts of fine things, and surely he'll be coming to dinner at the Lodge. I shall have to dig out all my special receipts to-night. . . ." The cook's thoughts wandered off and she became lost in the preparation of soufflés and joints for dozens of dinner guests, all of them members of the beau monde, of course.

"Maybe it's a curse that Miss Drabble or the marquess That Left put on us—well, *them*—for spoiling things," suggested the romantic Alice Patch, absently patting a green satin bow in her hair.

"Oh, Alice, for pity's sake, use your head!" William Tabbard practically barked at her.

Sarah shook her head. "Well, who can say what might have been? Perhaps we would have been there and perhaps not," she reminded Alfie and Tabbard logically. "And," she went on, "I think Irene is right. Who can say that we would have been happy there? You know, I have said to Galen more than once that I think we are just too sentimental about the Park." Several of the company made sounds of disagreement and she raised a hand. "Come. Those of us who were there"—she looked at Cornelius Pratt, her husband, and Alfie Sharp— "were very young, and the others—may they rest in peace—tended to remember only the happy times and to forget anything unpleasant. . . ."

"Now, Sarah . . ." Galen began.

She smiled at him and patted his arm lovingly. "Now, *Galen,* it is only natural for you to remember it all with such fondness." Sarah looked at her friends. "And so, we have always felt that we were missing something wonderful because we were not in service at Templeton Park."

A good deal of grumbling could be heard. "So, Sarah, are you telling us that we should not go to work for the marquess," Alfie huffed, "now that there is finally a marquess *there?*"

"Of course not, Alfie. I am only suggesting that we *all* of us may be expecting more than the poor man or the Park, for that matter, can give us. That is all."

Sarah Waters had heard the stories of life at Templeton Park and the marquess and Miss Drabble so many times over so many years that she very nearly felt as if she had been there herself. She had more than once been on the verge of speaking to her friends—and to her own husband as well—as she had just done, but had always pulled back, unwilling to cast a pall over their memories, if indeed they listened to her at all. But now, faced with the prospect of their going up the hill to work and being sorely disappointed, she had felt she must speak. Most of the group presently were willing to concede that actually working at the Park for its owner might not turn out to be as fine a development as they had hoped. Still, when the meeting ended a short time later, everyone was anxious to get home to savor the news with a husband or wife and to begin to prepare for the appointment with the marquess on the following day.

As Neville walked back to the Park, he reflected that he had not mentioned that Charles Templeton had, so far, failed to make much of a favorable impression on him. Well, of course, a gentleman's gentleman would never stoop so low as to spread gossip about his master, or to complain about his habits. Still, the former-shop-assistant-now-valet, had expected that a man of Templeton's stature and town bronze—folk in Painswick tried to keep up with the London doings of the only Marquess of whom they could boast, even if he were a nonresident—would dazzle with his polish, style, and elegant manners. But the sad fact was that, to date, the poor marquess had seemed not very much more than most of the quite ordinary men who had come into Mr. Tembo's shop. Neville had for years longed to work for a man of gentle birth, never daring to suppose there was any chance of his being valet to a peer. Such a man he could admire, so he believed, and the gentleman in his turn would appreciate the skills that he would bring to this all-important post.

Neville had worked for the previous five years for Mr. Walter Tembo. Mr. Tembo's establishment in New Street provided, according to the gold-lettering over the smart bow window with the glittering panes, "impeccable garments for the discerning gentleman." New Street had not actually been "new" for better than four hundred years, any more than most of Mr. Tembo's clientele could lay claim to the status of gentleman. Thankfully, the proprietor had early on realized that to flourish, or even to remain in business, he would have to stock the plain and practical clothing more suitable to the everyday life of countryfolk, and these items he sold in abundance. But he kept the sign over the window and continued to offer fine coats, shirts, and waistcoats, and these, too, were bought, albeit with considerably less frequency than the rest of his more mundane inventory.

Neville, whose cousin twice removed on his mother's side had been valet to the Marquess That Left, had listened as a lad to that fellow's tales about his long-ago employment with the nobleman and had wished for nothing more than to emulate his relative. He studied hard under Mr. Tembo, eagerly learning all those things that made a gentleman a gentleman, at least so far as his dress was concerned. He learned that a coat and trousers must fit just so, either to hide a customer's embonpoint or to show off his muscles. He discovered which fabrics were suitable for waistcoats and whether and when fobs and chains would be appropriate accoutrements to that garment. Tembo claimed to have worked in Weston's establishment in London where he had learned just how a gentleman of the haut ton ought to attire himself. He was an avid admirer of Beau Brummel, that supreme arbiter of men's fashion, who dictated that elegance in one's dress was achieved through simplicity and cut of the very best quality fabrics, and the tailor passed down these dictates to his enthusiastic assistant as if they were come from Mt. Sinai.

At thirty years of age, Neville was nothing if not quick of mind and ready and willing to grasp his chance when it came along, as he had always believed that it would. He had no sooner learned that Lord Templeton was staying at the Park than he had heard that the man's valet had taken a toss. Letting no grass grow under his feet, Neville had presented himself immediately at the mansion to inquire if its current master might require any assistance from a capable and hard-working fellow who knew a very great deal about a gentleman's habits and needs. The applicant hoped that he had been able to successfully conceal his surprise and glee when told by the marquess that his offer would be gladly accepted. And so, poor Neville, or Wainwright as his new master had come to call him, had been somewhat disillusioned to find that said master was not the top-of-the-trees dandy he had dreamed of and expected.

Mr. Rideout had, of course, waxed poetic about the sartorial splendor of Marquess Templeton. His coats were made from only the softest and best fabrics; his trousers conformed to his well-made legs without a wrinkle; his neck cloths, of the finest linen, were always perfectly tied, a job the master left to Rideout himself—and here Rideout had paused just the moment required to allow his acolyte a gasp of awe. All of this was necessary, he explained as if to an idiot, not only because the marquess was a gentleman of *impeccable* taste and discrimination, but because he mixed in "the most *privileged* social circles, don't you know, his attendance always being in demand at the bon ton's most elite events. Why, a ball or dinner simply is not *complete* without Lord Templeton. And as for the *ladies*, well, his manners, his dancing, his repartee, his looks, all ensure that he has his choice of any one of them, young or old."

But the ailing valet had made it painfully clear that he doubted poor Neville's ability to cater to Lord Templeton, let alone see that he was togged out as he should be. He had looked down his oversized nose at the younger man and, when he heard whence he came before appearing at Templeton Park, he had first been shocked; then he had guffawed—in the very coarsest way, Neville thought, although he dared not say so—at the cheek of a "mere clerk," as he had called him.

"I daresay, Wainwright, that by the time Lord

Templeton returns to London, which, by the way, I predict shall occur *much* sooner than he anticipates, he will be so desperate for *my* services that I shall find myself with a rise in pay the likes of which I have never dreamed!"

And all of this had, naturally, served to make Neville question everything he had ever been taught, certain that he had no idea at all of the best way to tie a neck cloth or how to keep his master's clothes clean and in good repair. Unfortunately, he had come to see very early on that none of that mattered much to Lord Templeton, who seemed to be more concerned with comfort than appearance and had yet to attend anything more stimulating than services at St. Mary's. Still, there was always hope. After all, the gentleman had not lately been at his best, as much of the time since his arrival had been spent in recovering from the injuries he had sustained in the carriage mishap.

Now, Neville rapped softly on the door and stepped into the library that had become his master's favorite part of the house. The room was of moderate size, small enough to be cozy and large enough to hold what the young man considered to be a vast quantity of finely bound books. These were accompanied by maps of lands real and mythical and an assortment of treasures that included an ancient astrolabe and various more modern sextants, a long-ago marquess having been quite keen on seafaring and exploration, even though he had never set foot on board a ship. Books climbed all the way up each of the two side walls, where narrow mahogany stairs could be rolled smoothly along brass fittings in order to reach volumes on the higher shelves. The roof on this part of the house sloped downward and large glass doors that comprised almost the entire outside wall, gave on to a view of the valley in the far distance and, nearer at hand, to a peaceful, small garden.

The late spring day was pleasantly warm and Neville spied the marquess outdoors. His master was propped against some cushions, long legs clad in kerseymere of an unremarkable shade of brown, stretched out along the length of an old teak bench. Templeton heard the sigh that escaped Neville's lips, but did not acknowledge it; neither did he try to contain a little smile, for he knew his appearance to be the cause of his valet's dismay. Templeton's shirt was nothing more than a simple cambric, unadorned by a single ruffle or stitch of embroidery. Its cuffs were unbuttoned, and while both sleeves had been rolled up, one had come down and hung loose in a mass of wrinkles around a hand that grasped a leather-bound volume. The collar of his shirt was spread wide in deference, as had been the unfastened sleeves, to the warmth of the day, and no neck cloth lay in intricate folds to relieve the Spartan character of the shirt or to make up for its state of déshabillé. As he read, Templeton's restless fingers had unknowingly rumpled his hair. Neville sighed heavily. His master certainly did not look like much of a marquess.

"Ah, Wainwright." An index finger kept his place in Wordsworth's *Poems in Two Volumes* and he looked up at Neville, blinking as the sun pierced the tree branches that hitherto had shaded his eyes. "Do you know where I might purchase a petticoat?"

Neville blinked back at him. "Did you say petticoat, sir?"

"I did, Wainwright. Do you know where I can purchase one?" he repeated.

"Er, well, my lord, I would suppose that one could

be had at Mrs. Kindle's Ladies' Bazaar." This establishment, just a few doors away from Mr. Tembo's shop in New Street, boasted that it could outfit my lady from head to toe, so Neville assumed that such a vast inventory surely must include the requested undergarment.

The marquess nodded, a smile playing with the corners of his mouth. "Good. Very good. Very well then, Wainwright, I should like you to go to ah"— he waved his free hand in a small and aimless circle—"Mrs. . . . Kindle's shop and buy me a petticoat. . . ." Templeton stopped midsentence, unable to hold back a laugh at the look on his valet's face, and began to rephrase his request. "That is, I wish you to purchase the garment so that I may give it to someone. . . ." Neville's scarlet countenance reflected little improvement at the receipt of this knowledge, Templeton quickly determined that, while his servant might be pleased that his master did not intend to use the petticoat himself, he was nearly as discomposed at the prospect of actually making the purchase of such an item. He took pity on him. "Never mind, Wainwright. I shall do it myself."

"Oh, no, sir. That is"—realizing he had just contradicted his master—"I shall of course do just as you ask, sir. I did not mean to . . ."

Templeton swung his legs to the gravel spread out evenly beneath the wooden bench and left Mr. Wordsworth behind him on the cushion. "No need. I do not mind going." He patted Neville's shoulder to emphasize that he had taken no offense at the servant's apparent demurral. "New Street did you say? I daresay I shall be able to find it. I shall go this afternoon."

Three

It had taken not much more than a few weeks for Lavinia to settle into her new home in Painswick. The old house was solidly built and structurally sound, but the lack of attention and care that came from years of alternating vacancy and less than fastidious tenants had left the property shabby and, in the eyes of its new owner, rather forlorn. She had spent what seemed endless hours supervising carpenters who repaired or replaced windows, doors, and walls, choosing paints and wallpaper, and overseeing the movement and placement of furniture. The surrounding grounds and outbuildings required just as much attention before the barn and stalls were, in her opinion, fit for occupation by those animals who did not live in the house.

Her sunny bedroom overlooked the garden that was spread like a multicolored carpet at the back of the house and, to the left, a large fenced pasture where Trillium, the goat who was the latest addition to the Taylor menagerie, Feathers, and Puck took their leisure. Several shade trees within the enclosure offered shelter from the milder elements, and clover and grass grew there in green abundance. The animals seemed content here, and Lavinia could be easy in her mind that she had done the right thing by moving them away from their familiar surroundings in London. The cats could often be seen stretched languorously along the fence, and the dog, Neptune, frequently crawled into the pasture to play tag with Trillium or to lie with his friends under the trees on warm afternoons. Phidippides stayed closer to Lavinia, but was learning his way about even better than she had hoped. He sometimes wandered off on his own to stretch out beside Orpheus's cage or in the quiet garden.

Orpheus sipped daintily from his water bowl and stretched his neck far back, beak pointed skyward, the better to speed the soothing liquid on its way. The little yellow bird had been warbling and tweeting for an hour and he was not at all used to such exercise. He shook his head rapidly and fluttered his feathers to rid them of the tiny drops of water that had splattered there as he drank, then settled more comfortably on his perch and sighed with contentment.

He liked the country. He had most definitely *not* liked the journey to get here, though, for it had been dark in his large, filigreed cage while the cover was on, as Lavinia had thought it ought to be for the first leg of their journey into the Cotswolds. Orpheus had been confused by the bumps and ruts and the unrelenting feeling of movement as they traveled, and his ignorance had made him frightened, which in turn, had made him fractious and painfully noisy. Lavinia wondered if people knew just how truly awful a canary could sound if it so wished. Thankfully, it had not taken her too many miles before she realized that removing the cover from the bird's little home might relieve his anxiety and give her some peace. He had blinked rapidly in the sudden light, then looked about him with quick little movements and soon settled. A short while later when Lavinia had slipped the cover back over the delicate wire of his cage to protect him from the dust that was rising in suffocating clouds from the turnpike, Orpheus had fallen sound asleep and did not make a peep of complaint.

It was a sunny afternoon in May, and Lavinia could imagine few things as boring as a discussion on what to feed a goat, but then she had known that Trillium's arrival in the household was bound to be a lot of work when she had taken her in. The undersized white goat had a dark brown mask that lent her a comically sinister appearance, especially when she crept, as she too frequently did, into the flower beds to feast on blossoms. Fortunately, she was endearing as well as wily and energetic, and liked to follow Lavinia as she worked in the garden, pushing her head into her mistress's hand for a pat. Little Trill had been so scrawny at birth that her neighbor, Mr. Stanton, had intended to drown the poor creature.

"She'll never amount to anything, never be a decent milker, but she'll eat me out of house and home. Just ask her mother." He had jerked his head in the direction of Angel, who stared placidly back as she suckled a demanding Trillium.

Lavinia, who had called to offer sanctuary to the animal, had entreated him, "But surely, Mr. Stanton, you would never be so cruel as to kill her? Why, just look at that sweet face."

The man had dismissed her pleadings with an earnest shake of his head. "Have to, Miss Taylor. Can't have anything here that doesn't pay for its own keep. That's the way of things. I take no pleasure in it, I promise you."

There had not been a hint of malice in his voice,

nor did he express any regrets now when he called at Greenbriar Lodge and saw how Trill thrived there. He had found Lavinia in what had been an herb garden, trying to determine if any of it might be salvageable. The two had been discussing Trill's diet for several minutes, with Mr. Stanton assuring Lavinia that the little goat should continue to flourish on the feed that she had been providing.

"And how are you getting on here at the Lodge, Miss Taylor?"

"Quite well, Mr. Stanton. I am very comfortable here."

He looked about and nodded. "Big place, this." She nodded back in acknowledgment. "And it's just you here? That's right, isn't it?"

She held back a smile, thinking how inaccurate it was that the female sex was said to produce the most notorious and incorrigible gossips. But she could easily understand the man's curiosity. Lavinia was still something of an unknown quantity in the little village, since she had not yet had much opportunity to get about and meet her neighbors, and Mr. Stanton, with a perfectly good excuse to call, probably had been deputized by his wife and a host of others to discover as much about her as possible.

"Yes, that is correct. Although with all my friends, I certainly do not want for company," she chuckled.

He leaned forward and stroked Phidippides's sleek gray head. "Well, Mrs. Beatrice must be taking good care of you. It's no secret that you deprived the village of some fine meals when you took her away from the inn, Miss Taylor." He teased her. "Now we must all be content with what our own kitchens can provide."

She laughed. "Mrs. Beatrice is a gift from the gods, Mr. Stanton. There is nothing that she does not prepare to perfection. I can easily understand why you miss her at the Swan's Nest."

After Mr. Stanton had taken his leave, Lavinia went to the pasture to check on the animals, then wandered into the back garden. She was, just as she had told Mr. Stanton, very happy in her new home. Its refurbishment, while not complete, was far enough along to allow her every comfort and, she had been pleased to find, to bear out her decision to purchase it. The effort had also kept her occupied. Lavinia had missed Uncle Amory keenly, but her friends and pursuits in London had helped to fill the void left by his death; her removal to the Cotswolds could have meant real loneliness had she not been so busy putting her new property to rights.

Now that the work was nearly finished, however, she was beginning to feel at loose ends. Lavinia had not yet made any real friends in the neighborhood and was too recent an arrival to have become involved in any village works such as the church or helping the sick, although she had every intention of participating in those efforts. Phidippides had stretched out in a shady spot on the brick path and was snoring loudly. Smiling at his contentment, Lavinia continued her rambling, stooping now and then to pull a weed or remove a blossom past its prime. She had supposed that, once village life made more demands on her time, this restlessness would go away, but lately she was less certain that this would be the case.

And it's just you here? That's right, isn't it?

For the last fortnight or so, a thought had been niggling at the back of her mind, one that she had not entertained for a long time: perhaps she ought to marry.

Later, long after the sun had set, Lavinia watched

fireflies turn on and off in arrhythmic syncopation outside her window. It might be quite nice to have someone to sit beside her, to hold her hand while they watched this delightful display. The give and take and comfort to be derived from a happy marriage were what she was discovering she craved in her life, now that she was settled here in Painswick. *I am not exactly on the shelf, so I hope that gentlemen would still consider me as a potential wife,* she thought. She wondered what it would be like to lean her head on a man's shoulder and share her thoughts and responsibilities and troubles with him, to consider the feelings and opinions of someone besides herself, something she had not had to do since Uncle Amory had died.

Looking around her at the candlelight illuminating rounded areas of soft yellow walls, she considered that perhaps a husband would not have wanted their bedroom to be painted yellow. Where else might they differ? Well, for one thing, she realized that not everyone would care for the rather spare style of furnishings that she favored; some folks, she knew, preferred heavier, more elaborate pieces— sphinxes and serpents and any number of winged creatures of every description. It was the sort of thing Lavinia heartily disliked, but she supposed that it was also one of those things on which she might need to compromise.

As she slipped a soft cotton nightdress over her head, Lavinia thought about the dozens of far more important matters on which a husband and wife could be expected to have conflicting opinions. Then she stopped. In her daydreaming, she had pictured a marriage where her feelings and preferences would be given equal weight with those of her husband, but that was not always the case, not by half. She was quite aware of marriages in which the man made all the decisions. Oh, he might indeed leave the choice of a room's color to his wife, but anything of real importance was decided by him, not by her. He could select his friends *and* hers, tell her how and on what to spend *her* money, choose where they would go and what they would do, and determine how their children would be raised. Why, if he felt so inclined, a woman's husband could beat her and there was little, if anything, that she might do about it, since she was little more than his property.

Lavinia drew up the covers snugly around her shoulders as she settled into bed, for the strong breeze that had come up made the night unseasonably cool, and smiled at the ghastly turn her thoughts had taken. *Honestly,* she chided herself, *this is 1818 after all and you are not some helpless green girl about to be married off by old-fashioned, uncaring parents to a monster who will treat you like chattel! You are of age, in possession of a considerable independence, and a good deal of common sense, all of which surely will prevent your contracting an alliance with such a creature.* Relieved by her own reasoning, Lavinia began to wonder just what sort of man she did want to marry.

Tall, she decided, without a care at all for all those important matters that had only just been occupying her thoughts. *He will have to be tall, for I am certain that I do not wish to look* down *upon the man I wish to look* up *to.* Lavinia had nearly achieved her full height, over five-feet-nine-inches, by the time she had reached her thirteenth birthday, and had been forced to endure the teasing of some of her friends, who christened her La-Vine-y-a, because they said she grew as tall as a vine. It was a name that, regrettably, had remained with her for a num-

ber of years. Even now, long after she had become
reconciled to and actually pleased with her height,
she thanked the gods of fashion for the flat shoes
that were *à la mode,* since so many of the men in
London had not been much taller than she was.

Charles Templeton is very tall, she remembered and
then wondered why she should have thought of
him, much less recalled any particulars about his
person. She told herself that she probably did so
because there were so few eligible men in Painswick,
and did not stop to probe for any other reasons
why he should have popped into her thoughts.

Of course, this yet-nameless husband must love
animals, otherwise, regardless of his height, there
would be no place for him in her life. *Templeton likes
animals—well, horses at least.* His own beast, Aristotle,
had been tethered within the shade of a tree for
his comfort when she found the marquess, and
there was also the concern he had expressed for
Puck when she had inadvertently pulled hurtfully at
the pony's reins. Recalling how he had snapped at
her then, Lavinia once again asked herself why Templeton should be on her mind. *Surely,* she told herself, *there are other men in the district who would make
good husbands. Yes, certainly there must be.* But she
knew that Painswick was decidedly short on unmarried gentlemen. *Hmm. I should have told Mr. Penn to
be sure to find me a place with lots of bachelors.* With a
little giggle that turned into a yawn, she decided to
give the matter further consideration later.

The next morning, Lavinia lingered over her
breakfast coffee, tapping a pencil thoughtfully on
the sheet of paper in front of her. She was planning
a party to help her get to know her neighbors better. An al fresco supper, she thought, would be just
the thing, with tables on the back lawn, and perhaps

archery boards set up for those who felt so inclined
before the meal. Lavinia herself had never tried it,
so knew little about the matter except that it looked
like it might be fun and she supposed it would be
a good way for her guests to get acquainted. She
wrote down "targets and other archery things," and
began absently tapping the pencil again. A moment
later, she chuckled. *Well, that makes no sense, you
know, the neighbors already know one another. It is* you
who are still the stranger in the village!

As for who to invite, Lewis Stanton and his wife,
Helen, were at the head of the guest list, since Lewis
had unknowingly inspired her to give the party and,
besides, they were her closest neighbors. The Stanton family had been in Painswick for generations
and their estate was one of the largest in the area,
second in size only to Templeton Park. Lewis was a
gentleman farmer whose practical opinions and
sound counsel were a sought-after commodity in the
neighborhood. Helen was the perfect complement
to Lewis, dispensing advice on domestic matters to
both new brides and established matrons.

Albert Breverton and his sister, Cynthia Weld,
would make good additions to her list. Their few
brief meetings, the last laughing as they dodged
huge puddles during a downpour that had turned
Gloucester Street into a small river, had been most
pleasant. Mrs. Beatrice had told her that the siblings
were devoted to one another, with Cynthia, the
elder by a mere seventeen months, having always
looked out for her younger brother.

"Even though he must be getting close to sixty
by now and more than able to take care of himself,
I should think," Irene Beatrice had explained with
a smile and a shake of her head. "Why, he didn't
exactly die of neglect all those years that Mrs. Weld

was married to her Frederick and living in Cirencester, now did he? Still, after Mr. Weld passed on, she came back here to keep house for her brother. Said she just could not see the sense of living all alone there—her two sons have gone off to live in America—and Mr. Breverton, living by himself here—he never married, you know—and I suppose that does make some sense."

Before long, Lavinia had added several more names to her paper, including widower Chester Stone and his children, Clarissa and Harold. He had been introduced to her after church by the vicar's wife and subsequently they had met several times after service at the tea table frequently set up on the church green. Lavinia could not say that she knew Mr. Stone at all well, but she believed she had detected a definite interest on his part, and she was not averse to knowing him better.

Finally, she penciled in the name of Dorothea Caton, a particular favorite, despite the fact that she did not know her much better than she did the others on her list. They had met at Mrs. Kindle's Ladies' Bazaar when they had simultaneously reached for the same bolt of checked muslin.

"Oh, dear, I am sorry!"

"Pardon me!"

They had both laughed, each holding the opposite end of the length of fabric.

"Now, now, ladies, I beg you will not come to blows here in my little establishment." Mrs. Kindle chuckled. "Only give me a moment and I promise to find something else just as fine as that dark blue. Ah! Here you are, this nice Nile green check is just the thing."

"Oh, yes, please." Lavinia nodded and released her end of the bolt, still laughing. "That would be lovely, Mrs. Kindle." She turned to her opponent and extended a hand not nearly as soft and white as it had been when it resided in London. "I am Miss Lavinia Taylor. I live at Greenbriar Lodge."

"I am glad to meet you, Miss Taylor. My name is Dorothea Caton and you can find me, should you care to now that you have seen how ruthless I can be when I cannot have what I want, not too far from you, in Bisley Street."

Dorothea Caton's tone was dry. Past middle age, but still quite fit and attractive, her cheeks shone with high color and her still-lustrous black hair was dusted only lightly with gray. She had a throaty voice that could be a bit loud, and her smile was unusually and engagingly wide.

"And good for you, Mrs. Kindle." She nodded in the dressmaker's direction, then looked back at Lavinia. "That green would look a sight better on you, Miss Taylor, than it would on me. I could never wear it."

Before Lavinia could respond to this assessment at least as it applied to herself, the other woman went on. "And is it not wonderful that I may truthfully pay such a compliment and still get what I want?"

Lavinia, at first, did not know how to take the lady or her words. Was she bold, amusing, honest? Deciding that Mrs. Caton must be all three, Lavinia laughed in agreement.

"Yes, Mrs. Caton, I must say that it is."

"Good, I made sure that you would not wish to come to cuffs with one so much older than you, Miss Taylor."

She could already sense that there would be little use in uttering the usual polite demurs at this statement. "I willingly accept your wise counsel, Mrs. Caton," Lavinia replied with a smile.

The two had chatted amiably for a long while as they browsed through Mrs. Kindle's pattern books and tempting fabrics and trims, each promising to call on the other soon. The very next day, Mrs. Caton had stopped at Greenbriar Lodge and was invited to stay to tea. Despite the number of years that separated them, the two women had a great deal in common.

Dorothea Caton was eager to hear a firsthand description of the latest goings-on in London, being especially interested in the plays recently staged in the theaters. Lavinia was pleased to satisfy her new friend's curiosity, relating all the details she could recall of her last visit to the theaters in Covent Garden and Drury Lane, where she had attended a performance of *The Merchant of Venice* with Edmund Kean in the starring role. Mrs. Caton had seen Kean once a number of years before in the provinces and had thought him promising, and she had been very pleased to read that he had found success in London. On a brief visit to the metropolis with her late husband, Kemble had been performing in *Macbeth* with Mrs. Siddons, and the evening had left so strong an impression on Mrs. Caton that her eyes still sparkled when she spoke of it. She and Lavinia shared their opinions of these and other actors and the plays they had seen until they had drunk an entire pot of China tea and consumed far too many apple tarts.

"I remember Kemble's deep, resonant voice. It was like magic." Lavinia nodded in agreement. "Such talent, my dear. Why, I defy anyone not to weep when he enacts a tragedy."

"I agree, Mrs. Caton. He has an almost uncanny

ability to virtually become the character he is portraying. Kean is the same way. You should have seen his Shylock. Did Mr. Caton also enjoy attending the theater?"

"Oh, indeed, yes. Every bit as much as I, thank heaven." An unspoken memory brought a bright smile to her face. "And, as I mentioned, we attended productions outside of London, of course, whenever we could, but once I had a taste of the plays performed in our capital, they spoiled me a bit for the rest."

Their talk turned to books, and they found they both had a great love of reading. Mrs. Caton spoke enviously of the bookshops and lending libraries that were so easily to be found in London.

"Ah, Miss Taylor, you cannot know—oh my, but you shall soon—how very tedious life can be in Painswick where we cannot boast a bookshop such as Hatchards! I do love our little village, for in all other respects it lacks nothing. But my dear, I ask you, how can a town, even one so small as Painswick, claim to be civilized if it has no place where one may purchase or borrow a book?"

This was a predicament of which Lavinia had until now been unaware. She had been so busy since arriving in Painswick that she had not yet had the time to finish reading those books she had brought with her from London. Now that Mrs. Caton pointed out this shortcoming, she realized that she had not noticed a bookshop in the village.

"Oh dear, that is unfortunate. Where is the nearest shop then?"

"In Stroud. And do not hope for much, because Mr. Broadbent's establishment would hardly be worth the trip if it had even the least bit of competition in the vicinity." She brightened. "Well, I am *so* very pleased to find that you enjoy reading, Miss Taylor, for we may borrow each other's books, you know. Oh," she added quickly, "that is, if you care to, of course!"

Lavinia just as quickly assured her guest that she would be quite happy to trade books.

"Do you exchange with anyone else in the village?" Lavinia inquired, hoping that the circle might be wider than just the two of them.

"Yes, with Albert Breverton and his sister, Cynthia Weld. They have a very nice library, although Albert's share of the collection runs pretty heavily to history and mythology." She sniffed.

Lavinia had shown her guest into her own small library and Mrs. Caton examined it with enthusiasm. "Such eclectic taste! Coleridge, Mrs. Radcliffe—ah, I see you have one or two I do not, wonderful!—Byron, Fanny Burney, Cowper, Wordsworth, Defoe. Oh, this is splendid, Miss Taylor. You must come soon to see what I have. Much of it was my husband's, who enjoyed a good tale. We used to take turns reading to each other on winter nights." She sighed happily.

"You must miss him a great deal."

Mrs. Caton nodded. "I do and that is a fact, even after four years without him." They had returned to the tea table and Lavinia called to her maid for another pot. "But I must say," she confided, "that I miss just being married almost as much as I miss my dear Theodore."

Lavinia took a sip of her fresh, warm tea, then set the cup carefully back in its delicate, flowered saucer. "Indeed?"

The older woman tilted her head a bit and smiled. "I daresay that sounds a bit . . . odd." She considered a moment and raised her brows. "Perhaps it is. It is only that I miss the companionship. I miss having someone who knows the things that I like and dislike, and I miss having someone to take care of." She gave a little laugh. "I fear that might sound as if *any* gentleman would do as a husband and I do not mean that at all."

"Of course not," Lavinia assured her.

"Have you never been married?"

"I have not."

"Hmm. But surely you had the opportunity." Mrs. Caton's kindly smile and tone redeemed her intrusion.

"Well, I . . . I cannot say that I was ever much tempted to accept. So many marriages I have seen were less than happy, and I never was sufficiently sanguine to feel that marriage to any of the gentlemen who offered for me might prove any better. It just seemed safer to remain unwed. Although heaven knows it is not easy to be an unmarried lady!" Lavinia chided herself for speaking so candidly with a woman she barely knew, something that, as a rule, she did not do, but Mrs. Caton's easy, kind manner encouraged frankness. "Since the passing of my uncle"—she had earlier mentioned her loss—"I have begun to feel a bit alone and . . ."

Her guest was nodding with an understanding smile. "Well, we shall have to . . ."

She was interrupted by a soft tap on the door. A maid entered, carrying a package wrapped in brightly printed paper and tied with a large, floppy, yellow satin bow.

"Pardon, Miss Taylor, this was just delivered for you."

"From Mrs. Kindle's shop; that is how she wraps her packages, you know." Mrs. Caton said.

"It cannot be for me. I only bought that ecru morning dress and it will not be ready until Thursday week."

"Do you know, Miss Taylor, I still think you should have had Mrs. Kindle make up that blue striped poplin we looked at, and the green as well. No woman can ever have too many gowns, and that shade of green on you . . ."

"Mmm." Lavinia had been tempted to have gowns made just as Dorothea Caton recommended, and a new habit besides, but had decided she could just as well make do with what she had. Funny, but she had not had much interest in fashion since she left London, a fact she put down to less need and, to be honest, less competition from other ladies of high fashion, a breed not very common in Painswick. But ever since returning from Mrs. Kindle's Ladies' Bazaar, she had regretted not purchasing the gowns and riding habit.

"In any event," Mrs. Caton said interrupting her ruminations with undeniable logic, "this box is much too small to contain such a dress, Miss Taylor."

"You are right, of course. What could it be?"

The maid shook her head. "But it has not come from the dress shop, ma'am, at least not directly."

Lavinia blinked. "Well, where did it come from, Margaret?"

"The man said he was from Lord Templeton, Miss Taylor."

Dorothea Caton's eyebrows shot up and she turned boldly inquisitive eyes on her hostess. Lavinia peeked at her and flushed. "Lord Templeton?" The maid nodded. "I see." Lavinia frowned. "Er, very well, Margaret, you may put it upstairs, please."

Mrs. Caton only barely suppressed a squeak of disappointment, for she could hardly press Lavinia to open the package in front of her. *Well,* she thought, *this is a turn up. It would seem there is more to Miss Taylor than meets the eye. And to the marquess, as well.*

A short time later, Lavinia sat in a chair by a window in her bedroom, the still-unopened parcel in her lap. She had half a mind to return it in the same condition in which it had arrived, but good manners and, although she hated to admit it, curiosity, precluded such bold action. With a sigh of exasperation, she untied the ribbon, which she then rolled up and put aside to add to her sewing basket later. Once the paper had been removed, she sat for a few moments with her hands on the box, wondering what could have possessed Templeton to send her anything.

Presently, Lavinia took off the lid and drew aside the tissue that covered the contents, inadvertently letting a small white envelope fall to the carpet; then she withdrew Templeton's gift. Furious, she rose from her chair, sending box and tissue onto the floor beside the card, and held the present aloft, momentarily speechless. The petticoat was snowy white linen, entirely plain until the bottom, where there were not one but two deep flounces here and their exquisitely embroidered with deep purple violets.

"Oh . . . oh! How dare he?" Lavinia sputtered and began to pace. "The effrontery of the man!" Stepping on the previously unnoticed envelope, she bent to retrieve it. Not surprisingly, the note's contents did nothing to assuage her nerves.

My dear Miss Taylor:
    May I hope that you will accept this small gift as a token of my gratitude for your invaluable assistance.

*I can only say that no other ladies of my acquaintance
would have possessed the ability to come to my aid as
you did. You will notice that this petticoat, which I
feel compelled to offer as a replacement, your having
so nobly sacrificed its venerable forebear, has two
flounces.*

*I must point out that this is not extravagance, but
practicality. In the event, heaven forfend, that you find
yourself again coming to the rescue of a discommoded
gentleman, you can safely forfeit a ruffle and not have
the garment become entirely useless to you.*

With most sincere appreciation, I am your servant,

Charles Templeton

For just a moment, Lavinia thought she might
have clouted the fiend, had he been present, *venerable* petticoat, indeed! And after daring to presume
to make her such a gift at all! But suddenly she saw
the humor in the situation and began to laugh
heartily. Templeton might be a rogue, but he was
an entertaining one, and she had a great liking for
people with a sense of humor.

Perhaps she ought to add his name to her guest
list. She would never wish him to accuse Lavinia
Taylor of being so toplofty that she could not see a
joke, no matter that she had to be less than ladylike
to accept such a gift from a gentleman who was a
virtual stranger to her, *and* be pleased about it into
the bargain. *But what of Mrs. Caton? What must she
think? Who knows,* she considered wryly, *polite society
in Painswick may be less discriminating than it is in London. Mrs. Caton may not have thought it gauche that a
man I hardly know*—for various neighbors had been
a topic of conversation during her visit—*had sent me
a gift and that I had accepted it, but she might be shocked
to find out what that gift was!*

Someday, Lavinia decided, she would have the opportunity to give Templeton a good trimming over this, but for now she would hold her tongue. Doubtless her other guests would be glad of the chance to get to know him. Moreover, her acquaintance with the recent arrival had come up in her conversations with Mr. Stanton, and surely he would wonder if Templeton were absent. Templeton himself might think she was trying to avoid him if she did not issue him an invitation, and she would never allow the man the satisfaction of believing he had gotten the best of her. True, she did believe that his behavior on the occasion of their initial meeting had been arrogant, abrasive, and uncouth, but she had also glimpsed humor and compassion. The circumstances of their encounter had been trying. Surely, Lavinia reasoned, his good qualities must exist in greater abundance than he had demonstrated at the time. In any event, it made sense to give him the benefit of the doubt. After all, one was bound to meet him constantly in a village of this size. And, if the truth were told, it would be interesting to see how the inept Lord Templeton was getting on here in the country. She hoped for his sake that he had managed to overcome the clumsiness she had witnessed in him.

Well, I seem to have little choice, Lavinia at last convinced herself. *There.* She added his name with a flourish and finally put aside the list.

Four

If Lavinia had been furious upon receipt of the petticoat, Templeton had been most pleased with himself for thinking of such a gift. While the bestowal of similar presents was not outside his experience, like most gentlemen, Templeton normally presented them to certain kinds of women, but never to ladies of his acquaintance. He had made an exception in Lavinia Taylor's case first because he felt the delicate subject of a lady's undergarments had been raised, so to speak, at their meeting, second because he felt it only proper that he replace what he had, effectively, ruined, and third because he wanted to get a little of his own back and he sensed that she was both proper enough to be angry with him and good-humored enough to see the jest.

It also occurred to him that, once in possession of such a garment, it might occur to Miss Taylor to give more thought to her appearance. He had noticed that her gown had been faded and her coiffure most definitely démodé. Of course, Templeton realized that this was the country and folk might not, generally speaking, be expected to maintain the high standards he was used to in town. Still, Miss Taylor had possibilities: nice eyes, good teeth, a fine figure, he *thought,* although it was difficult to be certain what was under that ancient gown she had been wearing when they met, and he had a natural objection to any woman's hiding her light under a bushel, as it were. It even occurred to Templeton that he would be more than willing, were the lady to ask him nicely, to give her some much-needed advice on how to dress and perhaps fix her hair. After all, life in London and especially life with Althea, had required that he be up to the minute in all the latest fashions for ladies as well as gentlemen.

Moreover, if he were going to spend any length of time in Painswick, as he felt more than inclined to do, he would need something other than his books and his property to keep him amused, and his forays thus far into village life, limited though they were, had shown him that opportunities for female company were meager and rested largely on Miss Lavinia Taylor and two widows well-above his own age.

If I am going to pay my attentions to Miss Taylor, I . . . Templeton stopped himself in midthought. *Pay attentions to Miss Taylor? What in heaven's name? It's one thing to pass the time, old man,* he lectured himself sternly, *that is all well and good, but paying one's attentions to a lady is quite another thing altogether!* It was not as if Lavinia could compare to the sort of female he was used to. She was not so pretty or sophisticated, and certainly not so chic as the London ladies of his acquaintance. He was compelled to acknowledge, however, that she was also not so sharp or brazen as they sometimes could be. It occurred to him that, on the whole, Miss Taylor might not be at all bad to know. He would simply make it entirely clear from the outset that his attentions were not intended to lead to any sort of permanent relationship, and he would be free to enjoy her company.

While the marquess was generously forgiving of Lavinia Taylor's social imperfections, he had failed to pay much attention to the changes that had been wrought in him. Poor Neville Wainwright was well aware of them, and he had not yet given up his attempts to reinvigorate Templeton's interest in his own appearance. Since his retirement to Painswick, Templeton's attire had become much less formal and deliberate. His intricate cravats tied in the Mathematical mode, Rideout's proudest accomplishment achieved only after weeks of practice, had been replaced by mere colored handkerchiefs tied in a loose, simple knot. His gorgeous, figured silk waistcoats had been usurped by fine but rather dull cottons that demanded far less meticulousness of habit from their wearer. Templeton brushed aside Wainwright's repeated entreaties to encase him in tight-fitting coats, and declined the poor man's attempts to wrap his closely shaven neck in the white stocks he had carefully ironed and which he was so eager to try his hand at tying. His explanation that his casual dress, which by the way, was of equally exceptional quality as his London clothes, was more comfortable for country pursuits made Neville feel no better, since it was his belief that a marquess, especially one who was also a Corinthian, ought to be doing more lordly things than examining the state of his hay barns.

More than Templeton's appearance had changed. His new life was taken up with estate matters, much to the delight and surprise of his agent, whose lot it had been to make all decisions himself after going through the motions of asking permission and advice on matters of substance. Templeton took to roaming his property on foot or on horseback and, before very long, became a familiar and welcome face to his tenants. His village neighbors were less known to him, although he had consulted once or twice with Lewis Stanton who was, he found, highly thought of by one and all, including his agent, Clarence Best. When he was not tramping through his fields or discussing roofs or land management with Best, Templeton spent hours reading, something he had enjoyed tremendously as a boy—he had a fond memory of reading a history of Rome when he was about twelve and confined to his bed for more than two weeks with the mumps. In recent years, other entertainments had left him little time for books, and so he had begun to discover the secrets of his extensive library with great delight.

Charles Templeton was, much to his own surprise and delight, very happy with his life in Painswick, much happier than he had dared to hope he might be away from the entertainments and distractions of the city. He did not yearn to return to town, went days without thinking of London or his friends there, and spent little time thinking, *I might be going to the opera at this hour* or *It would feel good to go a round or two with Welles at Gentleman Jackson's,* and he certainly did not miss Althea Hubbard. Unfortunately for Templeton, she missed him, or at least what she believed he could offer her, very much indeed.

"He never did!"
"You don't say!"
The ribbons on Margaret's white cap fluttered as

she nodded her head first toward Sarah Waters, then Irene Beatrice. "He did!"

"Oh dear. A *petticoat* did you say, Margaret?"

"I did." Another vigorous nod as Margaret described finding the petticoat on Lavinia's bed. "Had to have been the one that was in the box, you know, because I've never seen that in Miss Taylor's laundry. And then, I would remember those little violets at the bottom. *And* it's new besides; Miss Taylor's petticoats could do with some replacing, as I've already told her." Margaret had accompanied Lavinia from London, but had soon become great friends with the two older retainers.

"In *my* day, a gentleman did not give a lady undergarments."

"Nor in mine, Irene," pronounced Sarah Waters. "Tsk. Can you imagine?"

Both older women looked askance at Margaret, the younger by a good number of years, as if she might explain the motives and behavior of the generation that she shared with Lavinia and Templeton, but she shook her head vigorously in denial. "Nor in mine, I assure you!"

"And especially not unmarried ladies and gentlemen, Sally," Mrs. Beatrice further defined the solecism.

"Quite right. And it took my Galen a few years after we were wed before he dared to make me such a gift." Sarah smiled.

"They both are from London, remember. I have heard that town folk are much bolder, more forward, do you know, than we are here in the country. . . ."

"No, Irene, I cannot believe that such a thing goes on even there, at least not between *respectable* people. And we know that Miss Taylor and the marquess are most respectable."

"Mmm. True."

When Margaret had arrived with the news of the petticoat, Sarah Waters, who was housekeeper for the marquess, and Irene Beatrice had been sitting in the former's parlor, sharing stories about their new jobs.

"Was Miss Taylor angry about the petticoat?"

Margaret tilted her head to one side. "Hard to say for certain. At first, she seemed quite put out—before she even opened the package. I think she was also a bit embarrassed because Mrs. Caton was visiting when it was delivered. I happened to be passing her room when she opened it and I could hear that she was quite miffed. But afterward, she did not seem very much perturbed. As a matter of fact, she gave me these party invitations to deliver an hour or two afterward and there was one there for the marquess."

Her companions' eyes popped. "You don't say!" Sarah Waters exclaimed.

"Please, Sally, let's not start *that* all over again!" Irene laughed. "Well, you just cannot tell about people, can you? My guess is that she might fancy him, but she is still in a pucker about that sort of gift—whatever happened to sending a lady flowers, I should like to know—and will see to the gentleman in her own good time. She strikes me as that sort of woman."

Margaret added, "I think there must be a romance brewing. For I cannot think of another reason why he should do such a thing and why she should accept it."

"But I thought they had met just that one time,

when Miss Taylor helped him after his carriage accident."

"It would seem that they know one another a little better than that. Perhaps they have met since then and we below stairs just have not been aware of it."

The older women looked at Margaret and chuckled at this suggestion. "My dear child," Sarah explained as if to someone a bit slow to understand, "that is quite impossible. Servants know everything. Just ask the people we work for." She caught Irene's eye and they both laughed aloud.

"At least, they believe that we do." The cook paused. "If we knew all the things our employers thought we did, we should have precious little time left for work."

Sarah's thoughts turned to the more practical side of things. "Do you think that she will wear it, Margaret? The petticoat."

There was a sharp intake of breath as the maid expressed disapproval at such a thought. "I should think not, Mrs. Waters."

"Well why not?" Irene asked. "Since she has not sent the petticoat back, he already believes she's accepted it, as indeed she has! And remember she has no idea that anyone else knows what was in the box, so she would think that she could wear it without worry. Were you to bring up the matter, Margaret, she could simply tell you that she had purchased the garment herself at Mrs. Kindle's shop."

A soft rap on the door was followed by Galen Waters's voice. "My dear, may I come in? I have Neville with me."

The two men entered the room and nodded at the ladies present. "Ah, it is good to see our friends from the Lodge. Irene, Sarah told me you were coming to tea, and Margaret, how good to see you, as well. How are things getting on at Greenbriar?"

The group spent a pleasant quarter hour talking about everyone's satisfaction with their new positions, how much they liked their master or mistress and how "comfortable" things felt at their respective residences. At length, Galen said, "Ahem, I think you may be interested in what Neville has to tell you."

Neville looked a bit uncomfortable, but wasted no time in imparting his news. "Well, as I was telling Galen, I was that surprised . . ."

It did not take long for Neville to relate what he knew about the petticoat. "He went and purchased it himself, and the next thing I knew, he had young Tim running over to Greenbriar Lodge with this enormous package all dressed up like a"—he had been about to say "tart," and glanced at the assembled women and blushed—"like a . . . a . . ."

"We know what the box looked like, Neville," Margaret said coming to his rescue. "I've just been telling Mrs. Waters and Mrs. Beatrice."

Neville sipped at his tea and thought. *Imagine giving a lady an undergarment! And here in our little village!* Such behavior he had never expected from a peer. *On the other hand,* he asked himself, *why should you be surprised? The marquess has not exactly lived up to your other expectations.* He had been so flustered by Templeton's action that, had his master not needed him to see to his bath—a matter that took upwards of two hours, the marquess being quite as particular about his hygiene as he had ever been—he might have arrived below stairs to tell his news even before young Tim reached the Lodge with the petticoat.

As it was, Neville had met Alice Patch on his way

and, unable to contain himself, had told the maid all. Alice had reacted predictably enough. Only momentarily surprised at such forward behavior, she was quickly convinced that, if love were not blossoming in both the parties' hearts, then it must be just the marquess who was smitten, and wouldn't it be a terrible shame if they did not help matters along for the poor man?

"And what makes you think that Lord Templeton and Miss Taylor, if, in fact, we should even be speaking of them in the same breath that is, need or want our help, girl?" William Tabbard inquired of Alice between slurps of tea.

Templeton's servants were gathered as usual for their afternoon meal and the sole topic of conversation, thus far, had been the petticoat, already elevated in reputation to the status of The Petticoat. Since even the most content of the group had lately begun to tire of hearing how happy one and all found their lives at the Park, their master's gift of an undergarment to Miss Taylor was seized upon with alacrity even by those who pretended to have no interest in the suppositional romance.

It was a wonderful, if by now somewhat tired, fact that Sarah Waters's concern that her friends might be disappointed with their employers had been groundless, for the servants had found everything to be all that they could have wished. Galen Waters's garden was already showing signs of his efforts, and his lordship had told a beaming Cornelius Pratt that his presence and competence could rival that of any London majordomo. Jim Lewis's wife had all she could do to keep her husband from sleeping in the Templeton stables, so proud was he to be there, and Irene Beatrice was so happy with Lavinia Taylor that she thought she might burst. Even Alfie Sharp and the laconic William Tabbard had been heard to wax poetic about their new situations.

"I should think their need for our help would be obvious, even to an old curmudgeon like you, William," Alice now replied loftily. "They must be in love and we must help them find each other!"

"Good God!" Stephen Willard interjected. "Will you listen to the child, then?"

"I do believe that they can 'find each other' quite well enough without our assistance, Alice," Cornelius Pratt pointed out rather more gently than Stephen Willard.

"You just keep to your place, girl. Nobody needs help from the likes of you, especially not your betters. You remember that." William Tabbard had much less patience than Cornelius, particularly since the discussion was also slowing the progress of the bread down the table in his direction. "Find yourself out of a situation, if you're not careful."

"Now, what would the old servants have done in this situation, I wonder?" Alfie asked with a mouthful of muffin.

"Who cares?"

"Stayed out of it if they had an ounce of sense, I should imagine, Alfie!"

"Yes, Alfie. Just remember what happened the last time one of us interfered with them," Ursula Willard said with a nod of her head. "The master left and never came back!"

"No, no, Ursula, that was because we didn't, that is, they didn't—I will not say 'interfere,' because that is not at all what I mean. . . ."

"All right, Alf, say 'meddle' then." This from Jim Lewis who never could resist tweaking the older man's nose.

"I suppose it might not hurt to try." Everyone

turned to look at Sarah, who gave a little laugh. "Well, why not?" This was no small concession from a woman as practical as Sarah Waters. "I cannot say which way the wind is blowing. I do not think anyone knows if Miss Taylor returns the marquess's feelings or, indeed, if there are any feelings to return." She raised a hand to ward off Neville's imminent defense of his master. "I know, Neville. I am certain that you are about to tell us that the marquess is an honorable man and he would never behave in such a fashion if his heart were not engaged." He nodded. "And I hope you are right. Otherwise we shall all find we are employed by a rake." Her eyes twinkled. "I think we are all agreed that we should proceed on the assumption that he does have good intentions and, until we find out otherwise, that Miss Taylor does not find his attentions entirely unwelcome."

There was no noticeable disagreement and Jim Lewis added his thoughts. "Let us say for now that we shall just all keep our eyes and ears open to any opportunity that might arise to further relations between them."

"Well said, Jim. Very eloquent indeed." Cornelius Pratt absently ruffled his hair, still bright red even though he was in his sixties. "I certainly think we ought to do that. But"—he winked at Alice Patch— "I think a nice, firm nudge in the right direction might be in order." Murmurs of assent followed this suggestion. "After all, if they do not suit, the marquess and Miss Taylor will be no worse off for our efforts."

Once again, there was general agreement. Sarah did not inform her friends of the details that she, Margaret, and Irene had worked out after the departure of Galen and Neville from her parlor, deciding that there had been sufficient mention of unmentionables in mixed company for one day.

"Miss Taylor, I should like to introduce Mr. Thomas Darnall. He is nephew to my late husband and has been living in Italy for years; we have only just met, in fact. He is making a stay of a few months with us in Painswick while he decides where to make his permanent home," Mrs. Weld explained.

Lavinia bobbed her greeting to the tall, very well-dressed gentleman, who added a dazzling smile to his nod of acknowledgment. "Welcome to the neighborhood, Mr. Darnall. I hope you will enjoy your visit. Do sit still, Neptune," she patiently instructed the hound at her side. "How pleasant that you and Mrs. Weld can spend this time together."

"Yes, indeed, ma'am. My aunt tells me that you are rather new to the village yourself, Miss Taylor."

"That is correct, sir. I have been here for just a short time." She hesitated a moment. "I am having a supper for some friends at Greenbriar Lodge, that is my home"—she waved her basket behind her— "the day after tomorrow. Your aunt and her brother have kindly agreed to come and I hope that you will also, Mr. Darnall. We can both of us get to know our neighbors a little better if you do!"

"You honor me, Miss Taylor. I shall look forward to it."

"Well," Lavinia remarked to Neptune as they continued on their way to the baker's shop, "Mr. Darnall seems like an amiable gentleman, doesn't he? And wasn't it nice that Mrs. Weld took the time to make a proper introduction?" Neptune's expression indicated that he would be perfectly willing to agree with anything she might say for the small price of a pat on the head. Lavinia complied. "Good dog. He is rather handsome, too, don't you think so, Neptune? And well-spoken." Suddenly, she found herself looking forward to her supper party a good deal more than when she and Neptune had left Greenbriar Lodge. She looked down at the skirt of her afternoon dress that was at least two seasons out of date and grimaced. "Goodness! Whatever am I going to wear?"

Mrs. Beatrice had sighed repeatedly that she was too busy to spare the kitchen maid to pick up the Lodge's order of bread and Lavinia, who felt like taking a walk, had at last offered to do the errand. The delicious aromas of Mr. Clover's shop cloaked her as soon as she opened the door. Neptune, who was tethered to the post outside, gave a disgruntled "woof" as the smells wafted in his direction, and settled down to wait hopefully for his mistress. Mr. Clover's clerk was assisting customers while the proprietor himself proudly saw to the request of Charles Templeton.

"Will it be your usual, my lord? The apricot tarts? They look especially tasty today, don't they?"

"They do indeed, Mr. Clover"—Templeton smiled—"but I fear that if I don't try something else I will be coming dangerously close to a certain chap in London name of Alvanley. . . ."

"Beg your pardon, sir?" The allusion was lost on the baker.

Lavinia, standing close enough to hear this exchange, chuckled. Templeton looked over his shoulder and grinned. He took in at a glance her outmoded gown and less than perky bonnet, noting that both had once been of the first stare. "Miss Taylor." He tipped his hat. "How very pleasant to see you."

She gave him a nod that was proper and nothing more. "Lord Templeton." She turned to smile at the shopkeeper. "Mr. Clover, Lord Alvanley is a bit of a dandy who lives in London. He once took such a fancy to apricot tarts that he ordered his cook to provide one for him every day for a year."

"You don't say, ma'am!"

"I assure you, Mr. Clover, it is true. Alvanley is a true gourmand who has become rather portly over the years because of such indulgences," the marquess put in. He patted his trim midriff with a smug but infectious grin and eyed the trays filled with a variety of baked treats. "Perhaps I shall have one of those little cakes." He pointed to a round delicacy thickly covered with white sugar.

"Oh, those are quite good, sir. More like a biscuit they are, and filled with a lovely blackberry jam that the missus puts up every year. Folk do like them very much." Mr. Clover explained with justifiable pride. "And they're still a bit warm, too. Missus only finished baking them a short time ago."

"Well, that sounds much too good to miss, doesn't it, Miss Taylor? Will you join me?"

"Thank you, no, Lord Templeton. Although they do look wonderful, Mr. Clover, I must watch my diet you see."

"Ah. Pity." Templeton replied without an ounce of that commodity in his voice. Clearly he had never had to give his figure a moment's concern. "Oh, thank you, Mr. Clover." He handed over his coin, accepted the cake in both of his hands, and inhaled deeply. "Mmm, smells delicious!"

"Thank you, sir." Mr. Clover bowed his head and moved off to assist another customer.

Lavinia eyed him speculatively. "You are going to eat that now?"

"Of course. I come here two or three days a week for a treat. In the beginning, I forced myself to bring home what I bought, but soon I decided there was really no reason to delay the enjoyment. Actually, I've been telling Clover that he ought to consider putting in a few tables"—one arm swung to take in the customers' part of the shop—"the place is large enough. And I'll wager he could double his business."

"Perhaps he does not wish to double his business, sir."

"Don't be foolish, Miss Taylor, of course he does. What businessman does not? Why, he could serve coffee and tea, perhaps bring in more sweets. Or even ices!"

"Good heavens, he is a baker, not a confectioner. And he certainly is not Gunther. And this is not London, in case you had not noticed, sir."

"Humph. Well, I think it a very good idea." Templeton took a huge bite of the cake and shut his eyes in rapture. "Mmm."

"Oh!"

"What? Oh my! I am sorry, Miss Taylor. I seem to have, er, that is you have . . ."

"Blackberry jam all over the collar of my gown?" she managed through clenched jaws. Templeton's eager bite had caused the contents to shoot out the other side and land with a plop on Lavinia's pink gown. Really, the man was not only as clumsy as she had seen at their first meeting, but gauche as well.

"I am terribly sorry," he repeated. "Surely that is not one of your, um, best gowns, is it, Miss Taylor?" Templeton's command of the social graces seemed to have lost some of its polish since his removal from town.

"Indeed! Am I now to put up with your appraisal

of my gowns, sir?" That his assessment was correct only added to her chagrin.

He took a handkerchief from his pocket and put the linen square, now liberally sprinkled with sugar, into her hand.

"Obviously you think my gown not exactly, well, up to the minute." He held in a snicker. "Only, tell me, Lord Templeton"—Lavinia seethed as she wiped ineffectually at the collar—"if it is your intention to cause the ruination of my *entire* wardrobe piece by piece. For if it is, then I shall simply have everything delivered to the Park where you may get the process over with all at once. I assure you, it would be less bothersome for me that way!" She was trying to keep her voice from rising to a level that the other customers could hear.

"Well, then you would be able to replace it all."

She glared at him. "Is that supposed to make me happy?"

"It seems to make most people happy. I know that I enjoy it tremendously." By now, they had stepped outside into the sunshine where Templeton finished his cake and dabbed at his mouth with the berry-stained handkerchief that Lavinia had handed back. A thought occurred to him. "You have traveled to London?" he inquired, alluding to her accurate and ready description of Alvanley.

"I *lived* there until a few months ago, sir."

"Ah, really?" He was surprised.

She stood up straighter. "Yes, sir, I did. But, what has that to do with anything?"

"Not a thing. It is only that it explains your familiarity with Alvanley." *And the fact that you formerly took greater care with your appearance,* he said to himself. Apparently, she did not see the need to maintain a town level of dress and sophistication here in

Painswick. It occurred to him for the first time that he seemed to have adopted the same posture.

He flushed at the gracelessness that had spoiled her gown, for spoiled it was, and he begged her forgiveness again.

"Yes, very well. I suppose it is not a tragedy, for as you suggested, sir, it is hardly a new gown." She allowed him a very small smile, then thought better of it. "And I pray you, do *not* consider replacing it as you did my . . . petticoat. . . ."

"Ah, did you like the one I sent, Miss Taylor?"

"You are very coming, Lord Templeton. Gentlemen do not send ladies undergarments. Not even in London." Unknowingly, she echoed Irene Beatrice and Sarah Waters. "I ought to have been offended. In fact, I *was* offended, sir!"

He nodded meekly his acceptance of this stricture. "But you kept it, Miss Taylor." His lips curved into a lovely smile, and she could not have said for certain if this was borne out of stupidity or smugness, but she suspected the latter.

Lavinia gave a sharp intake of breath. "Well, only because I felt that to return it would only serve to draw out, you know to call attention to, the entire, um, process."

Templeton continued to smile. "Did you like it?"

"Well, yes, it was . . ." She recovered herself and sputtered, "You may be assured, sir, that I shall never wear it!"

He laughed. "As you wish, Miss Taylor. Are we walking the same way? Good, then you will not mind, I hope, if I accompany you. I was excessively pleased to find that you were not so angry that you would not invite me to your supper."

"Aha, so you surmised that your gift would make me angry!" she bantered.

"The thought had occurred to me, ma'am. But I did feel obliged since I had caused you to ruin a perfectly go—that is to say, ruin your petticoat, and then I had an instinct that you would enjoy the joke. Besides it is a perfectly good petticoat, you know, and I am deeply hurt that you do not intend to wear it!"

The man could be quite charming when he chose, Lavinia concluded. "Nevertheless, I shall not, sir. But I am pleased that you will come to my supper."

When he deposited her at the door of Greenbriar Lodge a few minutes later, Templeton pointed out that she had been so enthralled by his company that she had forgotten to make her purchases. Lavinia's dismay was alleviated by her decision not to tell the marquess about the sugar coating the tip of his nose or the smudge of jam deposited on his chin by the berry-stained handkerchief.

Five

The day was warm for mid-June, but a light breeze ruffled the air and kept the flies at bay. Behind the Lodge, tables had been set up under the shade trees where the guests would dine. A brightly striped marquee, its blue and green flaps drawn back with white ropes, would protect the platters of food on which Mrs. Beatrice and her helper were even now putting the finishing touches. Archery targets and bows and arrows had been set up on the far lawn where stray arrows might cause the least damage. Blankets, cushions and comfortable chairs were spread out under the trees with small tables at hand to hold drinks and food.

A deep bed of peonies of crimson, cerise, and white exhaled their heady perfume into the early summer air. Just behind the house, rhododendrons in full flower spread their dark green leaves and roses ran up walls, tumbled over fences, and stood erect, arms spread wide, brazenly showing off their myriad fragrances and petals of violet, pink, yellow, and white. Trill had abandoned her meal of blue clematis that clung to the fence to taste the straw archery targets. Angus, the stable boy, chased after the little goat, which dodged and ran, and it was impossible to tell who was having the most fun.

Two of the cats were stretched languidly on tables, one of them on his back, plump paws folded primly beneath his chin, hind legs extended to either side.

The kitchen was buzzing with activity and filled with tempting aromas.

"I need another bottle of Madeira, Susan," Mrs. Beatrice instructed her young assistant. "These quail are plumper than I'd dared to hope, and I need more of the wine to cover them properly. Oh, good. Thank you."

Susan Porter, who hoped to be a cook one day herself, watched Mrs. Beatrice's capable hands with rapt attention and nearly forgot to add the bacon to the bean casserole. Mrs. Beatrice raised her brows to look at the helper's efforts.

"Yes, good, Susan. That's it. Yes, you've chopped them just the right size." Praise being applied in this kitchen as meagerly as salt, Susan nodded her thanks and flushed a bit with satisfaction. "After you finish with that, you may go outside and see that the tables are ready."

"Yes, Mrs. Beatrice."

Preparations above stairs were not proceeding as smoothly as they were in the kitchen. Lavinia had been unable to decide which gown to wear, vacillating between a Nile green and white striped sarsenet and a soft jonquil tarlatan. They both were more elegant than the occasion called for, but she felt that her other dresses were no longer nice enough, and she wanted very much to make a good impression on her neighbors.

Lavinia wrapped her dressing gown tightly around her, for a cool breeze flew in the window and she was only minutes out of the bath. Biting her lip, she

considered the two gowns again and shrugged her
shoulders.

Margaret stood before her, a gown draped over
each outstretched arm. She glanced at the little
brass clock on the mantel. "Um, it is getting late,
Miss Taylor. Have to decide sometime," she teased,
"otherwise your guests will be here before you're
dressed."

"Oh, I suppose the green and white stripe, Margaret," she said at last. She tipped a napping cat
from a chair and sat down in front of her mirror.

Lavinia glanced into the mirror and caught a certain look in Margaret's eye.

"What is it, Margaret?" Lavinia looked from her
to the dress the servant held, her head tilted to one
side. "Is there something wrong with the gown?"

The maid immediately smiled and corrected her
posture. "Oh, er, no, ma'am."

Lavinia's dress selection was banded at the hem,
sleeves, and bodice with rich lace. Although well-
made and quite lovely in its day, the gown was several seasons old now, its fine fabric having lost the
enthusiasm it had once had for life. Lavinia had
not given her wardrobe much thought during the
last year of Uncle Amory's life and even less since
coming to Painswick, where her sparsely filled social calendar put no demands on the local modiste.
She had decided that this would be the most presentable of her things even if its very elegant lines
might be a bit out of place in her garden. But,
looking at it now, or it might be more accurate to
say, seeing it reflected in Margaret's eyes, she realized that it was not only too formal, but quite as
démodé as her others—most of the ladies she met
in the village were quite nicely turned out—and
not so very far removed from its eventual reincar-

nation as a dust rag. Lavinia looked at Margaret from the corner of her eye and gave a wry grimace. "A bit . . ."

"Mmm," Margaret agreed with disconcerting speed. "Still," she continued bracingly, "nothing for it now, Miss Taylor." She saw the pained look on her mistress's face as she bit her lip, and laughed. "It is not so bad as all that." She held out a petticoat, but as Lavinia stepped into it, her toe caught the hem and tore a hole in it.

"Oh! I am sorry, Miss Taylor. The hem must have been loose. Dear me, how could I have missed such a thing?"

Lavinia chuckled. "Never mind, Margaret. I must be getting clumsy in my old age."

"Not at all, ma'am." Margaret removed the torn petticoat. "Now, here's another one." She held out the garment.

"Not that one either, Margaret." Lavinia raised an eyebrow comically.

"Ma'am! I do apologize. Oh, dear, what a terrible abigail you must think me. And rightly so!" she exclaimed, looking at a gaping seam, her face the very picture of innocence. "And there is not enough time for me to mend it now. . . ."

"Never mind, Margaret. As you have been telling me, I need some new petticoats. Just bring me my other one; the one with the plain hem."

"I am afraid that one is in the laundry, Miss Taylor." Poor Margaret was beginning to wonder just how far she could go with this charade before she found herself without a situation. She had removed some stitches from one petticoat, torn another and hidden yet a third! "And we do not have much time left. . . ." She left the sentence hanging.

"Well, just put a stitch or two in the first one and . . ."

Margaret shook her head. "No, it might not hold. I could not send you out in such a condition, ma'am." She paused a moment, seemingly lost in thought. If Margaret did lose her position, she could become a screaming success on the stage. "But, why not wear that pretty new one that you bought? The one with the violets?" The maid gave no hint the she knew where the item had come from.

"No!"

Margaret blinked in surprise.

"I mean, I find that I do not care for it after all. Whatever made me purchase such a dreadful thing?" This was doing it up much too brown, but Lavinia could not stifle her reluctance to wear it.

"Forgive me, Miss Taylor, but what choice have you?" She tilted her head toward the fireplace and looked pointedly at the ticking clock. "It is nearly time. And, even if you do not like it, there is really nothing wrong with it. Why, it is extremely pretty, I think. The embroidery is superb. And I can understand completely why you bought it. Such a choice shows very good taste," Margaret suggested with a glance to see Lavinia's reaction.

To argue further would have wasted more time she did not have and made Lavinia look foolish. "Oh, very well." But she uttered the words with less than her usual grace, and added, "After today, you may have it, Margaret, since you seem to admire it so much!"

The maid smiled brightly. "Thank you, Miss Taylor."

Margaret began to do up the buttons of the dress, and smoothed it over the petticoat as Lavinia turned in front of her glass. "Good heavens, Margaret, do I actually look as bad as I think I do?"

"No indeed. There's honestly not a thing wrong with this dress, and your hair is lovely, if I say so myself." She grinned and picked at the round sleeves to puff them out more. "You just think about the beautiful new petticoat you're wearing. That will give you confidence."

Thank heaven Templeton cannot see that I am wearing the petticoat. Doubtless he would be excessively pleased with himself if he knew. He might even think I am wearing it for entirely the wrong reason!

"Margaret, tomorrow we go shopping," was Lavinia's dry response.

"Splendid, ma'am," the maid chirped. "Now"— she handed Lavinia her gloves and led her out the door—"you go and have a lovely time at your party."

The maid gave a heavy sigh as she sank onto Lavinia's bed. She had been as nervous as a cat about her subterfuge and was heartily glad it was over. Still, the plan might not bear fruit for, while she had been able to get Lavinia into the petticoat, she had no way to ensure that Templeton would notice it. *Well*—Margaret gave another sigh—*I must hope that matters work out as they should from here on.*

Sounds of laughter and teasing carried down into the garden from the broad lawn, where some half dozen guests were taking aim at the archery target, fitting arrows to bows and issuing good-natured challenges to one another.

"Gerard, you could not hit that center if I were to promise you a million pounds!"

"Ha! You haven't *got* a million pounds, Ingham."

His friend notched his arrow with great delibera-
tion, raised the bow in large hands and took careful
aim, sending his arrow straight into the heart of the
target some thirty yards away. Gerard Melbury's
young sister and his wife applauded with great exuberance. Laughing, he turned to Ingham with outstretched palm. "All right then, Dan, pay up, you
scoundrel!"

Dan Ingham threw back his head and laughed.
"I swear, Gerard, you've never made such a hit in
all your life."

"Well, that's a fact I cannot deny, Dan. Must have
been the thought of all that lovely blunt that did
it!"

When it had come her turn at the brightly
painted target, Lavinia had acquitted herself well,
albeit not as grandly as Gerard Melbury. She and
his wife, Anne, near her own age, had formed the
beginnings of friendship and had promised to visit
later in the week, and this development, together
with the general success of her party had put Lavinia in high spirits.

Everyone had accepted Lavinia's invitation. Those
who were not testing their skill at archery were
spread out on the lawn talking. Several children
played in the warm, dappled sunshine afforded by
some nearby trees, and their squeals and laughter
mixed with the voices of the adults. Her neighbors
were proving to be as friendly as Lavinia could have
wished, and she was pleased to have been able to
mention to Dorothea Caton that two people had
expressed an interest in joining a book circle,
should the ladies decide to form one. She was also
not surprised to find that her neighbors were, indeed, quite interested in getting to know the newly
resident marquess.

And he, evidently, was interested in knowing them. At least, what else could one surmise from his cheerful, open countenance and his readiness to chat with one and all, answering questions about the Park and London. At the first inquiry regarding the latter, Templeton's pulse had quickened. Did Mrs. Palfrey know about his reasons for leaving? But he had recovered himself quickly for, certainly, his questioner could not possibly know ought of his affaire with Althea. He had patiently answered her and all the others, talking easily and expansively about life in the metropolis and promising to entertain soon at the Park, since it had not been open to visitors for such a long time.

"Of course, it's nothing like your residence in London, though, is it? The Park, I mean, my lord," remarked David Lane knowingly.

"Do you make a long stay here, sir?" inquired Mrs. Hollis, doing her best to sound offhand.

With three daughters, all of them on the verge of marriageable age in a village with few good prospects, Mary Hollis was in no position to let *a marquess, for heaven's sake, Mr. Hollis,* slip through her fingers. She hoped to dispose of more than one of her girls, for surely a peer, and especially one as young and lively as this one appeared to be, would be entertaining any number of friends and relations. *You mark my words,* she had prophesied to her husband just the night before, *there will be plenty of visitors,* male *visitors to the Park, now that the marquess has come to stay. Our girls cannot help but find themselves husbands.* Her own husband found no quarrel with this expectation, saying only that *they had better be quick about it, for they are eating me out of house and home, and I do not intend to spend a fortune tempting husbands for them.* His wife had explained the con-

tradiction in his sentiments, pointing out that if
Fanny, Elizabeth, and Dulcinea—Mrs. Hollis had a
partiality for Cervantes—were so expensive to keep,
then it made sense in the long run to spend what
he must to see them resettled elsewhere.

"Life here in Painswick must seem awfully hum-
drum after the excitement of London, sir. After all,
there is little hope that our paltry entertainments
can compete with those to be found in town. Oh,
Miss Taylor, I . . ." Augustus Tolland's face reddened. "I assure you that I did not mean to imply
that your supper is not an event of great signifi-
cance here in our hamlet. . . ."

Lavinia raised a hand to staunch this encomium.
"Please, Mr. Tolland, I beg you will stop"—she
chuckled—"else you will turn my head with such
fulsome compliments."

But the poor man would not let himself be so
easily and quickly forgiven by a lady whose hospi-
tality he was at present enjoying, and one so lately
of London, where good manners, or so he had always believed, were strictly observed. "Indeed,
ma'am, you are too generous in your understanding. I only wish to assure you—er, not that you require *my* assurance, of course—that this"—he
spread his arms wide—"gathering is the finest of
which I have ever been a . . ."

"Oh cut line, Tolland, you are doing it up much
too brown," Mr. Stanton interrupted with a grin
and a roll of his eyes. "And perhaps you should not
be so quick with your praise. After all, we haven't
dined yet!"

"Lewis!" Helen Stanton exclaimed, mortified. But
everyone took Stanton's comment for the banter it
was intended to be.

"Quite right, Stanton." Templeton smiled. "This

ain't Carlton House, you know," he informed Augustus Tolland unnecessarily.

"Thank goodness," Lavinia interrupted with a small, theatrical shudder. "For if we were in his house, then we might see our *beloved* Prince of Wales."

Templeton nodded, overlooking her sarcasm.

"Have you been there, then?" someone asked. A dozen pairs of eyes fastened on Templeton, awaiting his reply.

"I have."

"You have met him? The Prince?"

"Well naturally, he's met him, dear, he has been to his *house.*"

"Oh and I suppose going to Carlton House is just the same as visiting our house, is it, Tom?" Elvira Rowley retorted with a laugh.

"Actually," Lavinia put in, "you might not necessarily see the prince if you went there, for he does not always make an appearance at his own entertainments, or sometimes he arrives very late and then stays for only a few moments." There were some in the group sufficiently ignorant of His Highness's quite notorious exploits, pecuniary and otherwise, and still others willing to overlook them, who thought his appearance in their midst would be the greatest favor. For the most part, however, Lavinia's guests began to express their displeasure with the heir to the throne.

"My, what bad manners! Have you seen him when you were there, Miss Taylor?"

"I have never been there."

"Ah, you have never been invited, Miss Taylor?" This from Templeton, who had a glint in his eye. For some reason, it niggled at him that she was so ready to express her knowledge and opinions of life among London's ton.

"I have not, sir. I only relate what I have heard on good authority. I did not travel in the prince's circles."

"Pity."

"Not at all, Lord Templeton," she replied cooly. "How could I miss the attentions of a person for whom I have neither respect nor regard? For our prince is, *I* think, a buffoon." There were murmurs of agreement with her assessment. "But I must think that you were numbered in the Carlton House set, sir, were you not? Do tell."

Once again, eyes turned toward the marquess. "I was invited to Carlton House once or twice, ma'am, but it happens that I am in complete agreement with your opinion of him."

"I see. You declined the invitations, then?" Lavinia's voice was sweet.

"No, Miss Taylor, I did not. That would have been rude, and my poor excuses for not attending easily found out."

Lavinia raised a brow of disdain, but refrained from saying anything more than a civil, "Of course," as the servants arrived to serve the supper.

A marquee covered two tables where her guests were served cold meats, casserole of beans and bacon, truffles with wine, quails in Madeira, asparagus, and peas. There were bottles of fine claret and pitchers of lemonade, and to conclude the meal, cherry tarts and syllabub. After being served, everyone sat informally at the tables set on the grass. Thomas Darnall had invited Lavinia to sit beside him. As they ate, he said, "Lord Templeton seemed to enjoy baiting you about the prince and Carlton House."

We'd Like to Invite You to Subscribe to Zebra's Regency Romance Book Club and Give You a Gift of 4 Free Books as Your Introduction! (Worth $19.96!)

If you're a Regency lover, imagine the joy of getting **4 FREE Zebra Regency Romances** and then the chance to have these lovely stories delivered to your home each month at the lowest price available! Well, that's our offer to you and here's how you benefit by becoming a Regency Romance subscriber:

- **4 FREE Introductory Regency Romances are delivered to your doorstep**

- **4 BRAND NEW Regencies are then delivered each month (usually before they're available in bookstores)**

- **Subscribers save almost $4.00 every month**

- **Home delivery is always FREE**

- **You also receive a FREE monthly newsletter, which features author profiles, discounts, subscriber benefits, book previews and more**

- **No risks or obligations...in other words, you can cancel whenever you wish with no questions asked**

Join the thousands of readers who enjoy the savings and convenience offered to Regency Romance subscribers. After your initial introductory shipment, you receive 4 brand-new Zebra Regency Romances each month to examine for 10 days. Then, if you decide to keep the books, you'll pay the preferred subscriber's price of just $4.00 per title. That's only $16.00 for all 4 books and there's never an extra charge for shipping and handling.

It's a no-lose proposition, so return the FREE BOOK CERTIFICATE today!

Say Yes to 4 Free Books!
Complete and return the order card to receive this $19.96 value, ABSOLUTELY FREE!

If the certificate is missing below, write to:
Regency Romance Book Club
P.O. Box 5214, Clifton, New Jersey 07015-5214
or call TOLL-FREE 1-888-345-BOOK

Visit our website at www.kensingtonbooks.com.

FREE BOOK CERTIFICATE

YES! Please rush me 4 Zebra Regency Romances without cost or obligation. I understand that each month thereafter I will be able to preview 4 brand-new Regency Romances FREE for 10 days. Then, if I should decide to keep them, I will pay the money-saving preferred subscriber's price of just $16.00 for all 4...that's a savings of almost $4 off the publisher's price with no additional charge for shipping and handling. I may return any shipment within 10 days and owe nothing, and I may cancel this subscription at any time. My 4 FREE books will be mine to keep in any case.

Name _____

Address _____ Apt. _____

City _____ State _____ Zip _____

Telephone ( ) _____

Signature _____ RN120A
(If under 18, parent or guardian must sign.)

Terms and prices subject to change. Orders subject to acceptance by Regency Romance Book Club.
Offer valid in U.S. only.

Treat yourself to 4 FREE Regency Romances!

lll..l..lll...ll.l.l..l.l.l..lll..l.ll..ll.l.lll..l

REGENCY ROMANCE BOOK CLUB
Zebra Home Subscription Service, Inc.
P.O. Box 5214
Clifton NJ 07015-5214

PLACE
STAMP
HERE

Lavinia had decided that she had been rather stiff-necked about Templeton's remarks, but now reconsidered based on this observation by a third party.

"Do you think so? I thought rather that he was teasing."

"Perhaps, ma'am." He hesitated for a moment before uttering this. "But I confess I felt it rather poor form for a gentleman to speak to a lady—and one who is his hostess into the bargain—in such a fashion. It may be"—he smiled shyly—"that I am too particular about these matters. And I am certain there is no harm done, for you are too good-natured, I think, to take offense."

Lavinia thought that Thomas Darnall's manners seemed more polished than those of the marquess. She thanked him for the compliment.

"Would you like to take a stroll when we have finished eating? Perhaps you will tell me about the flowers you have here."

She smiled back. "I shall be very happy to, Mr. Darnall."

Actually, Lavinia would have liked to remain seated for the duration of the party, the better to conceal her gown, or at least most of it. Her trepidations had been confirmed. The dress was too formal for the occasion, she had only to look about her at the other ladies' to prove that. Just as bad, it was clearly at its last prayers. She could not for the life of her have said why she had not replaced her wardrobe since moving to Painswick. Mrs. Kindle was a fine modiste, as good as any she had patronized in London, that much was evident from the attire of her female guests, most of whom must use that woman's services. And yet she had come away from her sole visit to the shop with nothing more than an order placed for a morning dress. Lavinia was certain that one or two of her neighbors had glanced at her in much the same way that Margaret had, and she was a bit embarrassed. Might the ladies present think she was trying to lord it over them with such a formal gown? Or were they thinking she did not consider them or the occasion important enough to wear something better?

As she and Darnall concluded their meal, Chester Stone appeared at their table and, hearing of their intention to have a walk, asked if he might join them. Darnall looked slightly less than happy at this prospect, but smiled and said gamely that the new arrival was more than welcome. Lavinia found that she quite liked having two gentlemen request her company. Trill wandered around the perimeter of the company and was made quite a pet of by several guests.

"Lord Templeton, have you ever boxed at Gentleman Jackson's saloon?" asked the Stantons' grandson, who had recently celebrated his fifteenth birthday, and was developing a case of hero-worship on the marquess.

"Yes, I go a round or two there occasionally with my friend, Welles."

"Honestly? What is it like there, sir?"

"Now, James, do not bother his lordship."

"But, grandmother . . ."

"He is not bothering me a bit, Mrs. Stanton. I was terribly curious about boxing when I was about James's age." He turned back to the boy. "How much do you know about boxing, James?"

"A bit, sir, but my parents will not allow me to go to a mill. And there was a first-rate one in Stroud just the other week, only my father would not take me or let me go with Freddie—he's my best friend."

Helen Stanton raised a heavy brow and pursed her lips in disapproval.

"Well, I should think not, James. A mill is no place for a gentleman, you know. The company often can be poor, and there is little relationship between what you will see in a public prizefight versus what goes on in a private boxing establishment such as Jackson's."

"But, sir, the Prince of Wales has attended mills," the boy pointed out.

"For a time, yes, but not for many a year. He found it much too violent. Once in Brighton, he saw a man by the name of Earl killed in the prize ring. He was so distressed that he awarded a pension to Earl's widow, and he has not been to a match since." *Take that, Miss Taylor,* he said to himself. "But, if you really are interested in the *art* of boxing, I could give you a pointer or two, I suppose. If you have permission, that is." He nodded in the older Stantons' direction.

Young James's expression had shifted rapidly from dismay to horror to excitement. "You will, sir?" He looked to his grandfather hopefully.

"Well, James, I think your father would consent," decided Lewis, whose son and daughter-in-law were visiting her parents in Cheltenham. "Although, I am less sanguine about your mother."

"Oh, thank you, Grandfather," the boy cried, avoiding his grandmother's gaze, knowing full well that she would remain on his mother's side in the matter. "Wait 'till old Freddie hears about this! When . . ."

"Do not pester him, James," she interjected sternly.

"But, Grandmother, Lord Templeton has stepped into the ring at Gentleman Jackson's! I just want to ask him about my stance. . . ." He cast a pleading look at Templeton, who gave in with a chuckle.

"All right, lad. Let's just step over here out of the way."

Lavinia stooped to pick a deeply colored laced pink and inhaled its faintly spicy fragrance.

"These grounds are most attractive, Miss Taylor."

"Thank you, Mr. Darnall."

"Yes, I quite agree with Darnall, Miss Taylor. The garden is lovely and much finer than mine, I must confess," Chester Stone added.

"Father!"

"Father!"

Stone's son and daughter ran screaming into their midst.

"Father, Harold is making fun of me! Make him stop!" Clarissa demanded.

Her brother shoved her rudely and she stumbled backward, more for theatrical effect than loss of balance, screeching in outrage, "Do you see?"

"Stupid! Go away and leave us alone!" A boy tall for his age, with a crop of thick blond hair, Harold stuck out his tongue at his sister and squeezed his eyes shut as he shook his head in derision. "Father, tell her to go and play with the girls."

"I hate you!"

"I hate *you!*"

Lavinia, Darnall, and Stone halted their stroll. The other guests in the vicinity did the same and stared at the pageant as the two obstreperous children continued their argument. Harold started to chase after his sister, and she ran screaming even louder than before, then hid behind her father.

"Help!"

"She's a stupid girl, Father. Cannot we send her away to school?"

Chester Stone smiled beatifically, seemingly undisturbed by the goings-on.

"Now, children, you must play nicely together."

His offspring only grew louder, a development few would have believed possible. Clarissa broke from the cover of her father's rather portly form and dodged past her fleet-footed brother, then tripped and tumbled onto the grass. She was up and tore off quickly, Harold again in close pursuit. The pair first ran back through the group of strollers, then headed toward the tables and diners picking at the last of the food.

"Harold! Clarissa! Behave yourselves, do." They ignored him. By now, their quarrel had been forgotten and they took turns chasing one another, noisily dodging behind trees, tables, and people.

Their father stood, hands on hips, chuckling as he watched. "Such unabashed enthusiasm."

Lavinia's eyes popped in amazement. Was he really going to do nothing to stop their misbehavior? One of the other children, a boy of seven, began to run toward them and would have joined in their antics had not his father seized him by the ear.

"Philip!" his father hissed as he dragged the child away, "*you* will remember your manners!"

The disruption did not bother James Stanton, who stood, arms raised in mock combat.

"How is this, sir?" he asked.

Templeton stood back, head tilted to one side, as if he needed to think before answering. "Mmm. Let me see. You should drop your right arm a bit and pull it in just a little."

"Like this?" James Stanton carefully adjusted his position.

"That's better. Now, raise your left—Oof!"

"My lord!"

Harold had crashed into the back of Templeton's legs, throwing him completely off balance and landing him on the grass, a very surprised look on his face. The children ran off laughing, without a word of apology or regret, leaving an overturned chair and a wobbling table full of crockery in their wake. Templeton got up and made light of the mishap, although he cast a baleful look in the children's direction.

"Oh, dear," Lavinia said. She seemed destined to find Lord Templeton sprawled on the ground. Poor man, he hardly looked his best in front of all their neighbors.

Darnall smirked in Templeton's direction. "Clunch," he said under his breath.

With relative quiet restored, her guests returned to their perambulations and conversation. Lavinia excused herself to see to her guests and assess the damages wrought by the Stone children. The Stantons' were not amused by the children's antics, having raised their son and two daughters with little patience for misbehavior, especially in public. Cynthia Weld, looking shocked, whispered something in Dorothea Caton's ear.

A servant retrieved a platter that had been toppled to the ground but saved from breaking by the soft grass. Chester Stone hurried up to his hostess.

"Oh, Miss Taylor, I do hope that the children have not caused any upset." He smiled winningly.

"Any upset?"

"The children have so much energy that I hesitate to curb it. Such vitality is a joy to see, would you not agree?"

His children's "vitality" could still be heard, as

their squeals emanated from the vicinity of the barn. But Lavinia did not fear for the animals, for she knew that Peach would ring a peal over the children's heads and send them off if they caused any sort of annoyance.

"Er, 'a joy,' well, Mr. Stone . . ."

Templeton caught her eye as he dusted off his trousers and joined them.

"Oh, Lord Templeton, I can see you are not angry with Clarissa and Harold."

Templeton blinked. Apparently his urge to read them a resounding lecture was not evident on his face. "Just a bit of mischief, you know. They are harmless." Stone smiled and went on. "Still, I promise you I shall take them to task for not stopping long enough to apologize."

Templeton was certain he heard Lavinia choke back a laugh. He glimpsed the Stone children come from the direction of the barn—Peach apparently having done his job—and begin running pell-mell toward the lawn, where a few people had resumed their archery competition. He bent his head in their direction. "You might want to see to them now, Stone. They could be tempting fate," he suggested dryly.

Stone glanced over his shoulder and shook his head with a grin.

"Should you not go after them, Mr. Stone? They could be hurt there." Lavinia asked, picturing one of them darting out in front of a flying arrow.

He sighed. "You might suppose so, Miss Taylor, but they never seem to come to any harm, thank heaven. Nevertheless, you are quite correct. Better safe than sorry! You will excuse me?"

As he moved off, Lavinia peeked at Templeton,

who gave her a long look from the corner of his eye.

"Yes, I am convinced that they never get hurt, they simply wreak havoc wherever they go, laying waste . . ."

"Damn, sir, whyever did you warn him?" Darnall asked as he strolled past to get another glass of wine.

". . . to everything in their path . . ." Templeton finished.

"Not as bad as that, surely?" Lavinia asked. "They have seemed well enough behaved before this."

He looked at her askance. "Those creatures are entirely without discipline. What can the man be thinking of?"

"Perhaps he is trying to make up for the loss of their mother."

"Humph. Well, if so, he is doing them no favor, you know." She nodded her agreement. "So, you are seeing a different side to Mr. Stone and his children today, are you? Do not go up into the boughs, ma'am. I have seen you with him after church more than once."

She gasped. "Have you indeed, sir? Am I to assume that you have been watching me?"

He looked at her for a long moment before replying. "Hardly. You may, however, assume that I have eyes in my head and since the four of you were not hiding behind the headstones in the churchyard, I observed you together." He paused again. "Whyever should you think I would be watching you, Miss Taylor?"

Since he took great care to look down his patrician nose and spoke in the most condescending tone, Lavinia found herself with a blush on her cheek.

"My lord, all Mr. Stone and I have done is talk."
She had no idea why she felt compelled to explain
her behavior.

He waved a dismissive hand. "May *I* assume that
any thoughts you may have had about Mr. Stone as
a prospective husband have been put to rest?"

"Husband?" She nearly screeched as loudly as
Clarissa, then lowered her voice to an urgent rasp.
"What makes you think . . . How dare you?"

"You need not be coy with me, you know. You
are not getting younger, after all, and it is natural
that you should wish to marry."

Lavinia stood poised to give him the set down of
his life. Then she saw the sparkle of mischief in his
eye and decided to play along. "So, you do not
think he would make a good husband, sir?"

"Not unless you can send those two monsters to
live in India, Miss Taylor."

"Just a bit harsh, I should think. I know they
should not have knocked you down, but you were
not hurt, after all."

"I am not referring just to the indignity that *I*
suffered," he responded stiffly, then grinned as he
added, "Go ahead, Miss Taylor, I dare you to tell
me that you could spend above an hour in the
company of those terrors without wanting to murder them. And we will not even discuss the sanity
of a parent who countenances such behavior.
Surely you could not wish to adopt such a family."

There was a rumble of unexpected thunder
quickly followed by another louder, longer one, and
the sky began to darken as heavily laden rain clouds
crowded in.

"Oh, no. I did not think it would rain, did you?"
Templeton's look told her that it was not his turn
to answer questions. Lavinia smiled at him pertly,

but she knew that she ought to have set him back on his heels with a few well-chosen words. "It seems, sir, that any discussion of my marital ambitions, *should I harbor any*, must wait for another time." She held out a hand to catch the first of the heavy raindrops. "But, perhaps, you will be good enough to help move us all inside?"

He twisted his lips. "With the greatest pleasure, Miss Taylor. But I repeat my observation: you are not getting younger, so I hope you are planning to wed *someone*."

Lavinia had the greatest urge to stick out her tongue at him, as Harold Stone had done earlier, but just then the sky split, letting loose a torrent of rain. There were cries of both dismay and glee from various parts of the garden, as people rushed past them toward the shelter of the house.

"I shall see to Mrs. Asher, Miss Taylor."

The marquess referred to the eldest of Lavinia's guests, a lady whose advanced age forced her to walk slowly and with the aid of a stick.

"Will you take my arm, Mrs. Asher? I should like to help you into the house, if I may."

"I am certain that I do not require assistance, Lord Templeton, but if you would like to, I shall be much obliged."

Margaret and Ellice ran toward them carrying umbrellas. Lavinia waved Ellice back to Templeton and Mrs. Asher. The other guests, apart from Clarissa and Harold who, given leave by their father, were enjoying the downpour, already were far ahead of them nearer the house.

"Oh, Margaret, thank . . ."

The maid smiled and said as she passed her mistress, "Yes, ma'am, I shall walk little Harold and Clarissa back, shall I?"

Lavinia could hardly say no and, anyway, it was not as if her gown, fast becoming drenched, was worth saving.

The cloudburst was so fierce that it had already produced puddles in the grass. Mrs. Asher, despite her demurral and the aid of Templeton's arm, was unsteady on her feet. For his part, the marquess was having some difficulty in holding the umbrella over the old woman's head and simultaneously helping her toward the shelter of the house. His pleas that she slow her pace went unheeded and, in a moment, she slipped on the wet grass. When Templeton ducked to avoid her flailing cane's connecting with his head, he inadvertently tugged on Mrs. Asher's arm, nearly tipping her over. Fortunately, he reacted quickly enough to save her, but not himself, and he landed in a heap for the second time in the same day.

"Good heavens, my lord, you are not much help are you?" the elderly lady asked him bluntly. "Are you hurt?"

Lavinia hurried back to them as quickly as her sodden gown would allow. *Not again.* Mrs. Asher was preoccupied with holding on to the umbrella, the wind having picked up considerably in the last few moments. Lavinia tried to help, but succeeded only in knocking the poor woman's cane to the ground and they nearly lost the umbrella altogether.

"For pity's sake, Miss Taylor, let it be. *I* am fine as sixpence, I assure you. *He,* I fear, is not." She nodded her head toward Templeton. "See to him, girl," she said with a brave smile, "before the two of you finish me off entirely!"

"Oh, I am so sorry, Mrs. Asher, I . . ."

"Get off with you, I said, before the poor man drowns!"

"Yes, of course, ma'am." *Lord help me, what an introduction to the neighbors.* She turned to the marquess. "Lord Templeton, have you hurt yourself?"

Templeton, attempting with little success to return to a standing position, now ceased his effort and stared at Lavinia, a huge smile spanning his face.

She stared back in annoyance and befuddlement. What could he possibly have to smile about at this moment? Darnall appeared just then, sopping wet, looked at Templeton, and shut his eyes in wonderment. He bowed before Mrs. Asher and held out his arm with exaggerated gallantry.

"Mrs. Asher, may I offer my services?" He turned his eyes heavenward in a broad comic gesture. "I think that gathering two-by-two would seem to be the appropriate action at this juncture." Mrs. Asher grinned in appreciation at his wit. "I shall be happy to escort you to the house, ma'am, since Lord Templeton does not seem to be, um, *up* to the occasion."

The older woman took his arm, enjoying the farce enormously. "Mr. Darnall, I should be forever grateful to you."

He turned to Lavinia. "Miss Taylor? May I assist you? No? Very well, you must swim to shore on your own. Mrs. Asher, we shall have to press on just the two of us."

"You are all kindness, Mr. Darnall. Is my bonnet on straight, sir?" In fact, her white straw hat with its pretty blue ribbons was ruined and hanging down dripping about her ears.

"Ma'am, you have never looked lovelier. Of course, I must remind you that I have known you only since this afternoon, but I defy any man to curse me if I am wrong. You are a vision! Shall we?"

They moved off slowly, arm in arm, heads held high and chatting comfortably, as if they were strolling of an afternoon in Hyde Park.

Their burlesque was lost on Lavinia, and she knew that it could not have produced Templeton's smile.

"What, sir, are grinning at?"

"Why, Miss Taylor, you *are* husband hunting. And, if I do not mistake the matter, *I* am your prey!"

"*What?*"

"Although you have a most unusual way of telling me, ma'am." Having finally pulled himself to his feet, he tucked her arm in his and they proceeded quickly toward the house, "Come, Miss Taylor, we shall be the last pair up the gangplank."

She pulled away from him and scowled, trying to maintain some dignity. "Take your hands off me, sir." The action caused her to slip on the grass, however, and he took back her arm to steady her. This time, she did not reclaim it. They resumed their flight.

"Allow me to explain my deduction, ma'am." He pointed at the bottom of her gown. "You are wearing my petticoat, Miss Taylor. Well of course, it is not precisely *mine*, is it? Not any longer. Not since I gave it to *you*, that is. But, the point is, why else should you wear it? If not because you harbor a tendre for me. Hmm?"

Lavinia looked down and gasped. When the light fabric of her gown became wet, the violets on the hem of the petticoat showed through, quite clearly betraying her secret.

"Oh, no! You do not understand, my lord. It was never my intention to wear this! And as for wishing to marry you, why I am happy to say that I have never entertained such an addle-pated thought. . . ."

He leaned closer and whispered in her ear, "Never?"

Six

. . . and now that you have read the whole tale, Edwina, you can easily understand why I should like to throttle the man. He is perfectly odious I promise you. I cannot say—entre nous, of course—that I have not been thinking of marrying, as I have told you in my last letter, but to think of marrying him! Such arrogance, Wina!

The thought occurred to Wina that she had never seen or heard her friend's conversation so punctuated with exclamations and underscoring as she had since the marquess had come into her life.

Oh, very well, I cannot lie to you, my dearest friend. I have thought of marrying him! But only once mind. Well, perhaps twice, but never above two or three times at the most. And I am convinced that I have never let on to Lord Templeton that I have thought of marrying, and certainly not of marrying him! And all because of a stupid petticoat, Wina. It is just too awful. . . .

Templeton did not fare much better than Lavinia, once left alone with his thoughts that night. He knew better than to blame himself for his less than dignified appearance at her party, but that was cold comfort to one who was theretofore used to appearing to advantage at all times. Miss Taylor's opinion was of no consequence, of course, but it was especially irksome that he seemed always to look the fool in her presence. He was a peer, after all, and one with a reputation with the ladies to maintain, but how was Lavinia Taylor to know this? He supposed, with all humility, that she had heard of him, since he was well-known in town, but she had not acknowledged this nor evidenced any partiality for him. Until today, that is, when she had worn his petticoat. He had half expected her to send Tim back to the Park carrying the gift back to its giver, but she had not. He wondered why she had worn it. Did her action signal that she had a tendre for him? Had she intended somehow for him to catch a glimpse of it? And then what? Perhaps she had worn it simply to have his gift near to her. He pondered this for several minutes before deciding that another obvious conclusion was that there was no particular reason why she should *not* have worn it.

Templeton put aside the estate reports that he had not been reading anyway and settled back more comfortably in his chair. The puzzle of the petticoat thus seemingly solved, he felt deflated for he had to concede that she had given no other sign of interest in him. But how dare Lavinia Taylor turn up her nose at him! She had made a point of letting him know that she had formerly resided in London, but she had not acquired an ounce of town bronze that he could detect while she was there. She ought to be over the moon at his presence in Painswick, but she gave no hint of such elation. He had been right about her from the beginning; she was nothing more than a country mouse. *And you're a damned fool,* he cursed himself, *else why should you care about such an unremarkable and unsophisticated female?*

But there was still his pride left to deal with. While he had never before set out to win a lady just for the sake of winning her, neither had he ever had to exert much effort to attract one; he had been too good a catch not to easily appeal to most females with whom he came into contact. Templeton's earlier plan to merely pass the time with Lavinia during his stay was no longer sufficient, but he did not need her to fall in love with him to assuage his wounded pride. No, he did not wish to woo Lavinia precisely, although he supposed she would make a fine enough mistress once she visited the right modiste and hairdresser. She might even make a suitable wife, were he in the market for one, but he was still too recently escaped from being legshackled to Althea to entertain thoughts along those lines. He merely wanted her to alter her opinion of him and to observe her realization of his eligibility.

Since coming to the country, he had achieved a sort of anonymity, especially with respect to his rank and station. The attention paid him by his neighbors, with the exception of young James Stanton, was more what they would have given to any sort of exotic animal that arrived in their midst, and he actually found this development refreshing. Yet, at the same time, he experienced a queer need for some bit of recognition of the man he was in London; it was, after all, what he had been all his life until just a few weeks ago. But how could he make her see what every other female of his experience had seen entirely on their own? Well, if he were still in London, he would simply charm her; few women ever resisted him, and he did not think that the country mouse would be any different.

But determining how to approach her took some thought. Eventually, he decided to see to it that they spent a great deal of time in one another's company; for if they became friends, surely she would come to appreciate his appeal. Templeton had never had a female as an actual friend before and the prospect intrigued him. He already knew that Miss Taylor was well read, for he had been part of a conversation with her and several others at the party, discussing books, where she had acquitted herself well. Moreover, he had no doubt that she held strong opinions on a host of nonliterary subjects. He was not intimidated or outraged by the intelligent, outspoken, and educated women that the ton frequently referred to as bluestockings, but then, he had not spent much time in their company. Still, the thought of having an intelligent conversation with a woman he had made love to appealed to him while it left most men he knew unmoved. He did not think Miss Taylor was either so academic or so bold as to be a bluestocking. *Still,* he told himself, *time spent with her would be, in one way or another, stimulating.* He did not then explore in just what other ways this might be so.

"My God, Will, did you see what happened to the marquess? He looked absolutely caper-witted the way he kept landing on his ass, though it's me as says it, and I'm no more than a laborer on his land. There was I, helping with the archery things and such, and I tell you, I was that embarrassed for the poor man." Alfie Sharp shook his head with empathy.

Will Tabbard grunted. "That's not going to help him, is it? I mean, I ask you, you cannot expect to attract a lady if you can't manage to stay upright, can you?"

The two men were enjoying their pipes and pints in the yard of the Swan's Nest, their work done for the day.

"Terrible thing," was Alfie's grim judgment. "What's to be done?"

"Can't have them going on like this, Alf."

"Certainly not."

Will took another mouthful of ale. "Suppose he decides to leave? What then? No, we have to do something. Let's talk with the others."

"Right you are, Will." He tapped out the dead ash from the bowl of his pipe. "Try your blend?" He held out a hand for his friend's tobacco pouch.

Dorothea Caton called on Lavinia a few days later to say that several more people had expressed an interest in participating in a book circle.

"Splendid!" Lavinia exclaimed with more enthusiasm than she might have felt before her supper party. The truth was that the Stones—all three of them—and Templeton had put her off the idea of marrying, at least for the moment. The thought of marrying someone as awkward and arrogant as the marquess or as indulgent as Chester Stone—not to mention being mother to his children—made her think that her single life was not so bad after all, so she had best make the most of it. "I am so pleased to know it, Mrs. Caton. Please, you will take tea? I was just about to call for some. Good. Now, tell me, who is to be in the group?"

"Mrs. Weld and Mr. Breverton"—here Lavinia detected the slightest hint of rose in her visitor's cheek—"Mr. Darnall, he says he is a great reader, you know, Mrs. Stanton, you and I of course, and Lord Templeton."

Lavinia stiffened at the mention of Templeton's name, but she did not remark upon it. "Well, what should be our next step?"

"We ought to decide on a book and arrange for our first meeting. I took the liberty of mentioning *Waverly* and, fortunately, everyone had read it and agreed it would make an excellent choice for our first discussion. You have read it?" Lavinia said that, coincidentally, she was reading it then. "Good. When shall we meet?"

They soon arrived at a date. It had been decided that the circle would meet at a different house each time, and Mrs. Caton, the titular head of the group, offered for hers to be the first.

"I shall send off a note to apprise them of our plan," she told Lavinia.

Lavinia spent the rest of her day at Mrs. Kindle's Ladies' Bazaar, choosing patterns, fabrics, and trims, and being fitted for an entirely new wardrobe. By the time she left the shop, she had placed orders for enough clothes to keep her in style even in London. Mrs. Kindle, thrilled to have the custom of a London lady, agreed to have the order completed as soon as possible. And so, the next day, when Templeton called, she was wearing her only new garment, the morning gown Mrs. Kindle had recently made up for her and which she had worn only once or twice before.

"Lord Templeton is calling, Miss Taylor."

She considered saying she was not at home, but realized she could not avoid contact with the marquess forever, no matter how much she wished to. She put aside her book and took off her spectacles. "Good day, Lord Templeton. How nice of you to call."

He grinned maddeningly. "Do you really think so, Miss Taylor? And I had made sure you would throw something at my head if I dared to put it into your drawing room."

"Indeed? Why ever should you have thought so, my lord? Oh, yes, Ellice, please bring tea and some of Mrs. Beatrice's cakes." Lavinia raised a questioning brow in her guest's direction. "You will take refreshment, I suppose?" She tried to keep the sarcasm from her voice, but was neither entirely successful nor entirely abashed by her lapse in good manners.

He was still grinning. "How kind of you to invite me, Miss Taylor. I should be honored. I may sit, then?"

His gibe made her flush, for Ellicc had stayed after showing Templeton in, and Lavinia had not asked him to sit before giving instruction to the maid.

"Of course you may, sir. That is, unless you prefer to drink your tea standing up. I think you will find *that* chair quite comfortable." She moved her arm gracefully in the direction of an armchair halfway across the room.

"Doubtless. But then we should have to shout at each other instead of having a polite conversation." He walked deliberately toward the satin-covered sofa and sat at the end opposite her. He continued to smile.

The day was quite hot and Lavinia was in no mood to bandy words with him.

"But then, I do not believe that we have *ever* had a polite conversation, so I daresay your proximity when we do converse is quite beside the point." She smiled stiffly.

Templeton was looking handsome and cool, although how he managed it she could not imagine, since her blood seemed to be approaching the boiling point. A fine lawn neckerchief was tied loosely about his neck and his fawn-colored coat and trousers were immaculate. Templeton, who was observing her at the same time, noticed a decided improvement in her appearance and was on the point of saying so in just those terms when he reminded himself of his mission.

"Ah, I cannot disagree, Miss Taylor. The fault has been, I fear, entirely on my side." She blinked in surprise. "Yes, I know, you are astonished at my admission. . . ."

" 'Astonished' is perhaps a bit strong. . . ."

". . . And that is most understandable, for I have been less than charming when we have met, ma'am. But I am prepared to mend my ways and can only beg that you will give me the opportunity to do so." Templeton did not pause long enough to let her respond. He had to win her over, but he knew that a woman as intelligent and clever as Lavinia Taylor would turn him out in a trice if he began to gild the lily. "Miss Taylor, I have been rude, difficult, ungrateful, and quite full of myself. Fact is, I do not know why you continue to speak to me at all."

Lavinia looked at him from the corner of her eye, then glanced down thoughtfully. This was not the man she knew. *That* Templeton was just as rude and tiresome as he had just confessed. So, which then was the real Marquess Templeton? The one whose reputation she had heard of in London was not exactly ramshackle, not by London standards anyway, which could countenance practically any behavior in a gentleman or a peer before it dubbed him a rakeshame.

Why, look at someone like Richard Barry, the seventh earl of Barrymore, a shameful creature whose heyday was a bit before her time. His exploits were so excessive that he had been nicknamed "Hellgate" because of his dissipation. He was an expert driver, and sometimes driving home in the early hours in his high-flyer phaeton, would break the windows on the street with his whip, a bit of playfulness he called fanning the daylights. No, the London Templeton at least was a finished man, one James Stanton probably described to his friend, Freddie, as an out-and-outer or a trump. She remembered that he helped to set London style and was an acquaintance of the Regent and no doubt a regular at the gentlemen's clubs, but he was not a member of the dandy set. Those men, who had too much time and money on their hands, set themselves up as arbiters of all that was socially acceptable and were in the habit of speaking and behaving offensively and outrageously. It was not unknown for such men to push others into the gutter as they passed on the street or to deliberately insult a lady or a member of the clergy. Of such sins she knew she could absolve Templeton. Lavinia sighed. She supposed she must learn to get along with the man.

She smiled. "Overdoing it just a bit, sir, but your apology is accepted. Truth to say, on occasion, I may have given you cause to be short-tempered."

"I am certain that you never . . ." He caught her eye and flashed that grin again. "Yes, you did, Miss Taylor." She threw back her head and laughed, just as he had intended she do. "But I should say that we were well-matched, would not you? And now, let us shake hands and be done with abject apologies and get on with being friends."

Lavinia took his outstretched hand, then pulled back suddenly. "You must take back your awful remarks about my husband hunting *and* you must say that you do not believe that I wish to marry *you!*" She grinned now, rather impudently, but she was serious all the same and he knew it.

"Miss Taylor, anyone with eyes can see that it is the gentlemen who will hunt *you* in the marriage market, not the other way round."

She put her nose in the air and gazed at him from under hooded lids, waiting.

He stepped in quickly. "And a woman as intelligent and as lovely as you could never possibly wish to marry a fool such as I."

"Well said, my lord." Her smile was all contentment. "Ah, here is the tea."

"Nothing in the post, ma'am," Ellice said softly as she set down the old silver tray.

"No?" The disappointment was evident on her face. "Thank you, Ellice. Do you take sugar, my lord?"

"One, please." He inclined his head in the direction of Ellice's erect retreating back. "You were hoping for a billet-doux, Miss Taylor?" he teased.

She decided that if she took exception to every provocative or outré remark the marquess made they should be forever at daggers drawn. "Oh no, sir, nothing of the kind. I have been awaiting a letter from my brother, Samuel; he is at Oxford."

"Ah." Templeton sipped his tea, prepared to be the kind of good friend who listens.

"He is very young to be there, but you see he is so bright that it would have been a shame to make him wait. He is also a notoriously poor correspondent, and I have not had a letter for three weeks—no wait, nearer four. He was supposed to be traveling for a few weeks after the end of term with a friend, and was to finish in London, but I thought I would have heard from him by now. Another week and I shall progress from miffed to worried." Lavinia passed him a plate of cakes scented with almonds and saw his look. She laughed at herself. "I am sure that you think me a doting sister and you are correct! There is just him and me, no other family, and I have looked out for him since our parents died."

"I see." He was noncommittal.

"Sam can be . . . a bit impetuous, and I am sometimes concerned that he may get into some difficulty."

"And you do not think that perhaps you ought to leave him more to his own judgment, at his age? Let him stumble a bit, as young men will?"

"I suppose I am overcautious at times, but he has been in a scrape or two and . . ."

He laughed at her gently. "That, my dear Miss Taylor, is one of the greatest occupations of a young man. I speak as one who got into many more than his share in his day and, as you can see, I have lived to tell about it."

She caught him up on this immediately. "Yes, but that is just what I am afraid of, you see. Oh no, I did not mean that the way it sounded." Lavinia smiled and sighed. "I suppose you have the right of it. I *know* you do. If I let him be, he will survive. Whether *I* shall," she concluded dryly, "is another matter altogether."

He decided to change the subject. "I see you were reading *Waverly* before I came in. I read it last year, and have just finished *Guy Mannering* by the same author. Are you enjoying it, Miss Taylor?"

They discussed the novel for some minutes, Lavinia confessing that she liked Scott's work less than she did that of Coleridge and Byron.

Templeton picked up on her mention of the author's name. "So, Miss Taylor, you concur then that Scott did write this book, even though it was published anonymously?"

They chatted about books and authors for some time. When the marquess took his leave a short time later, he thought to himself that the upcoming book circle discussions might be more stimulating than he had hoped. Thomas Darnall was coming up the path to Lavinia's house as Templeton was coming down. The former allowed a smirk of studied surprise.

"Ah, Lord Templeton. Upright today. Almost something of a novelty for you, isn't it?" He laughed.

Buoyed by the success of his visit with Lavinia, Templeton did no more than smile and lift his hat as he passed. Darnall frowned at him and rapped his white thorn cane sharply on Lavinia's door. A while later, the two were driving the short distance north to Painswick Beacon, from which considerable height they could enjoy the cooler air and the fine views across the Severn Valley.

As the days passed, Lavinia was both pleased and relieved that she had ordered a new wardrobe, for more and more of her time was occupied with the marquess and Mr. Darnall. As Lavinia wrote in her next letter to Edwina, she had not enjoyed such popularity since they had debuted in the metropolis. Templeton called frequently and even remarked politely upon her changed appearance, but his visits clearly were of a platonic nature. They often chatted about London, both confessing that they did not miss it a whit, and discussed the latest gossip about the Regent and the Princess of Wales.

The Prince of Wales and his latest escapades were always a source of gossip for everyone—the press and the populace shifting their loyalty between him and his wife, with feelings generally running against whomever was displaying the most outrageous conduct at the time. The two were, at the moment, in a dead heat with regard to unpopularity. Their daughter, the Princess Charlotte, had recently died in childbirth, but feelings of sympathy for both parents were largely displaced by their misbehavior. Her mother, Princess Caroline, continued to live indecorously in Italy, while the prince was still trying vainly to bring divorce proceedings against her, this time so that he might remarry and sire another child, since he would rather die before he got another on his wife.

Thomas Darnall, a gentleman who was all that a woman might wish for, figured prominently in her letters to Somerset. He was handsome, charming, thoughtful, intelligent and, evidently, well-fixed financially. She had great fun on their walks and rides; he was eager to get to know the neighborhood and more than once surprised her with the knowledge he had amassed in a short time about the village and its environs. And she had not yet seen him fall down, tip over his carriage, or spill any food on her gown. Even Templeton spoke highly of him.

There had been an elaborate picnic recently with several of her neighbors, including Darnall, his aunt, Mr. Breverton, and Templeton, who had organized the outing. Everyone had gathered on the riverbank, sitting on blankets and cushions under trees whose branches stretched out over the water, as if trying to reach the arms that extended across from the other side. They had been singing and were discussing the upcoming cricket match, wondering about or predicting the winners and talking of past matches and first-class bowlers.

Templeton's footman, Tim, spied his master stepping carefully down the bank to retrieve a bottle of ale that had been left to cool in the water. Having been told by Mr. Pratt and the others to take particular care that the marquess was not embarrassed again by any mishaps, Tim followed. The downward slope was slight but a bit slippery, owing to Tim's previous trips to insert then remove other bottles, and in his eager attempt to overtake Templeton, he succeeded in losing his own footing. Arms windmilling with the effort to regain his balance, he slid down the bank, colliding with an unsuspecting Templeton, who was none too sure of his own balance, and sent him face first into the water.

All eyes turned at the mighty splash, and a number of folk rushed to the bank to offer help. Fortunately, the water was not deep enough to carry away the marquess, and Tim, calling out in a needless panic, was able to pull him out with little effort. The water was muddy enough to cover Templeton from head to toe with grime, however, making him look quite as ridiculous as he supposed he must. He slogged to the perimeter of the gathering.

"Er, I no longer seem to be appropriately dressed for this occasion," he said wryly. "If you will forgive me—and this disruption—I shall return to the Park and make myself more presentable."

There were murmurs of sympathy and dismay as Templeton mounted his horse and rode off. Lavinia turned to find Mr. Darnall, face averted and shoulders trembling with mirth.

"Mr. Darnall! Surely you are not laughing at the poor marquess?"

"Forgive me, ma'am. I do know it is unkind of me, but you must concede that he seems to make himself a figure of fun so very often! I am beginning to wonder if he just craves the attention!"

"Oh, that is unkind, sir!" Still, Lavinia could not entirely contain a little smile. *Honestly, indignities seem to follow him like a dark cloud!*

"Tim, I'll have your guts for garters!" Galen Waters wanted to throttle the inexperienced young servant. "How could you be so careless? We told you to watch the marquess and make certain nothing unpleasant happened to him this time, and just look what's happened!"

Will Tabbard was helping Galen remove some rocks so that a new rose bed could be planted. "Things is even worse than they was," he fairly screamed at the hapless Tim.

By the time that the servants had gathered for their supper, word of Templeton's latest escapade had run through the ranks. Jim Lewis had been one of the first to learn of it, the groom being at hand to take Aristotle once his master had dismounted.

"We *told* you to look out for him!" Jim cried.

The poor lad only hung his head, too ashamed to look at the others. "I'm sorry. I tried . . ."

Alfie Sharp chimed in. "You *tried,* well . . ."

"Now just one minute, you lot!" It was Sarah Waters and she was more angry than Galen or anyone else had seen her in many a day. She put an arm around Tim's shoulders and squeezed. "Don't you pay one bit of attention to any of them, Tim, you hear me?" She rounded on the men, looking at each of them. Will Tabbard, Alfie Sharp, Jim Lewis, her husband, even Cornelius Pratt had spoken sharply to Tim. "You should be ashamed, all of you! You heard what happened. He told you it was an accident, poor little duck." Tim felt his shoulder squeezed even harder. "How can you blame him for that?"

They had the grace to look discomfited.

"Here, Tim"—Jim cuffed him playfully—"you heard Mrs. Waters, pay us no mind. If it had been me there, I probably would have fallen into the water with him!"

"Ahem! Well, I suppose you did your best there, Tim, and ain't no one can fault you for that. Not even us, eh lads?"

"That's right, Alfie," Mr. Pratt agreed. "Now you go on and see if Mrs. Waters can convince Mr. Pride to give you an extra dish of pudding. You earned it, my boy." He smiled at Tim, who gave him a shaky smile in return and moved off with Sarah, who threw a dark look back at them.

"Well, he's done it again, hasn't he? I mean, I thought a *marquess* had more, well, agility, if you get my meaning," Galen said. "How is Miss Taylor ever going to look at him without laughing? We shall have to watch him constantly before the man stumbles into his own grave!"

The others nodded and chuckled, although the situation was not amusing.

"I think you are right, Galen." Neville had entered halfway through the discussion. "I do *my* best to see he is turned out properly, although the lord knows he does not give me much help or encouragement, and then he goes and makes a cake of himself all over again."

"Gentlemen, please! I would remind you that

none of these incidents has been the marquess's fault. We shall all just have to be more vigilant."

"How, Mr. Pratt? We cannot follow him about wherever he goes."

"We must do just that, Neville, or as near as we can."

Seven

The first meeting of the Painswick Book-Readers' Circle met at Mrs. Caton's fine old house in Bisley Street two days after the picnic. A heavy rain began pounding relentlessly at the windows and on the roof shortly after the members had settled into the green-papered drawing room. Mrs. Caton's maid served wine, and soon the meeting was called to order.

"Well," Mrs. Caton ventured, "we are gathered to discuss the novel, *Waverly,* but I have no idea how we ought to proceed. Has anyone participated in such a group before or have any ideas to share?"

No one signified that they had any such experience. "I think we should just begin, Mrs. Caton," Helen Stanton replied practically. "Someone can comment on an aspect of the novel; then the others may build on that, as it were."

"Mrs. Stanton, since you have been so good as to give us your guidance, perhaps you will be the first to speak?" the marquess suggested.

"Why, thank you, Lord Templeton. I should be more than pleased to do so. Ahem"—she sat up in her chair and placed her wineglass on the mahogany side table—"ahem. I quite enjoyed the way the author has his characters speak in their own regional dialects, I suppose you would call it. Such a wonderful way to put the reader in the setting." She smiled at the group.

"Oh, I agree most definitely, Mrs. Stanton," said Lavinia. "I have never seen that done before and . . ."

Templeton put in eagerly, "that is because it is not often done, Miss Taylor. I found it a bit disconcerting at first, but eventually, I, too, felt more deeply steeped in the Highlands and the Jacobite rebellion."

Lavinia raised the subject of the author's true identity. Several agreed with her and Templeton in believing him to be Sir Walter Scott, and a lively discussion followed on the subject.

At the Park, Cornelius Pratt and several of the other servants shook their heads worriedly. "Still coming down in buckets, Sarah," pronounced Galen. "Good lord, what will happen to him, do you suppose?"

"No telling, Galen," Alfie replied dismally.

"Well, dear, we could hardly have sent Neville or Tim to sit in Mrs. Caton's parlor and talk about books with the others, could we? We shall just have to hope for the best." Nevertheless, Sarah looked concerned.

"Mr. Darnall, you have not said much. Did you not like the book?" Helen Stanton asked kindly.

"I, oh . . . I cannot say that I cared for it much, ma'am. Rather prosy, I thought." He cocked an amused brow at the company. "And long. *Very* long." He laughed and turned quickly to Albert Breverton. "How did you find it, sir?"

"Actually, I find that when I really enjoy a book, I do not wish it to end, so it cannot be too long for me," Mr. Breverton confided, rubbing his palms together enthusiastically.

"Mmm," Dorothea Caton said rather curtly, "perhaps. But the author did go on, didn't he? He probably could have made the book somewhat shorter. Do you really mean to say you find such a long book enjoyable, Albert?"

Mr. Breverton blinked. "Well, that is just my opinion, Dorothea."

There had been a decided chill in her voice that might have made the other guests uneasy if it had not been dispelled by the entry of Mrs. Caton's maid with the refreshment tray. Templeton did manage to get through the evening and all the way home without the assistance of anyone on his staff, much to everyone's relief.

The next day, he took Lavinia driving and let her take the ribbons for quite a distance as they bowled down the country road and alongside the river.

"You are doing quite well, Miss Taylor, for all you said you had only a little experience; you handle my cattle well."

"Thank you, my lord. This is a very nice rig." Lavinia grinned with pleasure. He noticed the dimple in her left cheek for the first time.

"Please, let us dispense with the 'my lords.' Call me Templeton, as my friends do." He watched her closely.

"Very well. Shall you call me Lavinia, then?"

"If you would be kind enough to permit me that liberty, ma'am."

She nodded. "These are fast trotters, Templeton.

I have seen you run them down this very road."
She peeked at him from the corner of her eye and
smiled. "May I open them up?"

There was that dimple again. She was quite fetch-
ing in a deep rose-colored carriage dress; another
new frock, he realized. He looked at the sparkle in
her eyes and laughed. "Go ahead, but go easy at
first. They do not know you, remember."

A short time later, they slowed their pace to allow
horses and passengers to catch their breaths, and
Lavinia relinquished the reins to Templeton.

"Oh, that was most exhilarating!"

"You acquitted yourself well. Their mouths are in-
tact"—he tipped his head toward his cattle—"as is
my carriage."

"And us!"

"That is also of utmost importance, Lavinia," he
responded gravely. "I would tell you that you are a
prime whip, madam, but I fear it would go to your
head."

"Oh, tell me anyway, Templeton, please!"

They were slowed almost to a walk, having just
come out of a sharp turn, much like the one where
his accident had occurred all those weeks ago.

He faced her squarely. "All right, Lavinia, you are
a prime whip. There! Are you happy?"

"Yes! Thank you, Templeton. That means a great
deal coming from a bang-up London driver, you
know."

"Imp! When we met—oh, somewhere near this
very road, if I make no mistake—you called me
ham-fisted!"

She blushed and laughed. "I do believe I did. But
you told *me* that I did not know how to drive at all
because I hit one or two ruts!"

"One or two! Why, you managed to find every . . .

Ah, Lavinia, I do not wish to argue with you. The day is too fine and you are too lovely to spoil either with an argument."

They exchanged a long look brought to an abrupt end by the unheralded appearance of a dogcart from behind them. Luckily, the driver reacted quickly enough to avoid catastrophe. The driver was Jim Lewis, equally as skilled with the ribbons as his master. Still, there was sufficient ado in the form of cries from all parties involved before everything came to rest safely. Templeton jumped down from the carriage, then assisted Lavinia to alight.

"Jim, are you all right?" he called to his groom.

"Right as rain, Lord Templeton, and that sorry that I gave you such a fright." He got down and went immediately to his horse. "There, Mike," he crooned, "are you hurt?" He examined the animal, who appeared to be unharmed. "You'll do, just a bit frightened, aren't you? And who wouldn't be, I ask you, the way *I* was driving?" Jim spoke as if his master and Lavinia were not standing beside him, his attention entirely focused on Mike. He recalled himself suddenly. "Oh, my lord, I beg pardon."

Templeton smiled. "Not at all, Jim. First things first. He does seem to be unscathed." He patted Mike's broad neck.

"He is, my lord, no thanks to me."

"Do not be so hard on yourself, Jim. I was at fault for being all but stopped in such a spot. No way you could have known I was there."

Jim gulped and said nothing. Actually, he had known Templeton was there, or at least in the general area, since he had been following his carriage at a far distance since the marquess had left the Park.

"Where were you going?"

"Going? Oh, I was on my way to Stroud to see the corn chandler, sir." The story had been concocted before Jim had left the Park in the event that Templeton saw him.

"Ah. You may be off then, Jim. I'll just move us out of the way." He helped Lavinia back to her seat and climbed up beside her.

"Er, no hurry, my lord. I can just follow behind you until you get back to the Lodge and then leave." Poor Jim was desperate to carry out his assignment better than poor Tim had his.

Templeton and Lavinia gave him puzzled looks. "That would make no sense, Jim, especially as Miss Taylor and I have not yet finished our drive. I would not wish to keep you from your duties." He pulled his vehicle just off the road to allow Jim to pass and nodded at the servant. "Good day to you, Jim."

"You'll be all right then, my lord?"

"I beg your pardon, Jim?" What in heaven's name had got into the man?

The ice was getting much too thin. "Nothing, sir. Just wanted to be certain you didn't need me for anything. Good-bye, my lord. Miss Taylor." He nodded and drove off.

Templeton looked after him for a moment. "Odd. I have never seen Jim behave so strangely. If I did not know better, I would say he had been following us."

"Hmm. Speaking of strange behavior, Templeton, did you happen to notice anything odd last night at Mrs. Caton's. I had the distinct impression that there was more to that exchange between her and Mr. Breverton than we saw."

"Oh, then you do not know?"

"Know what?"

"About Mrs. Caton and Breverton."

She shook her head. "What is there to know?"

"Only that many years ago they were very nearly betrothed. Well," he amended quickly, "at least they were *very close.*"

"You don't say!"

He nodded. "Of course, this was before Mrs. Caton, Miss Lawson she was then, met Mr. Caton. I gather that Miss Lawson had hopes, but Mr. Breverton was too slow off the mark. Eventually, she met Theodore Caton when he visited here and she married him."

"Poor Mr. Breverton. And he never wed anyone else? How sad!"

He shrugged. "Perhaps, perhaps not. Who can say if they might have been happy together, Lavinia? In any event, God knows it's taken him long enough—she's been back in Painswick for years—but my guess is that he's trying to woo her all over again."

"And you think she is rejecting him, Templeton? Is that why she bit back at him like that?"

"I haven't any idea. But it would be nice, don't you think, to see them together?"

"I do, for they both are good people and I am quite fond of Mrs. Caton."

"I quite agree, but I was speaking more in generalities. I only meant, is it not better for people to be together?"

It seemed to Lavinia as if the marquess must have been reading her recent thoughts. "So, Templeton, you subscribe to the Noah's ark notion that Mr. Darnall suggested the other week?"

His lips tightened and he shook the reins to quicken their pace. Why must she bring him into their conversation? "Let us leave Mr. Darnall out of it, shall we, Lavinia?"

* * *

"Jerrold, I am worried about Lavinia." Edwina put a supporting hand to her aching back and tried to stretch. She was much bigger in this pregnancy than she had been with any of the others and she was dreadfully uncomfortable.

"Why, dearest, is she ill? Has something happened to her?" There was genuine concern in her husband's voice.

She waved her friend's latest letter. "No, Jerrold, it is what is *about* to happen, I think, that concerns me. . . ."

"Now, Edwina—"

"*Listen,* Jerrold. I mean that I am concerned because of what she is about to do."

"Edwina," he began patiently, for he had found that patience was definitely the watchword during this pregnancy, "what could Lavinia possibly be planning that worries you?"

"She is going to be married!"

"She is? When? You have not said a word before this. I did not even know she was betrothed. To whom?"

"That is my point, Jerrold."

This was maddening. "*What,* er, what would be your point, my love? I am afraid I am all at sea."

His wife nodded as if this were no more than one might expect of a complete blockhead. "I am talking about the man she will *marry.*" Edwina realized that she was beginning to speak with her words underscored, as Lavinia had of late been writing. She sighed. *Bless him, Jerrold has the patience of the angels with me.* "The problem is that she is going to marry the wrong man, Jerrold. There."

"Is that all? I . . ."

" 'Is that all?' How can you be so cavalier about it? Lavinia is just as dear to you as she is to me."

"She is indeed," he spoke truthfully. "I am only trying to say in my poor way, darling," he drawled, "that you are worrying over nothing, since Lavinia is intelligent enough and old enough to know whom to marry. For heaven's sake, Wina, calm yourself, you'll worry the baby." He pointed at her belly. "Who is she marrying, by the way?"

"I do not know."

"What!"

She patted his hand. "Now do not get up on your high ropes, Jerrold. You see, no one has proposed yet." Her husband groaned in confusion and she added quickly, "But I believe they both will."

"So, you mean that she has a choice, then? Well, good for her."

"Perhaps. It appears that two gentlemen admire her and I think that she is encouraging the wrong one. Here"—she pointed to one of the pages in her hand—"she speaks of this Mr. Thomas Darnall and the poor Marquess Templeton."

"The 'poor marquess?' "

"Yes." She rose and crossed to Jerrold's chair, waving a page under his nose, then snatching it away as he reached for it. "Marquess Templeton. I *have* mentioned him before, Jerrold." She cocked a brow.

"Er, yes of course, Wina. Templeton." He tried to sound informed.

She laughed. "Jerrold, you are hopeless. But, to return to *Lavinia's* poor choice in men," she teased him, and he bowed his head in mock acknowlededgment, "Marquess Templeton sounds the perfect choice to me. He is handsome. . . ."

"Is not Mr. Darnall good to look upon?"

She made a show of consulting the letter. "Yes, dear, he is."

"Ah."

"He—the marquess, that is—is rich. . . ."

"Darnall would be a poor man? Oh no," he corrected himself, "that would be the marquess, the 'poor marquess.' Darnall is not in funds?"

"No, he would appear to be quite well-off."

"Mmhmm."

"Templeton is intelligent. . . ."

"But Darnall, evidently, cannot even read," her husband teased.

"Well, now you mention it, it is my guess that Mr. Darnall never even read that book."

"What book?"

"*Wayland.* No wait, *Waverly.*"

"Why should you care if he has?"

"Oh, never mind. As I was saying, Templeton is witty. . . ."

"While Darnall, one infers, is obtuse."

She nodded vigorously, then made a face. "Well, not precisely. That is not unless one gives him credit for his tasteless remarks about the poor marquess."

"Oh, yes, the poor marquess again. Tell me, what can Darnall possibly say that is tasteless about a man who is so clearly a paragon?"

"Ahem. Well, he has spoken so whenever Lord Templeton has fallen down."

"Fallen down? *Whenever* he has fallen down? Good God, woman, how often does he do this?" Jerrold Somerville was having difficulty holding in his laughter.

"Several times, actually, but it was never his . . ."

She was interrupted by the sound of Jerrold's guffaws and his palm slapping the arm of his chair. "Several times? Ha! Ha!"

"Really, Jerrold!"

"And you fault Darnall for making light of the man's, um, foibles? Ha! Ha!" He laughed all the harder.

"If you would only listen, you would understand. Do you want our friend to wed an unkind man?"

"No, darling, I do not. But neither do I wish to see her spend the rest of her days with one who has difficulty standing up, even if he is a marquess."

Eventually, Edwina convinced her husband of the rightness of her opinions, although it required a great deal of teasing from him and as much patience on her part before she was able to do so.

"You see, she does not think that Lord Templeton admires her in that way. She believes they are nothing more than friends."

"Probably all she wishes to believe, seeing how clumsy he is. I would choose Darnall myself."

"Jerrold, please be serious," Edwina pleaded.

He sobered. "All right, dear. But how do you know that Templeton *does* want her as more than his friend?"

"Jerrold," she said carefully, "a woman *knows* these things."

He gave a heavy sigh. "Of course, dear."

"If it were not for my condition, we might be able to travel to Painswick and . . ."

"Edwina . . ."

"I know, Jerrold." She smiled at him fondly. "Honestly, I would not interfere in that way. Lavinia must make up her own mind, just as I did." Edwina kissed his cheek. "But, I have dropped the odd hint for the marquess in my last two letters. For all the good it seems to have done." She shook her head.

He patted her hand. "That's all you can do, Wina.

Now, tell me how you are feeling this afternoon. Still tired?"

"But surely, Mrs. Caton, you just misplaced the snuffbox."

Dorothea Caton's look told Lavinia what she thought of this suggestion. "I do not take snuff, Miss Taylor, so there is little likelihood that I moved the box in order to misplace it. It belonged to Theodore. It was lovely, enameled with a scene of Venice and studded with aquamarines, and it reminded me of him. Oh, thank you, Mrs. Kindle." She accepted a parcel containing a silk shawl embroidered in soft browns and reds, and she and Lavinia departed the shop.

"When did you realize it was missing?"

"A day or so after our book circle met."

"Dear me. Do you suspect that one of your servants took it?"

"Good day, ladies." Gerard Melbury tipped his hat as he passed. "Lovely weather."

They greeted him, and Mrs. Caton resumed her tale. "I do not know what to think. My servants have been with me for years. Well, except for young Amy, the between-stairs girl I took on a few weeks ago. Her family is badly off, but I cannot think she would do such a thing."

"If this were London, I should not be at all surprised by this, because burglaries and all sorts of crimes are so common there. Why, one can hardly walk down the street at night without the fear of being set upon by footpads."

"Yes, I have heard some appalling stories, but here in Painswick, I must say such things are most unusual."

A thought suddenly occurred to Lavinia. "But then, who else could it be but one of us—those of us in the circle?"

"Oh my, no, I would never suspect such a thing, Miss Taylor! It must have been an unknown thief who got into the house. I was able to learn that Wendell, my butler, forgot to lock the front door on that evening, perhaps on other occasions, as well; you see, I have long thought that he may be sipping my brandy in his pantry. I have given him the sharp side of my tongue, you may be sure. I believe that the thief took advantage of that opportunity—the unlocked door—and stole the snuffbox."

"Was anything else taken?"

"Not that I have noticed. Why?"

"Only that it seems rather odd that he would take just that one item. . . ."

"It was very valuable."

"Still, why not take other things at the same time? I noticed that you have some beautiful silver that any self-respecting thief might love to have." Lavinia gave a crooked smile.

"Hmm. Yes, you are right, it is surprising."

"Have you notified the constable?"

"Oh no! I do not wish to do that, so much trouble, you know. I feel that it must turn up. The thief might be caught somewhere else, taking something in Stroud perhaps, and then my snuffbox will be returned to me."

Lavinia refrained from pointing out that, even if the miscreant should be caught, there was no possibility that the box could be returned to her, since its rightful owner would not be known.

Two days later, Mrs. Caton, no closer to finding the thief and the snuffbox and looking haggard, was telling Mr. Darnall of her loss after Sunday services. They were soon joined on the church lawn by Darnall's aunt and Mr. Breverton who was, indeed, hopeful of reigniting the spark that had once glowed between him and Dorothea Lawson.

"Whatever is wrong, Dorothea?" Cynthia Weld asked. "You do not look like yourself."

Mrs. Caton explained.

"I have been telling Mrs. Caton that I cannot fault her decision not to involve the constable. I have heard that investigations into matters such as this theft can be most unpleasant, even for the victim, if you can imagine such a thing, and so seldom result in recovery of the purloined items. A pity, but there it is," Darnall explained.

"Dorothea, I am sorry to learn that you have been robbed," Mr. Breverton said sympathetically. "Is there anything that I can do?"

"I hardly think so, Albert. But you are kind to inquire." She smiled stiffly.

"I am always at your service, Dorothea, you know that. Cynthia, I would like a word with the vicar. You will all excuse me?"

Templeton had invited Lavinia to supper a few days following the service and they talked at length about the theft of Mrs. Caton's snuffbox.

"Well, I suppose I cannot really blame her for not reporting the crime. Darnall is quite correct; these things are rarely solved. Nonetheless, it bothers me to just let the thing go like that." He waved a hand in emphasis of his feeling and narrowly missed colliding with Godfrey who was leaning over his shoulder to refill his wineglass.

"Oh, I am sorry, my lord!"

Lavinia snickered and Templeton glared at her. She finished nibbling on an olive and placed the pit at the edge of her plate. "So you do not know about the investigation?" she asked him in the tone of one who has learned the latest news first.

"Investigation? No, Lavinia, I have not heard about it. Do tell."

"Mr. Breverton has decided to look into the matter."

"Mr. Breverton? You cannot be serious." She assured him that she was. "But that is ludicrous. What does Albert Breverton know of such matters? He will be wasting his time."

"He cannot do any harm, especially since Mrs. Caton will not let the authorities try to recover the snuffbox."

"My dear Lavinia, he will make a mull of things, you mark my words. He will not have any idea how to go on and will end up just looking ridiculous."

"Indeed? Templeton, I remind you that you have managed to look ridiculous on more than one occasion that *I* know of, and you had not been attempting anything so enterprising and selfless as the restoration of property to its rightful owner."

"Well, bless me, aren't you the proper preacher, ma'am! If I had a thick skin, I should not be wounded by such cruel remarks. . . ."

"Templeton, if you did *not* have such a thick skin, you *would* have been wounded—by all the spills you have taken since you arrived in the district," Lavinia drawled. Templeton could not help but laugh at her bon mot.

"A capital hit, madam, capital. I still say that poor old Breverton cannot but end up looking the fool. Hardly the sought for outcome if, indeed, he has set his cap again at the fair Dorothea. However, I must believe that is why he has decided to attempt to find the thief."

"Do you think that is so?"

"Why else undertake such a thankless task? But never mind Mr. Breverton or the mysteriously missing snuffbox. Tell me, have you heard from your brother yet?"

Lavinia was pleased that he remembered. "I have not, but I have taken your advice to heart, sir, and have determined not to worry."

"Good for you, Lavinia."

Nonetheless, Templeton was beginning to worry himself. It was thoughtless and cruel of the young sprig not to keep better contact with his sister, particularly since he must know how she fretted about him. He determined to send a letter off to Lawrence Grover, asking him to make some discreet inquiries about Samuel Taylor's whereabouts.

The cricket match was held on the village green on a steamy morning in July. The sides were made up of townspeople who only played occasionally, and they presented a motley appearance clad in their old or everyday clothes. A huge number of people were gathered, eyes on the pitch and quietly applauding for one side or the other.

"Here, here now. They're in trouble today, 'cause here comes Noddy Drummond!"

"Best bowler in the valley!"

"Right. Pray for 'im, lads, our Noddy's got a real rib-tickler for your boy!"

Lavinia was at Thomas Darnall's side, obviously enjoying the match and, it appeared clear, her escort's company. Templeton exchanged pleasantries with them.

"Templeton, good match. Care for a wager?" Mr. Darnall asked eagerly.

"It is, but I think not, Darnall. I seem to have lost my taste for betting." He did not explain that he had left it in London at White's club.

"Oh, be a sport, we'll make it small stakes. A pound says Benton doesn't do any better this inning than last."

The marquess shook his head. "I prefer just to watch."

"Oh, but this adds spice to the whole thing, you know," he persisted. Lavinia cast them a puzzled glance, too involved in the match to have heard the particulars of their conversation. "Just a flutter." Darnall pressed him.

"I don't think so." Templeton said evenly. "See to Miss Taylor, man, you're ignoring her." He nodded and strolled off, leaving a grumbling Darnall behind. He stopped to purchase a paper of nuts from the grocer's boy before heading in Albert Breverton's direction.

"Mr. Breverton, enjoying the match?"

"I am indeed, Lord Templeton. I was a good bowler in my day, if I do say so myself. I was a devilish right-armer." He flexed his arm. "All in the follow-through, you know. Ah, yes, we played many a great match right here on this green. Ever play?"

"Not much, sir," he smiled. "I was a very poor batsman. My schoolmates would have paid me not to play if I'd continued."

After the match had concluded, Noddy Drummond having been just as murderous as his supporters had predicted, Templeton and Mr. Breverton sought the cooler air under the trees beside the river.

"Have you made any progress in finding Mrs. Caton's snuffbox, Mr. Breverton?"

The older man gave him a sidelong glance. "I expect you think that I'm an old fool."

"No, but I do think you have set an impossible task for yourself. But then, Mrs. Caton is worth it, I suppose?"

He did not pretend to be confused by this observation. "She is. So, you see I had no choice." His gaze was level. "I would do anything for Dorothea. But you already knew that; it is a small village."

"It is, Mr. Breverton, but the town is not talking, if that concerns you."

He nodded. "Good. Still, it would not matter. I was fool enough to let her go once; I want to rectify that mistake, but she will not let me. She is afraid I think. And perhaps a bit angry still, despite that she was happy with Theodore Caton. He was a good man."

Albert Breverton, a slight man of few words, had just spoken more than Templeton, or anyone else for that matter, had ever heard him speak, and the marquess acknowledged his gratitude for the man's confidence.

"I understand. Has she, um, warmed up at all?"

"Not to say *warm* exactly, not yet. But I have great hopes, sir!"

"And do you also have great hopes of solving this mystery?"

"Happens I do," he replied quietly.

Templeton choked. "You do? How? Who is it?"

"All in good time, my lord. All in good time. I am nearly there, but I must tread carefully."

"If you are getting close to a thief, Mr. Breverton, you had better tread carefully. He may be desperate if you corner him."

Mr. Breverton nodded his understanding. "I must be off now, sir."

Was it possible that he did know something? "Wait . . ."

"Good day to you."

Templeton stood, scratching his head and smiling. He could not believe that Breverton had the faintest clue about the whereabouts of the snuffbox, but he wished him well in his crusade to win back Mrs. Caton. He walked slowly back to the Park, wondering if he might not be able to perform some chivalrous act to win Lavinia, because he would see Thomas Darnall in hell before he would let him have her.

Eight

Lavinia and Mr. Darnall sat on a stone bench in the gracious shade of an ancient oak tree.

"Lavinia"—he had begged leave to use her given name two days previous when he had proposed marriage—"I do not wish to press you, for I know that I promised to wait for your answer. Only tell me that you have thought on my proposal and have not decided to reject me—at least not yet." He smiled at her.

Oh, dear. She had considered his offer. The truth was, she had done little else in the past two days and, while she had not decided to reject him, neither could she bring herself to decide to accept his suit. She did not love him, it was that simple. Certainly, she liked him a great deal, she had since first meeting him and she was, after all, a good judge of character. Still, she did not harbor deep feelings for Mr. Darnall. Lavinia knew that she *ought* to accept him; indeed, she had almost convinced herself a dozen times that she *would*. Just this morning she had chided herself not to be a goose, mentally ticking off all the reasons why she ought to take Mr. Darnall for her husband.

He is a good man who says that he cares for you. He is kind, he says he has a good income, although you both

*could live extremely well on your own money, and he is
tall! And then there is the unavoidable fact that no one
else is coming down the path to beg you to be his wife!
But then, who else might there be? Templeton? Ha! The
very idea is laughable. Not only because he clearly has no
desire to wed you, but because you have no desire to wed
such a buffoon! Just accept Mr. Darnall and be done with
it!*

Yes, she would. Lavinia smiled back at her suitor.
"Mr. Darnall, Thomas, you honor me. I . . ."

Crunch! Crunch! Crunch!

Startled, Lavinia and Mr. Darnall looked around
to find Trillium chewing blissfully on the hat that
she had stolen from the bench where Darnall had
left it.

Crunch! Munch!

Lavinia only just managed to choke back a snort
of very unladylike laughter. She might be used to
the animals' occasional misbehavior, although that
did not excuse it, but certainly other folk were not,
and she knew that Mr. Darnall might be displeased
by this development.

"Trill!" she called out, rising from the bench.
"Trill, bad, bad girl! Oh, Thomas, I *am* awfully
sorry."

But Mr. Darnall did not seem to hear her, for he
had risen, too, and was crossing in great, angry
strides to where the goat stood, a few yards away.
"Damned creature!" he bellowed. "Give me my
hat!" Trill turned, kicked up her heels, and
bounded off toward the meadow, the hat still in her
mouth. Darnall stopped, hands on hips, staring after her.

Lavinia could contain herself no longer. "Well, I
do understand why you are angry, Thomas, but
surely there is little point in getting the hat back

now, for it is ruined. . . ." She gasped at the look
he gave her as he turned, for his face was purple
with rage and he shook his fist in emphasis.

"That animal," he ground out slowly, "should be
shot! Do you countenance such antics, Lavinia? It
is inexcusable! It is the outside of enough! She
ought to be destroyed so that such a thing cannot
happen again!"

"I do apologize, for you are quite . . ." Lavinia
froze. " 'Shot?' " she repeated, shocked.

"Yes, madam. And I will do it for you, if you . . ."

"You"—she closed her eyes for a moment in an
effort to control her emotions—"Mr. Darnall," she
said quietly, "if you dare to harm Trill, *I* shall shoot
you." His eyebrows shot up. "And do not think for
even a single moment that I would hesitate to do
so. I do appreciate that you do not find her misdeed
amusing, and I shall, of course, replace your hat.
No"—she held up a hand to forestall him—"do not
say a word. Have I made myself clear?" She did not
wait for a reply. "Need I mention that I do *not* accept your proposal, sir? It is evident to both of us,
I think, that we, that is you, I, and the animals *including* Trill, would most definitely not suit. Good
day, Mr. Darnall."

Lavinia called on Mrs. Caton later to try to take
her mind off her altercation with Mr. Darnall and
to ask if the snuffbox had been recovered.

"It has not, Miss Taylor, and I am still that upset.
It makes me angry to think that someone came into
my home and just took what he wanted."

Mrs. Caton's maid entered and announced that
Mr. Breverton and the marquess had called to see
her.

"Oh, yes, Prudence, you may show them in."

Lavinia caught the merest hint of surprise on her face. Apparently, the gentlemen had not been expected.

Mr. Breverton strode into the room with more authority than he had ever exhibited, while Templeton followed wearing a somewhat confused look.

"Dorothea, I hope we do not call at an inconvenient time," Mr. Breverton said. Even his voice was stronger than before, and he looked quite pleased with himself.

"Not at all, Albert, Lord Templeton. Do please sit down. Dorcas, bring tea, please."

Templeton took a seat close to Lavinia. "Templeton, are you all right? You look, um, puzzled," she asked.

"I am," he whispered back as his hostess and companion exchanged pleasantries. "I was on my way to call on you and ran into Breverton. He took my arm—Lavinia, I swear he's a different man than the quiet one we have all come to know—and practically dragged me here. Wouldn't tell me why. Only said it was important and that he had been on his way to get me. I ask you!" He chuckled.

Dorcas left the tea tray, but as Mrs. Caton leaned forward to pour, Mr. Breverton put a hand on her arm.

"Dorothea, never mind that now. I cannot wait any longer while we all sip tea politely. . . ."

She frowned. "Really, Albert, one must observe the civilities."

"Hang the civilities, Dorothea. Do you want your snuffbox back or don't you?" He reached into his pocket and, with a huge grin, held out the snuffbox to her.

Cries of surprise came from everyone, but none

was louder than Mrs. Caton's. "Albert! You have found it! How? Where? Who took it?"

He laughed and patted the hand she had placed on his arm. She looked at the box a moment, then back at him.

"Breverton, good for you!" Templeton said and Lavinia seconded him. "You told me that you had an idea, but to say the truth, I was not sure whether to believe you."

"That is why I wanted you to accompany me here, my lord."

"You were right in your suspicions, then?"

The older man nodded vigorously. "I was. Unhappily."

"Why, Mr. Breverton? Please, never say it was someone we know," Lavinia put in.

He nodded again. "I am very much afraid it was, Miss Taylor. Mr. Darnall took it."

"Never say so, Albert!"

"Mr. Darnall!"

"Albert, you are so clever. How do you know that he took it? Oh, I suppose that is a stupid question, for obviously, you got it from him."

"I did, Dorothea. And I must admit that it was not terribly difficult to find out the truth. You see, for all his charm, I never quite took to Mr. Darnall. It seemed to me from various little things he said that he was not as well-off financially as he would have us think."

"I never noticed anything like that," Mrs. Caton said.

"Well, it was easier for me, you know, since he lived with Cynthia and me. Of course, he must have planned to eventually sell the snuffbox. He probably intended to steal more—perhaps from others of us as well; that would be why he had not departed once he had taken the box. So bold. Thank heaven he did not do anything worse." He paused so that his audience might ask him to elucidate and they gladly complied.

"Don't you see? He could have cheated us in other ways. He might even have tried to marry Miss Taylor in order to gain control of her fortune, for example."

Lavinia gasped involuntarily, then quickly covered her mouth with her hand.

"Exactly, Miss Taylor." Mr. Breverton nodded at her. "We must be grateful that he did not offend you in such a way. I do not mean to suggest that any man would not have every proper and real reason to wed you, ma'am. But Darnall is a bad 'un, and I am convinced you would have seen him for what he was immediately and sent him on his way."

Lavinia flushed.

"Mr. Breverton, what has Darnall to say about all this?" the marquess inquired.

"Nothing yet, sir, for he does not know. I must confess that I took the liberty of looking through his room this morning when he went out riding and fortunately found the box. He has not yet returned and thus, does not know it is gone."

Lavinia asked, "Have you spoken with the constable, sir?"

He shook his head and looked at Mrs. Caton. "Not yet. Cynthia will be very distressed to learn what Darnall has done and bringing in the law will make things worse."

"Albert, you know that I never wanted the constable involved in this. Can you not just send Mr. Darnall away with the threat of arrest if he does not go? Cynthia never even has to know what he did, and I can just say that the snuffbox had been misplaced after all, and has turned up again."

Mr. Breverton smiled at her. "You are all kindness, Dorothea."

She dismissed this praise with a wave of her hand. "Not at all. It is *you* who have earned all the credit, Albert, by discovering the thief. Thank you, my old friend. My lord, will you accompany Albert when he confronts Mr. Darnall? I do not want to risk his being hurt by that terrible man."

Templeton assured her of his agreement. Mr. Breverton sat down beside Mrs. Caton on the sofa and they looked, unspeaking, into each other's eyes.

"Lavinia, it is time for us to leave."

The words broke into her thoughts. "What?" She had been far away in thought and now looked up at Templeton, who stood waiting before her. "Oh, of course."

They said their good-byes, although neither Mrs. Caton nor Mr. Breverton seemed to pay much attention.

Late that afternoon, Templeton received a letter from Lawrence Grover. His friend began by stating that his inquiries about Samuel Taylor were "in hand" and that he would write Templeton further as soon as they were completed. A paragraph or two provided the latest news in London, and he chuckled at his friend's deft turn of phrase, then sat up much straighter in his chair.

> *By the way, you might be interested to know that, according to the town gossips, Silvester Hubbard has at last had enough and is divorcing Althea. No doubt having broken off relations with his own inamorata,*

he actually expected to find his lady wife at home in the evenings. I am told by a reliable source that learning she was cuckolding him with Ralph Preston was the last straw. How Mrs. Hubbard could stomach a rake-hell like Preston, only she could tell us, however, the lady has taken herself off to the country, probably in an attempt—a bit late, one is forced to note—to curb the scandal that is brewing.

Templeton shook his head, thankful once again that he was out of his liaison with Althea and away from town. He felt no pity for her. Hubbard's action, though hypocritical, was no more than she deserved if she had continued her faithless ways even after her narrow escape with Templeton.

"My lord? Mrs. Althea Hubbard is calling."

Templeton shook his head. He must have nodded off here in the sunny window after he had read Grover's letter, otherwise why would Pratt be mentioning Althea? He must be dreaming.

"What did you say, Mr. Pratt?"

"I said that there is a Mrs. Hubbard here, sir."

Then it was real, not a dream. Templeton's blood ran cold.

Althea Hubbard floated into the room as if it were her own, not waiting any longer for Mr. Pratt to admit her. Her arms were outstretched.

"Templeton," she said sweetly, engulfing him in an embrace.

"Althea."

She pulled back and smiled into his face, then pouted. "Are you not happy to see me, darling?"

Darling?

She leaned forward again, her perfume wrapping around him just as her arms had, and kissed his cheek. This was amazing, he was still holding

Laurie's letter in his hand and here the creature stood. And looking as beautiful as ever, he could not help but notice. Her mahogany-colored hair was arranged in what he was certain must be the very latest fashion, her complexion was as perfect as porcelain, and her costume, a muslin in the softest orange imaginable that very likely no other woman could wear, was stunning. Still, there was something different that he could not put his finger on. She watched him looking her over and smiled a cat's satisfied smile.

"Well, Templeton, I hope that I do not disappoint."

"Althea, that would be impossible," he replied truthfully. "Shall we sit? Now, do explain what you are doing here." He had never been so bold, so rude in his life, but he knew better than to mince words with Althea Hubbard.

She decided to laugh at his stern face. "First, my dear . . ."

"Ahem." Mr. Pratt had come back into the room. "My lord, which room shall I give to Mrs. Hubbard? I should like to have Ursula put away her things. And which one to her maid? Mrs. Hubbard's maid, that is." This last was added in the unlikely event that the marquess might have entertained the notion that Ursula had somehow employed a maid of her own.

Templeton's jaw dropped. It had not yet occurred to him that Althea had brought anything with her, much less her maid, because it had not yet occurred to him that she intended to remain at the Park. Clearly, she did intend to do so. The face he turned to her was dour. It was late in the day and he could hardly send her off to the Swan's Nest at this hour. *Only for tonight* he said first to himself and then to her, low enough so that Mr. Pratt could not hear. He gave the necessary directions to Mr. Pratt, pointed out that the number for dinner would be larger than expected, and asked that wine be served.

After Mr. Pratt had left on his several errands, Templeton turned back to Althea and tried to sound more polite than he had.

"You did not answer my question, Althea. Why have you come to Painswick?"

"Oh, but darling, I have not come to *Painswick* at all. You know perfectly well that I loathe the country. I have come to *you.*"

"Humph. I repeat, Althea, why?"

She was not ready to cease her game. "Because I have missed you, of course."

"Oh, Althea, cut line. Our last meeting would not have left anyone in doubt but that our affaire was over. I have a very clear recollection of a perfume bottle flying dangerously close to my head, therefore I cannot think why you should miss me."

She ignored this. "I am famished, Templeton, cannot dinner be served early? And may I have it in my room? It is generally served early in the country, after all, so that should not present much difficulty. Coral and I have been traveling for *days,* and I wish to dine and wash and go to bed." She gave him an arch look from under thick lashes.

Glad for the opportunity to delay dealing with Althea until the next day, Templeton quickly agreed. "But tomorrow we must make arrangements for you to stay elsewhere."

Her only answer was a cryptic smile. "Ah, Pratt," she said, as the butler returned with the wine, "I shall go to my room now. Have Cook—did Mr. Pride

come with you, darling?—send up my dinner as
soon as he can prepare it. What is it, by the way?"

Mr. Pratt's tone was all that was proper. "As I understand it, Mrs. Hubbard, Mr. Pride is serving a
very nice joint with parslyed potatoes, peas, and turnip. I hope that will suit."

She wrinkled her tiny nose. "Turnip. I detest turnip. Do ask Mr. Pride to give me something else.
Perhaps asparagus?"

The butler looked at the marquess, who merely
closed his eyes and gave a small wave of his hand
to signal approval.

"Very good, madam."

"Have water heated, so that my abigail can prepare my bath. Oh, and please bring my wine to my
room. I shall drink it now."

"Yes, madam."

"Thank you, Mr. Pratt," Templeton said as the
pair exited the room. *Heaven help me, what have I
done to deserve this? And what am I going to do about
it?*

The residents below stairs were no less disturbed
than their master.

"And did you see all those valises and bags?" Alfie
was incensed. "How long's she staying?"

"Yes, when is she leaving?" Ursula asked. "Rudest
lady *I* ever met."

Sarah Waters, whose patience was already at its
lowest ebb in years, chimed in, "She was not expected, that much is certain." Mr. Pratt nodded his
agreement. "Because the master would have told
us. What sort of lady just turns up on a gentleman's
doorstep?" She could not wait to tell Irene Beatrice
all about this.

Mr. Pratt was never one to gossip about his betters, but he could not resist informing all those assembled in his butler's pantry that, "The master did not look best pleased, I can assure you."

"She and her pointy-nosed abigail," Alice Patch complained, "have me runnin' and fetchin' like I'd no other duties to attend to, Mr. Pratt. That maid of hers has airs above her station, if you was to ask me." She straightened her immaculate white apron with a sniff of disapproval. It was unpleasant to be ordered about by another servant, but class lines were as well-defined and strictly observed among the servants as they were above stairs. "You did hear what Mrs. Hubbard said about the sheets, Mrs. Waters?" She watched Sarah carefully, for this was bound to raise the older woman's hackles.

Sarah put down her teacup and folded her hands primly in her lap. She sat up straight as an arrow in her chair and squinted at Alice. "What," she asked, her voice dangerously low, "did she say?"

Jim Lewis gave Alice a surreptitious kick in the ankle and hissed, "Don't be tellin' tales, Alice. Mrs. Waters doesn't need to hear such things."

"Ouch! You don't have to kick me, Jim! And why shouldn't Mrs. Waters hear?"

"You are right, Alice. Now tell me, what did she say?"

Alice cleared her throat. She seldom held the floor in this way. "She said as how they didn't smell fresh."

There was a collective gasp. Mrs. Waters's housekeeping standards were the highest, and no one had ever dared to question them before now.

"Not fresh," she repeated slowly. "I'll have her know that those linens, like *all* the linens at the Park, are laundered regularly, and I've got half a field of lavender in those cupboards to see that they smell clean. Why . . ."

"Now, dear . . ." Galen Waters felt it was time to interrupt before his wife had a fit. There were few things that miffed her like uncleanliness, so for someone to question her housekeeping was tantamount to suggesting she had committed murder.

"Galen! Can you imagine? Not fresh, she says!"

"Now, now, Sarah. She is from London after all, and only God knows how they keep clean there. I do not suppose that she is accustomed to having things as nice as you've done them here."

"Well . . ."

Cornelius Pratt joined the effort. "He is right, Sarah. Pay the woman no heed at all."

Presently, Neville came into the room and sank gratefully into a chair, heaving a sigh of tremendous relief. His colleagues waited for his report.

"Well?" Will Tabbard prodded him several moments later.

"Let him be, Will," Jim said.

"I have never seen the marquess in such a temper." He looked at his friends and shook his head.

"Yes, that was quite obvious at dinner," Joseph interjected. "Didn't eat hardly a thing and barked at me like he never did before."

Neville nodded in sympathy. "He was no better just now. Bit my head off, he did, just because I asked if he wanted the window left open or not."

Disapproving "tsks" emanated from around the small room.

"What did he say about *her*?" Mr. Pratt inquired. "Did he mention Mrs. Hubbard?"

"Mention her? He fair raved about her, although I could not understand most of it. He kept saying something about divorce and going back to London." He shrugged. "Most of it did not make much sense, except that he is most definitely *not* pleased that she is here."

"Why is she here, I wonder?" Galen Waters asked no one in particular.

"Yes, and just when it appeared as if things between him and Miss Taylor might be moving along in the right direction."

"This is bound to put the cat among the pigeons," Alfie Sharp intoned, and no one disagreed with his prediction.

Templeton slept only intermittently, but by the time the sun stretched above the horizon, he had decided to send Althea on her way that very day. No questions, no arguments, no delays. He hoped she would return to London or at least leave the village of Painswick entirely, but he would content himself if she simply removed to the Swan's Nest. What had possessed her to come running to him in her time of trouble? If Hubbard were going to go through with his threat and divest himself of her, what did she hope to accomplish by coming here? She could not have honestly expected him to give her his protection.

There was no purpose in asking himself what had attracted him to Althea Hubbard in the first place. The answer was plain enough for any man to see. What was considerably less evident was why, once he had ascertained her marital status, he had not turned on his heel and walked away. There had been plenty of other available women he might have turned to. Some were prettier than Althea and some even would have become his mistress, just as she had done, if he had asked them to. Instead, he had chosen to have an affaire with a married woman, and here he was, still paying the price for it. Well, he had reminded himself more than once during that long night, he deserved no better. He had taken another man's wife when he ought to have been looking for one of his own.

And what of the woman whom he was, day by day, becoming increasingly certain he wished to wed? What of Lavinia? How would she react to this? Well, he assured himself, she was hardly naive; she had lived her life in London after all, and one did not manage that without knowing how the haut ton lived. Still, that might ensure that she understood what had occurred when he lived in London, but it could be cold comfort if she did not understand why Althea was here now.

Templeton was in the morning room early for his breakfast. It was improbable, he knew, that Althea would rise at such an hour, but he wanted to be ready in the event that she did. He ate slowly, not that he had much of an appetite. By ten o'clock, he had read the newspaper, buttered and eaten three more pieces of toast than he wanted, and several times asked Mr. Pratt if he heard Mrs. Hubbard on the stairs. He had not.

By half past ten, he was considering the merits of a walk in the gardens, when Althea's abigail, Coral, entered soundlessly and made her curtsy to him. The young woman was plain to the point of homeliness, an attribute that he knew Althea required in her female servants. She could bear competition from no one, despite the fact that her beauty easily outshone that of most other women, highborn or low.

"Good morning, Lord Templeton. Mrs. Hubbard

is not feeling quite the thing today and begs that you will excuse her."

His lips twisted in a grimace of defeat. He recognized her game immediately. If she delayed until her presence at the Park had become routine, it would be that much more difficult for him to ask her to leave. Well, he would play her game, but not for long.

On the following morning, he breakfasted alone since Althea still had not risen, and found another letter from Grover in his post.

My dear Templeton:

I had not expected so speedy a response to my inquiries, else I would have waited and included this information in my last letter, but your request proved much easier to fulfill than I had anticipated. That was good for me, less so I fear, for your Miss Taylor, since her brother's folly has made him rather well-known in certain less salubrious sections of the town. I shall be brief, as doubtless you will wish to act as quickly as possible.

Young Sam Taylor arrived in town some weeks ago with his university chum, Phineas Troy who is, unhappily, as gullible and foolish as he. They managed to run through their luck—and funds—by frequenting every semirespectable faro bank, then tried to recoup their losses in the hells, including a particularly notorious one in Jermyn Street. I need not tell you how their luck ran there, my friend. A seasoned man of the town has no hope against the sharps in such a place, let alone two flats down from Oxford, who also spent more than their share of time disguised.

In a word, Templeton, the cubs are rolled up. The duns are out in full force, and rumor has it (the gos-

*sips yet again—where would we be without them?)
that soon they may be in danger of losing a great deal
more than their purses. My friend, I should think there
is little time to lose. If I may be of further service, you
need only to ask.*

Grover

Damn! He hated to think how this news would
upset Lavinia. And after he had assured her that
her brother was not getting up to anything dangerous. *If I had Samuel Taylor here, I would thrash him
soundly for worrying his sister like this.* What should he
do? Ought he to tell Lavinia, or ask Grover to intervene—or perhaps he might travel to London and
handle the matter himself. *But no,* he reconsidered,
*I have no right to insinuate myself in her family matters—
well, no more than I have done already, or to usurp her
authority, such as it may be. And then there is Althea;
will I be able to rid myself of her before I go? I shall have
to tell Lavinia what I have learned, although God knows
how, and offer my assistance, should she care for it.*

Lavinia broke the stem of another rose as she
tried to insert it into the large porcelain vase. Deciding that her blue mood lent itself more to the
expansive outdoors than to more fragile items inside, she took Neptune and Dover—an old, white
stray who had recently joined the family—outside
for a romp. A look at the darkening sky warned her
of coming rain, but she was undeterred.

Lavinia had never felt more foolish. Her hereto-
fore dependable character judgment had failed her
utterly in the matter of Thomas Darnall, for she
certainly could not give herself credit for turning
him off when he had threatened Trill. It had barely

occurred to her that Mr. Darnall might be a fortune hunter, something she should have considered in view of her prior experience with similar men in London. And if that were not bad enough, she had never suspected that he might be a thoroughly bad lot, who would steal from the likes of Mrs. Caton. She did appreciate that she could not have been expected to know all of these things, but they galled her all the same. Had she been so desperate to find a husband that she had not sufficiently considered the qualities of the man who had proposed to her?

The dogs tore around her in circles, and she obliged their request by throwing two large sticks as far as she could. They bounded away and returned momentarily with their prey, pleading for the game to continue, and she tossed the sticks again and again, until she was tired from the effort even if they were not. She felt better for the exercise and the air. As she strolled now at a more leisurely pace, Lavinia resolved to take an interest in village matters, such as the school. She had meant to do this some time ago, but had always had some perfectly good excuse to put off involvement.

Well, she would not delay it any longer. It was time she earned her keep, so to speak, in the village and the work would also help to keep her mind off of her troubles. She must accept that her wish to marry was not, apparently, going to come true, for there were no other eligible men in the village. Well, not if you eliminated Mr. Stone, which she had done immediately after her al fresco supper. Mr. Ingham was rather young, she thought, so was Martin Bennett, and Francis Nolan was too old. Mr. Breverton, she smiled to herself, appeared to be spoken for, at least that was the impression she had taken with her when she had departed Mrs. Caton's house.

There really was no one else, unless she counted the marquess and, charming though he might be, she could not see herself married to someone so ungainly. She had explained this to Edwina in one of her last letters, in response to her friend's less than subtle hints that she encourage Templeton. *And even supposing that I wished to marry him, Wina, I would never jeopardize our friendship by setting my cap for him.* Although, she reminded herself, she had almost married a thief and a liar, and alongside such qualities, mere clumsiness paled.

Lavinia knelt to examine the paw that Dover was favoring, and removed a sharp pebble. "There. Enough for you, then, my boy. No more running about today. We shall go back and soak this paw in warm water. Can you walk on it, do you think? I hope so"—she ruffled his ears—"for you are far too big for me to carry."

The dog rose gamely, but his limp seemed to be even worse and he sat down again and gave her a dejected look.

"Oh dear. You must wait here then, Dover, while I go back and get the carriage. I will not be long, I promise," she crooned to him.

"What is wrong with him?"

She jumped at the sound of the voice. Templeton's voice. "Templeton, you frightened me. I had not heard you coming."

"My apologies, Lavinia," he said, smiling, and knelt by Dover's side.

"This is Dover. He picked up a pebble, which I have removed, but now his poor paw is too sore for him to walk on all the way back to the house. I've just been telling him that I shall fetch the carriage to carry him home, but he looks so forlorn."

He looked into her concerned face, his eyes twinkling. "Yes, I did hear you explaining to him." He turned back to Dover. "Did you understand, old man?" The dog made no reply, although he did begin to wag his tail in appreciation of all the attention. Templeton turned to Lavinia, feigned worry on his own face, and teased her mercilessly. "He is an old dog. Perhaps he is deaf and did not hear that you do not intend to abandon him." Templeton leaned closer to the dog and raised his voice several decibels. "Dover old man, can you hear me?" It appeared that Dover could, as he turned away and brushed one paw over the offended ear. "It seems he does, Lavinia. Dover, Miss Taylor just wants you to know that . . ."

"That will do, Templeton." She laughed at his antics.

He examined the injured paw. "There is no serious damage, but it would not be good for him to walk such a distance. There is no need for you to go for the carriage, however. I think I can manage him." He gathered up Dover in his arms, lifting him gently and stood. "There, Dover, that's not so bad, is it?" Clearly, Dover had no objection to the proceeding.

"Oh, are you certain? He is not too heavy, is he?"

"No, Lavinia. I shall do very nicely, I promise you."

"Er, actually, Templeton, I was thinking about Dover. You, um, will not drop him, will you?"

"I am not going to answer that, Lavinia," he replied dryly. "Are you coming?"

They walked companionably for several minutes with Neptune prancing to lead the way.

"It certainly was lucky that you happened along, Templeton."

"In truth, ma'am, I am only returning, albeit to Dover, the courtesy you extended me in my distress all those weeks ago."

"I see. But how did you find me here?"

"Oh, one of your servants directed me. I had called to see you at the house. I have something to tell you," he said carefully, "some news."

They had almost reached the door and she turned to him with a laugh. "Never say so, Templeton! What is it this time? Has the vicar murdered his wife? Have Mr. and Mrs. Stanton been planning to blow up the Swan's Nest? Pray, what base behavior has come to light today in our *peaceful* little village? Oh, Ellice," she said to the maid who opened the front door, "put water on to heat, please. I need to see to Dover's paw."

"Er, where do you want him?"

"Oh, in the kitchen, if you would not mind, Templeton."

"I'll see to his paw, Miss Taylor," Ellice said when Lavinia had told her of his problem. "That way you and Lord Templeton will be able to visit."

"But . . ."

"Thank you, Ellice," Templeton said and steered Lavinia gently out of the kitchen.

She sat in the window seat in the morning room and looked at him expectantly. "All right, Templeton, evidently your news cannot wait. I suppose it is of some importance?"

He sat next to her and took her hands, speaking gently. "Lavinia, it is about Samuel."

Lavinia blanched. "Sam?" She gasped. "Is he hurt? Dear God, Templeton, is he . . ."

"No, no, my dear, he is very much alive, I promise

you. And well." This last might no longer be true, but he could not tell her that, not yet at least.

"Thank heaven. Then . . ."

"Only let me tell you, Lavinia." He squeezed her hands and smiled. "I hope you will not be angry, but I was concerned for you and I took the liberty of having some inquiries made in London about your brother. He is putting up with a schoolmate—Phineas Troy, do you know him?"

She shrugged. "I have met him once. He is the young man Sam was traveling with."

He nodded. "Yes, well, it does not seem as if they have gone very far afield, Lavinia." He paused, trying to gauge her coming reaction. "As near as I can tell, they have been in London the entire time, for . . ."

"Oh?"

"Yes. Lavinia, my friend has informed me that Samuel and Troy have lost a great deal of money gambling."

"Gambling! Samuel? But he does not know a thing about gambling, Templeton," she protested.

He could not explain to her that older sisters seldom are aware of half of what their brothers get up to, certainly his sisters never had, and were, frankly, better off that way. He settled for pointing out that, perhaps Samuel's ignorance of the matter had contributed to the substantial losses he had suffered at the tables. Lavinia stared at him, for a moment lost for words.

"Had he much to lose, Lavinia?"

"Well, his fortune is substantial and it provided him with a very generous quarterly allowance."

"Mmm. I suspect he had been saving it up for a while."

"But why? Why would he throw away his money like that? It is so foolish!"

"I cannot answer that, Lavinia. Look, the lad is done up and . . ."

"Then why has he not written to me? Or come here?"

"Very likely he is too ashamed to tell you what he has done." Although he did not say so, Templeton believed that Samuel probably would contact her soon; he would have little other choice if he wanted to satisfy his debts before the next quarter and buy back his liberty, doubtless curtailed of late by those who might be looking to do him harm.

"Then I shall send him the money he needs and he can come home. You see? It is not so complicated, after all."

"But you do not know where he is," he prompted. "With your London house sold, we do not know where he might have gone. Does Troy have anyone in the city with whom they could stay?"

She shook her head. "Not that I know of. Oh, dear." Lavinia had been pacing the room and now sat down again beside the marquess. There were tears in her eyes. "Templeton, what will become of him? Will . . . those people . . . try to hurt him?"

He could not lie to her, but he could trim the truth. "It is possible that these men are angry enough to try. . . . Now, my dear, calm yourself. I said *possible*. My friend writes that he is attempting to ascertain their whereabouts—Samuel and Troy's. I have written back to him just this morning to try to look out for the lads until . . ."

She began to weep quietly. He put his arms about her and leaned her head on his shoulder. "But he could be anywhere in that awful city." All her dislike of London, for reasons completely unrelated to her brother's difficulties, was evident in those words. "I must go there."

"Lavinia."

She looked up at him. "Will you help me, Templeton?"

"You have only to ask, my dear." He dared to touch his lips gently to her forehead, and she did not draw back.

"I must go to London. Will you come with me?"

He could not believe what she said. She was not concerned that he would fall or otherwise disgrace himself or jeopardize her brother. She had asked him to help her just as if she honestly believed that he could! How could he tell her that he could not? For Lavinia Taylor was not the only woman to have begged his help this day, nor the only one who had wept on his shoulder.

When Althea had not appeared by eleven o'clock, an exasperated Templeton had knocked on her door.

A few moments later, it was opened by Coral, who spoke in a whisper.

"Yes, Lord Templeton?"

"I wish to speak with your mistress, Coral."

"I am afraid that is not possible, my lord."

"Not possible? Why not? Is she *still* unwell?"

"Yes, my lord. She is resting. If you will excuse her, sir." She began to close the door.

"In heaven's name, Coral, the distance between London and Painswick is not so great that it should incommode Mrs. Hubbard for this long."

A weak voice came from within the room. "Templeton? Is that you?" it asked unnecessarily. "Coral, you may allow the marquess to come in."

"Too good of you, Althea," he drawled, then drew in his breath sharply as he got a closer look at her. Althea was standing by the window still in her night shift, and the sunlight clearly illuminated the roundness of her belly.

"Coral, you may leave us," she said.

"You are pregnant!"

Althea lifted her brow and smirked. "Thank you, Templeton. I had wondered why I have been unable to keep down my breakfast of late."

"I had no idea."

"Good God, man, say *something* intelligent," she snapped. "Of course you had no idea, for you did not have a hand in the making of this one." She put on the dressing gown that Coral had left on the chair by the window. "Oh, Templeton, what am I to do?" She sobbed, covering her lovely face with her hands.

He led her to the chair and knelt down beside her. A damsel in distress and he did not have the vaguest idea how, or indeed if, he could help. "Well, um," he began, "who did have a . . . that is, who is the father of your child? I suppose it is that good-for-nothing Preston." She glared at him. "No use denying you had an affaire with the man, Althea, I had it just the other day in a letter from Lawrence Grover."

"That prosy old woman," Althea said.

"And apparently right in this instance," he pointed out.

"But not about this." She put her hands on the contours of her stomach.

His look was puzzled. "Who then?"

"Silvester."

"Silvester! You cannot be serious! I cannot believe you!"

"He *is* my husband, Templeton, and not entirely bad to look at."

"And you are his wife, Althea, but that has meant little to either of you for some time. It had not occurred to me that you two, ah . . ."

She brushed the tears from her cheeks. "And I do not intend to acquaint you with the details, sir! Suffice it to say that this child is not a bastard. I only wish that I might say the same for its father." She sniffed loudly and smiled a little, evidently pleased with her wit.

"I do not understand your problem then, Althea. Why have you come to me?"

She gave a deep sigh. "Because, *my dearest*, Silvester is not any more willing to believe me than you were."

"Do you mean to say that he began this divorce action after you told him that you are pregnant?"

She nodded glumly. "He believes that the child is Preston's. But it is not. Our affaire, Preston's and mine, was of a very short duration, and so I know without question that he is not the father, only I cannot convince Silvester. Of course, I need not tell you that I do not care two shillings what Silvester believes and what he does not. Nor do I have any desire or intention to be a loyal wife or have him be a loyal husband. But I do care where my child and I shall live, and if that fiend divorces me, I shall be disgraced."

"What do you mean to do? You cannot remain here, Althea." She began to protest and he held up a hand. "No, I am sorry, but it is impossible."

"You cannot make me leave."

"What?"

She tilted her head and laughed. "You cannot

make me leave," she repeated. "And if you try, I shall tell everyone that you are the father."

"But that is ridiculous. I could not possibly be the father, you said so yourself. I have not been in London since . . ."

She waved a hand dismissively. "That will mean nothing, I promise you, *my lord*. Before anyone thinks that logically, if anyone in this godforsaken hamlet is capable of logic, that is, your name here will be tainted. Besides, have you not left your grand estate since you arrived here, for even a few days?" She could see that he had. "We shall see who is lord of the manor then, won't we, Templeton?"

"Surely you do not plan to remain here forever, Althea." He'd had no idea that she could be so vindictive.

"I do not wish to remain here at all." She looked around the room with distaste. "How could you think so? As I have already reminded you, I despise the country." She gave a little shudder for emphasis. "But unless I have someplace else to go . . ."

"Althea, if you think that I am going to set you up, you are quite off the mark. I told you in London that our relationship was finished and I meant it. Now, in the spirit of what we once shared, I am willing to let you stay for a few days while I handle some business that takes me away, but then you must be off to Silvester. Or, wait, didn't you tell me once about a cousin in Birdlip? Perhaps you could go to her."

"I shall not dignify that suggestion with a response." Templeton was just as glad, now that he thought of it, Birdlip was much too near. She put a hand to her head and shut her eyes. "Very well, I shall be completely honest with you. I am frightened. I have never been so frightened in my life.

Women do sometimes die in childbirth, you know. And it is not as if I have a husband who will comfort me. And I do not have a place to live and I have no idea what will become of my child if Silvester does divorce me. And . . . and"—she began to sob again—"I am so very afraid of being alone, Templeton. Oh, please do not leave me!" she begged.

"I am sorry to say that I cannot accompany you to London, Lavinia, not at this time. There is a matter that requires my attention here."

Lavinia straightened up and blew her nose. How could she have been so presumptuous? Her problems were not Templeton's problems after all. She should be grateful that he had taken as much of an interest as he had, otherwise . . . She did not want to think about what might have happened if he had not learned of Samuel's plight.

"I quite understand. Please do not look so glum, sir!" She managed a small smile. "I shall go on my own."

"What? Never. Er, that is, you cannot, Lavinia. That would not be at all the done thing."

"Templeton, I remind you that, until recently, I spent my entire life in London."

"Yes, my dear, you did. In Hamilton Place, if memory does not fail me. And in the Burlington Arcade. And at Lady So-and-So's for tea. And at Hatchards and Fortnum's, at all the proper places. But you did *not* frequent the kind of place where your brother is likely to be living on his remaining meager funds." That was a mistake, and he hurried on. "Nor the kind of place or *persons* with which you must come into contact if this nasty business is to be sorted out."

Lavinia was touched that he had worked himself into such a pucker over her well-being, but that was not rescuing Samuel. She supposed that this Grover would comply with his friend's request, but she could not knowingly impose upon a stranger, nor trust that he was dependable enough to solve her problem.

He took her silence for agreement. "Good girl. Now, as I said, I've asked Grover to look into the matter further, and I know that he will intervene on your behalf until we can go there—you and I— perhaps in ten days or a fortnight?"

"That was very thoughtful, Templeton. All of this was—have I thanked you? This Mr. Grover must be a fine friend to do all of this for you and, indirectly, for someone he does not know." She had to find out Grover's address, but she knew Templeton would never tell her if he suspected she would go off to London on her own. "You have known him long?"

"For many years."

"He must miss you. I imagine you spent a great deal of time together in London. Driving, for ex- ample, or . . . going to your club. Is he a member at . . . White's is it?" She had heard him mention that establishment to Mr. Darnall.

"Yes, he is. In fact, he helped me to be accepted there; not everyone gets in, you know. A true gen- tleman, Grover is, and a better friend no man could wish for."

Nine

In light of her brother's circumstances, London seemed to Lavinia even more unpleasant than she remembered. She did not blame the metropolis for his predicament; she held him entirely responsible for that, but she did believe that it offered too many temptations, too much opportunity for an inexperienced young man to come to grief. The carriage clattered through the green elegance of Mayfair and then Piccadilly, finally drawing to a bone-shaking stop in front of Grillon's hotel on Albemarle Street.

Soon, she and Margaret were out of the jostling crowd in the street and in the quiet of their rooms. If she had to be in London, Lavinia supposed that Grillon's was the best and safest place to be. It was respectable and elegant, even Louis XVIII had chosen to stay here for a short time on his way to Paris a few years earlier. The room was most pleasant, and the chambermaid who assisted her was cheerful and ready to pamper a tired and somewhat fractious guest.

"Here's plenty of towels for you, ma'am, and if you'll be needing anything else, you've only to tell me. My name is Gloria." She was a tiny thing with chestnut hair, bright blue eyes, and a ready smile.

The maid had a no-nonsense air about her that Lavinia liked.

"Thank you, Gloria. What can you tell me about the hotel dining room? Is the food palatable?"

"Yes, Miss Taylor, it is quite good. All our guests remark on how tasty it is."

Well, that was one potential problem out of the way. "Good. I am going to White's club later, Gloria. Will you be able to get a cab for me?"

The chambermaid laughed. "Mercy, ma'am, you can't go there. That club is just for gentlemen. They won't let you in, you know."

Lavinia did know this and she had not yet determined how she would get inside. But get inside she must, and she hoped that Mr. Lawrence Grover would be there and be able to provide her with Samuel's address. "Yes, Gloria, I realize that, but there is a gentleman there I must see and . . ."

A romance! The dearest thing to Gloria's heart. She considered a moment as she wiped a smudge from the large standing mirror beside the desk. "Well, ma'am," she said at length, "I may be able to help you there. It happens there's a young man in this very hotel, by the name of Cyril Punch, who sometimes runs errands to the club—for our gentlemen guests, you know. He is very well turned-out is Cyril, on account of dealing with all the fine gentlemen both here and there, and he could find out for you if your man is in the club. Would that help?"

"Gloria, that is just the thing!"

"Grand. I'll go and see if he is in the house, Miss Taylor, and bring him up shortly if he is. That be acceptable to you?"

A few hours later, Lavinia found herself sitting in a cab outside White's in St. James's Street, while

Cyril Punch made his inquiries inside. She had expected the wait to be interminable, but only ten minutes had elapsed when she saw a handsome gentleman walking at Cyril's side toward the carriage. The younger man stepped discreetly to one side.

"Miss Taylor?"

"Mr. Grover?"

The man smiled. "I am. Young Mr. Punch here says that you want to talk with me."

Lavinia nodded. "Will you join me, sir?"

The carriage rocked slightly as he climbed in. They shook hands.

"Mr. Grover, you may know who I am. . . ."

"I do, ma'am. Templeton asked me to find out what I could about your brother. Did he tell you?"

She acknowledged that he had. "But I need more information, sir. I must know if you learned where Sam is staying." She kept her voice from betraying her emotions.

"Miss Taylor, does Templeton know you are here?" He shook his head slightly, as if he could not quite believe she was sitting before him. She raised her brows in question. "Forgive me. I thought, given his interest, that you . . . Well, my mistake. Still, I must ask. Are you alone here in London? Do you expect to take care of this muddle on your own?"

"Mr. Grover, you are kind and your concern is most appreciated, but you have not answered my question. Do you know where my brother is?"

"I do." Grover looked uncomfortable. He had only been given the information a few hours earlier and had called at the address, but not found the young man in. He had not yet passed this information on to his friend. The letter was to have been written that night. Well, he could hardly keep the information from Taylor's sister. "He is in Ormond Street, Miss Taylor, number twenty-seven."

Ormond Street was a pathetic place. The garden that had once graced its precincts was long ago overgrown with weeds and contained all sorts of debris, and its houses, like their occupants, were in disrepute and disrepair. As the carriage rolled slowly down the street, searching for number twenty-seven, Lavinia's face reddened with anger at the sad pass to which her brother's heedless behavior had brought him.

"Whoa there, Beauty. Good girl. Here it be, ma'am. Number twenty-seven," the jarvey called out to her.

She remained in the safe and relatively clean confines of the cab for several moments, looking at the grimy building, trying to get up the nerve to step outside.

"You did say number twenty-seven, didn't you, miss?" prompted the driver.

"Margaret, you wait for me here." Lavinia stepped out, strode quickly up the three steps and rapped on the door. It was not until after she had knocked a second time that it was opened to reveal a dilapidated foyer and an equally decrepit woman.

"Well?" the woman croaked.

"I, um, I wish to see Mr. Samuel Taylor."

The woman, presumably the landlady, stared at her boldly and did not reply.

"Mr. Taylor does reside here, does he not?"

"I'm Mrs. Vernon. Mrs. Rose Vernon." Lavinia wondered why the woman felt it important that she know her given name. For that matter, she wondered why she introduced herself at all. "I be Mr.

Taylor's landlady." The woman looked Lavinia up and down as if she were goods in a shop window. "Who are you then?"

Lavinia was losing patience quickly. "See here, Mrs. Vernon, who I am is no concern of yours. Is Mr. Taylor in or not?"

"That's for me to know and you to find out, lovie. And you're not going to find out until you answer my question. Now, who are you?" she repeated, her voice rising in volume.

There was nothing for it but to answer the old woman's question. "I am Miss Taylor. Miss *Lavinia* Taylor," she could not resist adding. "I am Mr. Taylor's sister."

Mrs. Rose Vernon looked her over again, taking in her soft blue silk carriage dress, stylish bonnet, and kid boots. She nodded. "Good."

"Now may I please come in?" Lavinia was convinced that Sam was at home, else why would this crone want to keep her out? She put one foot over the threshold.

The woman stepped into Lavinia's path, blocking her progress. "Not until you pays his rent you don't." She held out a weather-beaten hand.

Lavinia blinked. "Rent?" she whispered.

"That's right, lovie. Rent. He hasn't paid any these last two weeks, and unless you want to catch him up and give us a little something to go on, if you get my meaning, *he's out in the street,*" she fairly screamed.

Obviously, Mrs. Rose Vernon intended to capitalize on Lavinia's fortuitous appearance on her doorstep. Lavinia paid what must have been at least an entire month's rent, so outrageous was it, and finally was allowed to enter the house. The interior was no better than the outside, worse once she took into account the smells and lack of sunlight, the latter owing to the layers of grime on the windows. On second thought she decided, the absence of light was a blessing; what she could make out in the dimness would not have been improved by illumination. Lavinia held her arms close to her body and kept a death grip on her reticule, both from fear of being robbed and a kind of chill she felt, for all that the house was close and quite warm.

The woman pointed toward the stairs. "Up one flight, fourth door on the right."

Lavinia nodded. She held her skirt about her ankles to keep it from brushing the dusty stairs, some of which had the filthy, threadbare remnants of carpet. Gripping the banister, she drew back from its surface, sticky with neglect. She half turned on the step.

"Mrs. Vernon, for the exorbitant price you charge, this place ought to be clean."

"Miss Taylor, the price I charge keeps my trap shut when certain people, certain not very *nice* people, comes here lookin' for my boarders." She gave a heartless, sly grin. "Keeps it shut when the rent's paid, that is." Her laugh was a cackle.

Oh God. Had she already let in someone who meant to do Samuel harm? Would she find him inside his room beaten or worse? What did such men do to people like Sam? Her hand shook as she knocked on the door. She waited. Was he not in after all, or was he lying there . . . She rapped again much harder.

"Sam! Are you in there? Samuel!" Lavinia tried to keep the panic out of her voice, but she knew she was not very successful.

The door opened a crack, just enough to allow a

glimpse of the caller by the occupant; then it was pulled open wide.

"Lavinia!" He glanced up and down the corridor and fairly pulled her into the room.

It was not small, but that was the only thing that might be said in its favor. Obviously, Mrs. Vernon did not clean here either, since it was as dirty and dark as the public part of the house. The paper had long-ago peeled from the water-stained walls, leaving here and there the faded shred of rose and ivy. There were two small beds with tattered covering neatly folded into place and an ancient candle stand and dish without a candle. A single chair that had once graced a lady's boudoir was too flimsy and battered to hold anything more than three neatly stacked books. A valise sat on the bed, but did not appear to contain much, although Lavinia could not see any other evidence of Samuel's belongings.

Lavinia took in all of this with a glance. Her brother stood stiffly, expressionless, in an attempt to stave off any negative criticism she might wish to offer. She swallowed what she wanted to say and instead asked, as though she were inquiring the time of day, "Where is Phineas, Sam? Is he not with you?"

He turned away for a moment, then met her eyes boldly. "No, Phineas left. Two weeks ago, I believe it was."

She looked closely at her brother then and saw the fear in his eyes, saw how drawn he was. His hands were trembling. From fear or hunger? Probably both, she decided.

"Sam," she burst out. "You look awful. You have not eaten in days, I am convinced! And what do you mean Phineas has left?" Lavinia could no longer contain her tears and she pulled him into

her arms. He had lost weight. "My poor Sam. What
has happened to you?"

He held onto her for a minute, then looked up,
eyes moist, and patted her cheek. "I'll come about,
Sis, no need to worry about me."

"No need to . . . The first thing we shall do is
leave this . . . place."

"I cannot. We owe Mrs. Vernon the rent." Evidently, Phineas had gone off without paying his
share of the bill. "And I can't leave without paying
her. That would not be right."

"I have paid that . . . Mrs. Vernon." He looked
at her with a question in his eyes. "The creature
would not let me in otherwise, Sam." Her lips
twisted in a wry smile. "Never mind. I shall tell you
everything after we quit this awful place." She took
his arm. "Come, you are going to love Grillon's."

Soon, Samuel was ensconced in his own room at
Grillon's. Once he had bathed, he and Lavinia repaired to a quiet corner of the dining room where
he ate like one who had been starved. Lavinia, too,
found her appetite had returned.

"Now that you are looking a bit more the thing,
Samuel, you can tell me the whole story." She gave
him a stern look that told him clearly she would
tolerate no roundaboutation.

Samuel touched his napkin to his lips and grimaced. "You are not going to like it, you know."

"Sam, I already do not like it, so you might as
well tell me."

After listening to great tales about the gambling
tables from certain classmates, Samuel and Troy had
decided to forego their original plans to travel
abroad and instead try their luck in the city. The
more well-known and reputable clubs turned them
away, either because they were not members or were

too young. It did not take long, however, before
they found any number of establishments that did
not care about their ages and were willing to accept
"such respectable gentlemen" into their circles.
Once this had been accomplished, it had taken the
two young men very little time to lose virtually all
the money they had.

"We had been putting up at one of the better
hotels." He grinned sheepishly. "I do not mean as
fine as this, but still a far cry from Mrs. Vernon's
establishment. It was not very long before the clubs
and houses we had been frequenting denied us admittance because our funds had dwindled. That is,
we could no longer play for such high stakes as we
had," he explained at her puzzled expression. "If
the owner of a faro bank knows you aren't a high-
flier, he is not as interested in letting you into his
game. In any event, once we were really down on
our luck, we had to find another game." He caught
her eye. "Well, we could not go back and tell our
classmates that we had lost—they had done splendidly, you see. . . ."

"So they would have you believe."

"I . . ." He looked at her with sudden realization
written on his face. "Good God, you mean they lost
as well, don't you?" She shrugged and smiled at
him and he gave a bark of laughter. "It seems
Phineas and I were incredibly stupid, Lavinia. Well,
we believed we had nowhere else to go but, um, the
hells." He peeked over at his sister to judge her
reaction to this.

"Yes, the gambling hells. I have heard of them,"
she said dryly "And so have you, Sam. They are
notorious for parting gamblers with their money.
They are even more unscrupulous than the legiti-
mate tables you had been playing at. How could

you have been so foolish?" Lavinia knew that this was exactly what she should not have said, but she could not help herself; she had kept this in too long.

He flushed with shame. "I know, Lavinia. There is no good explanation. I can only tell you that Phineas and I were desperate. We could not tell our families what we had done. We just wanted to recoup our losses."

"And you ended up losing everything you had left."

"Yes."

"And then some, am I correct?"

He blinked in surprise. "I am a complete flat, am I not? I have not even asked you how you found out about any of this."

"I was worried about you, Sam. It had been so long since you had written and that is not like you. A friend in Painswick had a friend here make some inquiries. And so I am here." She shrugged her shoulders.

"And so you know that I—and Phineas—owe money to one of the owners. There is this place in Jermyn Street. The chap who owns it, Mr. Roland, well, he's not someone you would wish to know, Lavinia. He claims I owe him, um, four thousand pounds." An enormous sum for one of his years and experience. Samuel could not look at her.

"Four thousand pounds?" she echoed.

He nodded. "But it was not so much, Lavinia. Honestly, I know it could not have been above fifteen hundred. . . ." She continued to gape at him. "I know, I know. But you will concede that is much less than four thousand. You see, he has added on Phineas's share, that's about fifteen hundred as well, and the rest is interest."

"But how have you been living, Samuel? Well," she caught herself, "I do realize that you have not been living very well, but you have had something."

"I, ah, have sold some things. My watch fob . . ."

"The silver one I gave you on your last birthday?"

"Yes. I pawned it with Hamlet, the jeweler in Cranbourne Alley."

She nodded. "The one they call The Prince of Denmark."

"Yes. And then I have been selling some of my clothes." He grinned. "I do not have much left but what I stand up in, Sis." She did not look amused. "And today I was going to sell my books. I heard there was a chap in the next street who allows pretty good money for books."

"So, Phineas just left you to deal with all of this on your own, did he? A poor friend, Sam."

He did not disagree. He would settle things with his friend later.

"And why did you not write to me? Don't you know that you can tell me anything, Sam? Instead, you have been suffering here alone."

"I was too ashamed to tell you, Lavinia. And even you must agree that my suffering is no more than I deserve for being so stupid."

"I cannot argue with you. Do not think that just because I've come here to help that I am not displeased about what you have done, Samuel. I am very angry indeed. Whatever were you thinking of? You lied to me"—she ticked off his sins on her fingers—"you gambled, and you could not even confine yourself to the so-called respectable places to do so and went to the hells. Sam, how could you have been so gullible? How did you think to ever extricate yourself from such a disaster?" Samuel listened quietly while his sister rang a royal peal over his head.

She patted his hand. "Even so, I still wish you had let me help you. What have you told this Mr. Roland?"

"I have not been able to get anything like what I need to satisfy him. I go to Jermyn Street to see him once or twice a week; that way he knows I have not fled as Phineas did—he was furious about that—and I've been telling him that I will be coming into some money. He does not know where I live—lived—so I have been safe. But it is a debt of honor, Lavinia, and one I must pay."

She did not dispute the point with him. "You are quite right, Sam. You must repay him, even if he is an unconscionable knave. But you do not have to pay him such shocking interest, nor Phineas's share. Let us think how we must proceed."

Samuel felt better already; then he remembered that he had forgotten to mention Anna.

"Well, he won't leave her, not from what I have overheard. And heaven knows she isn't going anywhere. So where does that leave us, er, him?"

Mr. Pratt had no good answer to Galen's question. "We must hope that Miss Taylor is willing to delay going to London until the marquess is free. After all, this is his best opportunity to show her that he is capable of handling serious matters."

"But she cannot wait for long, Cornelius," Sarah Waters reminded him. "It is her brother's safety that must concern her now. It is time that the master decided which lady it is more important for him to please," she said, lips pursed in disapproval. "From the talking that snip Coral has done—her mistress should hear her!—Mrs. Hubbard's husband is going to divorce her. She says that Mrs. Hubbard and the marquess had the London gossips' tails wagging at one time, but that was over before he came here! So why, *I* should like to know, has she come here with her *baggage*."

"Thinking he would take her in, I suppose," Neville suggested.

"If her own husband wouldn't keep her, why should Lord Templeton? She can't imagine to pass it off as his!" Mr. Pratt was shocked.

"You don't suppose he would take her in, do you? They might even move to London; I've heard her say that she hates the country."

"No, he never would. At least, he would not bring her to London. That's where her husband is, after all," Neville protested.

"I'll tell you this much, Neville," Sarah Waters snapped. "I will not work for that woman, that much I promise you. She is a harpy, that's what she is. Hasn't a kind bone in her body. Always making demands and shouting at folks. I ask you . . ."

A soft rap on the kitchen door heralded the arrival of Irene Beatrice.

"Good afternoon, Irene," said Sarah. "How do you manage to slip out of your kitchen at this hour of the day?"

"Not much to be done, with Miss Taylor away. Only the staff to cook for."

"Away?"

"Miss Taylor is away?"

"Where has she gone?" But Mr. Pratt thought he already knew the answer.

"Why, London." She looked at her friends' concerned faces.

"When did she leave, Irene?" Neville asked.

"Day before yesterday, it was. Early in the morning. Why?"

Her friends explained. "Oh, dear, that is not good at all. Why, the poor man is missing his chance to look good in front of Miss Taylor because he's here holding *her* hand. Tsk, tsk."

"We shall have to get him to London, that is all."

"All right, Nev. How do we do that, exactly?"

"We'll send a message from Margaret. 'Margaret' will say her mistress needs him and that he should come right away. He doesn't know her handwriting, so he won't suspect."

"Hmm." Mr. Pratt mulled this over. "It might just work, you know, Neville. It might just work."

"Grand. Irene, you get a letter off to 'Margaret' now, so that she knows what's afoot," Galen instructed her. "Sarah, you write 'Margaret's' letter. Neville, you bring Lord Templeton the 'message' from Margaret. Play it up, boy, we have to make him believe that he has no choice but to go."

"Althea, I am pleased that you are feeling better this afternoon. You are looking well, positively blooming, I should say."

"Oh, cut line, Templeton. I look wretched and we both know it, even if I have been able to stomach my food today. And if you have come to flatter me and tell me again that I must go, you are wasting your time."

"As a matter of fact, I have not, Althea, although the thought does occur. No, I have come to tell you that *I* am going away, for a short time at least, and so you are welcome to stay here. For the *present.*"

She was no less querulous than she had been since

her arrival. "You? Where are you going, Templeton? I don't want to be left alone, I told you that."

"Yes, my dear, well you never have been able to stand your own company, but that is another story. I am going to London. There is a friend who needs me there."

"There is a *friend*"—Althea's tone was acidic—"who needs you here, my lord. Perhaps you had forgotten."

Templeton sighed. "Alas, how could I?"

"What did you say?"

"Nothing, Althea." The marquess smiled. "This is another friend who has asked for my help, and I must go to her." Templeton had been distressed when he received Margaret's "message" through Wainwright. He had berated himself for forcing Lavinia to go off on her own to deal with Samuel's problem. Here she was in need of his assistance and he was determined not to fail her this time.

"Her?"

"Yes, her. Now, I do not expect to be gone for very long and, as I said, you may remain here during that time. But when I return, you will be going either to Birdlip or the Swan's Nest; you may choose."

"And a veritable clutch of choices it is, Templeton," she drawled.

In his own carriage, Templeton reached London in record time. He put up at the Pulteney in Piccadilly, Grillon's having no rooms available. Lavinia had not been in when he arrived. In light of his failure to help her when she asked and the apparent surreptitiousness of Margaret's message, it occurred to him that she might just refuse his assistance, no matter how badly she required it. It was best then, he decided, to return later in the hopes of finding her in, rather than leave a message. In the meantime, he strolled over to White's.

Lawrence Grover came in shortly after Templeton arrived and they took a glass of Madeira together.

He told the Marquess of Lavinia's finding him and that he had provided the address she required. "I was surprised to find Miss Taylor here on her own, Templeton. I had assumed that you, if not some other of her family, would accompany her."

"She has no other family, Grover, and I was unable to bring her here then. I did ask her to wait until I was able to get away."

"How could she wait? She believed her brother to be in danger—as he may well be."

"You are right and if I were able to do it over again, I would do otherwise. I not only let her down, but may have let her walk into danger. She is very important to me, Grover."

"Indeed?" His friend smiled. "I never would have noticed, old man," he teased.

"Lovely, is she not?"

Grover inclined his head. "She is. And determined. She would have her brother's direction of me if she had to reconvene the Inquisition to get it! But tell me, why didn't you come with her? What urgent business demanded your presence in Painswick? Recall that only recently you had no interest in, or ties to the place; now suddenly when a fair damsel needs you, you cannot leave!"

Templeton chuckled. "Grover, you make it sound just as absurd as it was. Only wait until I tell you why."

Ten

"Margaret, what do you mean she has gone out? Where has she gone? No, do not tell me," Samuel said with alarm. "I never imagined she would do such a hen-brained thing, as to go to meet him alone."

"I tried to stop her, Mr. Taylor. And I tried to go along with her, but she would not listen," Margaret said. "You were not in when she left and I did not know what to do. I am so sorry."

He cast his eyes heavenward. "I met up with a former neighbor from Hamilton Place and he went on and on. I could not get away. Do not feel this is any fault of yours, Margaret, for you are not to blame. Lord knows that my sister has a mind of her own. Anyway, if it is anyone's fault, it is mine. If I had not got myself into such a scrape, she would not be with Mr. Roland trying to get me out of it." He sat down, head in hands and ran his fingers through his hair desperately. "She did not say where they were to meet?"

Margaret shook her head.

"Very well. I am going to his club in Jermyn Street. If they are not there, perhaps someone can tell me where I can find him."

"Oh, Mr. Taylor, are you certain that you should?"

"I do not know what else to do, Margaret."

Margaret had received Irene's note that the marquess would be journeying to London, but so far as she knew, he had not yet arrived. "Sir, there is someone on his way here. A friend of your sister. He will be able to help us."

"Who are you talking about, Margaret? And why would he come here?"

"It's a gentleman, a marquess actually, from Painswick. Well, actually, he is from London. And she wanted him to come with her from the beginning, only he couldn't. . . ."

Samuel soon had the story, at least as far as Margaret knew it. It sounded to him as if Templeton might have a tendre for his sister and he was heartily glad of that; he wanted to see her settled. Still, he did not know when Templeton would arrive, and he could not count on someone else to get them out of this mess. He had caused it and he would be the one to extricate them.

Lavinia had sent Cyril Punch around to Mr. Roland's establishment in Jermyn Street telling him that she wished to discuss with him the matter of Samuel Taylor's debt. In Mr. Roland's gambling rooms, dukes lost their fortunes alongside draymen who lost their children's supper, and ladies of the haut ton bet the brooches given them by their husbands alongside prostitutes who offered the earrings given them by the same men. The difference between the hells, Roland's or anyone else's, and the gambling in men's clubs and private houses was the general honesty of the latter. Then, while gamblers could be left without a feather to fly in either place, the clubs settled for ruination if family fortunes fell short, henchmen of the hells would have their due in blood and bone.

Jeremiah Roland had survived in London's underworld with his fists and his sharp wits and, some ten years previous, had risen to the ownership of one of the city's most infamous gambling hells. Years of rubbing elbows with the well-bred had improved his speech and his taste in clothes. He was still a cunning, cruel, and ruthless man, fairly tall and once not bad to look on, but since achieving his dubious status, Roland had run to fat, strolling his rooms to spot the fool who dared try to cheat him and letting his minions extract his revenge and collect his wagers. He read Lavinia's note with a lascivious grin that displayed rotten teeth and gaps where rotten teeth used to be.

He eyed Cyril. "And who might you be, my lad?" Cyril told him. "Not your name, you numbskull! Why should I care what your name is? I *mean* where are you come from?" Roland waved the note in Cyril's pale face. "Where does *she* come from? Who is she, *stupid?*"

Cyril took offense at his tone, but while he liked to think that he was handy with his fives, he was no fool. "She's his sister—Samuel Taylor's sister. And . . . and she's staying at Grillon's."

"Is that right?" Roland examined his fingernails for a moment. "From out of town, is she?"

"Aye, she is. From Gloucestershire."

"I see. Money there, would you say, Cyril my lad?" He fixed him with a cold eye.

"Oh, I am sure that I don't kn . . ."

Roland seized Cyril's collar and shoved him violently up against the wall. "You 'don't' what, Cyril? You don't want to give me the wrong answer, *do* you? She's staying at Grillon's, so I already know she ain't poor!"

"No, Mr. Roland. She has money. Plenty of it, looks like."

Roland let him go. "That is so much better, Cyril." Cyril wished he had not told the man his name; it gave him chills the way he said it. "Now, you go back to the hotel and you inform Miss Taylor that Jeremiah Roland will be happy to meet with her this evening to discuss terms." He thought a moment. "Yes, tell her ten o'clock right here."

Despite Margaret's protestations, Lavinia had taken special care with her appearance, although she could not have said why she thought it politic to do so. Her evening dress was made of a Bishop's blue *gros de naples,* a fine silk whose corded surface appeared almost striped. The corsage, edged all around with a twisted band of yellow and white silk above rows of pearls, fell into a high vee in the back. Narrow sleeves were set low on her shoulders, and she wore white satin slippers embroidered with deep green ivy. Her blond hair was woven with satin ribbons and dressed in soft curls that framed her face. She had been tempted to wear a domino to conceal her identity, but decided that doing so might offend Mr. Roland. In any event, it was unlikely that she would be recognized.

The hackney cab stopped at Roland's establishment in Jermyn Street and, once again, Lavinia remained inside, too nervous to get out. This driver was not as polite or as patient as the one who had delivered her to Ormond Street.

"Here you are, lady." And, when she did not respond, "Look, we're here in Jermyn Street, just like you asked. Now will you be going in to have a run at the tables or do you want to go someplace else? I have to be off."

Lavinia alighted and paid him, but was not certain what to do next. The premises looked unremarkable, at least from this vantage point. People were passing up and down the street and many entered the building. Each time, she tried to get a peek inside, but it was too dimly lit and the door closed too quickly for her to see. She twisted her reticule and, chewing on her lower lip, tried to steel herself to go inside.

"Come with me." A deep voice made her turn and she pulled her arm from the grasp of the man who addressed her. "You are Miss Taylor lookin' for Mr. Roland, aren't you lady? Or are you here to do some other business?" He looked her up and down brazenly.

For one mad moment, she was not sure which of the alternatives was worse. Her indignation won out and she drew herself up to her full height. "Other business? How dare you? I'll have you know that I *am* here to see Mr. Roland."

"Good. Then come with me, like I said in the first place." He grasped her elbow again and led her toward an elegant carriage standing nearby.

"What is this? I am to meet Mr. Roland here. He said nothing about going elsewhere, and I am not going to get into any carriage."

"You will if you want to see 'im, 'cause he isn't here." The man stood aside, massive arms folded with infinite patience while she decided. He rocked back on his heels. "It's all the same to me." Of course, it was not, since Roland had warned the man that if he failed to deliver Miss Taylor it was at his own peril. "You can come with me and see him or you can go on back where you came from."

"Well, where are you taking me?"

"To Mr. Roland's house. It isn't far, right Jeb?" he called to the driver on the box, who confirmed his statement.

"Oh, very well." Reluctantly, she let him assist her into the carriage and sat back, thankful that he had not joined her inside. The carriage did not travel far, still in the dark it made many turns through increasingly unfamiliar streets, and Lavinia was soon lost. Presently, she was surprised to find herself at the door of a handsome town house in a quiet square. Light spilled on the front step, as a dour footman held open the door.

He nodded and led her wordlessly into a parlor. The room was beautifully furnished with a thick carpet on the floor that preserved the quiet. French doors opened onto a back garden fragrant with the heavy scent of old roses. The footman left, closing the door behind him with a soundless click, leaving Lavinia alone in the empty room.

Samuel hated to go back to Jermyn Street; he hated it every time he went there to meet Mr. Roland to satisfy him that he had not fled the city. Still, he would do anything for his sister, just as she, apparently, was even now doing for him. But Sam's recent visits had been during the day, when a different man was on duty at the door, properly alerted by Mr. Roland to admit one who had not money to play. This chap, a massive man who possessed a remarkable memory for such things and was paid to do so, remembered Sam only as one of a host of young men who was out of funds and no longer welcome inside. Samuel tried to walk past him non-chalantly and was halted in his progress by a large hand grasping the collar of his coat.

"Where you goin'?"

"Why, I am going inside. Where does it look like I'm going?" Sam felt it best to try to bluff his way through. "Please let me go."

"Oh, no you're not." The huge hand tightened on his coat.

"Do unhand me. I wish to go inside, I tell you."

"And I wish to go to Carlton House, but I ain't. Just like you ain't going in there!" The giant pulled Sam back in one powerful motion and tossed him onto the ground as if he did not weigh a thing.

To his credit, Samuel rose immediately and approached the man again. "You do not understand, I *must* go in!"

The giant placed his arm across Samuel's chest. "That's what they all say!"

It occurred to him that, if he had any money or anything of value, he might have been able to bribe the man, but he had nothing left. He could only appeal to his heart.

"Please, listen to me. I am looking for my sister. She was to meet Mr. Roland here. She must be inside with him now and I . . . I have to find her. Surely you have seen her. She is very pretty and tall with fair hair."

"Oh, yes, my lad"—he rolled his eyes—"those *ladies* run pretty thick around here." He pointed past Samuel's shoulder. "Look, there's one! She do for you, son? Ha! Ha!"

He had pointed to a cyprian of the lower order, and although she did have fair hair, neither it nor her rosy cheeks had come to her as naturally as Lavinia's. Sam's face grew red with fury. He was worried about his sister's safety and this lout was making rude jokes.

Several customers who were coming out of the establishment had overheard the giant's remarks. They stopped to look at Samuel and laugh, either because they were happy to have won a few pounds or because they had lost and were glad to see someone else being dealt a bad blow by fate. He tried to enlist them in his cause, to no avail.

"Here comes another one, lad." One man nodded at a whore staggering toward them, her bosom only barely contained by her bodice. "She's even better!" The crowd laughed as the woman approached them and leered at Samuel.

"Here now, gents, the lad don't have the money for any fun, he's just looking, that's what he told me!" The giant roared at his own joke and the prostitute swung her reticule drunkenly at Samuel for "enticing me all the way over here for nothing!"

"Now get out!" The giant gave Samuel a vicious push into the gutter. "And stay away if you know what's good for you!"

"Well, what's all this, do you suppose, Grover?" asked Templeton, who had overheard the last of Samuel's pleas and realized who he must be.

"It appears to me, Templeton, that a man with a very large head and, apparently, a very small brain, has assaulted this young man."

The crowd, which had been on the verge of disbursing once their prey had been dispatched into the street, now stopped to watch the new arrivals.

"I do believe you are right." Together, Templeton and Grover helped Samuel to his feet. Templeton strolled toward the giant. "You! Do you know who this young gentleman is?" he drawled.

"I don't know who he is and I don't care. All I

do know is he ain't got a farthing to his name and he ain't getting near this here establishment," he growled, rolling his hands into merciless fists and looking down at the tall Templeton in his most intimidating manner.

"No, no. You're wrong, old boy." He turned to where Grover stood, Samuel at his side, the former watching in barely concealed amusement. "Isn't he wrong, Grover?" His friend agreed that he most assuredly was. "There, you see? Even Grover here knows you're mistaken, and he is not the brightest of fellows. I'll wager that even these good men know that you are wrong." He waved his arm behind him to encompass the crowd that had grown since Templeton's arrival on the scene. Glad of the chance for some real fun, they all called out their agreement. "Oh my, old fellow, there doesn't seem to be a soul who thinks *you* are right. Pity."

"Be off with you!" said the man, as much embarrassed as angered by this fool's game. "Now!" he roared in Templeton's face.

The marquess pretended that the giant had not spoken, let alone nearly blown his head off. "And since you don't know who this young gentleman is, I shall tell you. He is my friend." By the time he uttered the last four words, Templeton's voice had stiffened from drawing-room polite to hard and uncompromising.

"I don't care!" the man bellowed. "Now get ou . . ."

Before he could finish, Templeton hit him with an unexpected and fiercely punishing right.

"Shouldn't we help him?" Samuel begged Grover.

"Whatever for, Mr. Taylor? I promise you, Charles Templeton has boxed with the best of them. And won. He has no need for my help or yours."

By the time the giant drew back his arm to retaliate, Templeton had hit him again, then again, toppling the man to the ground, where he lay momentarily stunned, as the crowd, more than one of whom had been harassed by the man, cheered.

Wouldn't James Stanton love to tell Freddie about this! Templeton thought with a smile. He bent over his victim. "Now, you will first apologize to *my friend.* Then you will tell him and me where we may find his sister. No, I beg you, do not attempt to strike me, for then I should indeed have to hurt you. Is the lady inside?"

The man rose, groaning and holding his midsection. "Don't know what you're talking about."

"Ah, but you do." Another punch penetrated his belly.

"Argh."

"Just so. You were saying?"

"She ain't in there."

"Where is she?"

"Gone off in a carriage," was all he would say; it was more than his life was worth to betray his employer.

"Oh, come, do be a good lad. I honestly do not want to hit you again. But I will," Templeton finished sweetly.

"She's gone to Mr. Roland's house."

Templeton's face became ashen and Samuel cried out as he heard the words. "I hope for your sake that you know where that is," he said quietly.

The giant nodded and slowly gave him the address.

After finding out how long ago Lavinia had left for Roland's house, he rejoined Grover and Samuel, the older man having explained their arrival to the younger.

"Come, we have no time to lose."

As they rode toward Roland's address, Templeton explained that he and Grover had called at Grillon's shortly after Samuel had left and learned from a very distressed Margaret where he had gone.

"I am just sorry that I did not arrive sooner. No, if I am truly honest, I must say that I am sorry I did not accompany your sister here in the first place, as she asked me to do."

"Well, sir, and I must say that I am sorry for causing her such trouble in the first place." Samuel shook his head in shame.

"Good God, please let us dispense with all the breast-beating. I suggest that we decide how we are going to proceed once we arrive at chez Roland," Grover exclaimed dryly.

Lavinia stood in the center of the room, unmoving, for several minutes. She was frightened and had no idea what she ought to do. She considered pulling the bell cord to summon the servant again, but what would she say to him? He had been uncommunicative upon her arrival, and she thought it unlikely in the extreme that he would divulge his master's whereabouts. Obviously, she was meant to cool her heels waiting until he deigned to grant her an interview. Not surprisingly, Lavinia felt uneasy in the strange house, virtually alone, she supposed, with the unknown but certainly unscrupulous, Roland. And if she needed help—as Margaret had promised her that she might—what then? Would the other members of the household staff come to her aid? This assumed there were other servants, but she had seen no one. She shivered, for the house felt cold and vacant.

Lavinia sighed and looked around her once more. The open doors let in a soft breeze from the garden and she inhaled deeply of the aromatic roses. Hoping the familiar smell and sight of the flowers would help to calm her nerves, she stepped into the garden. The moon was waning and the small space was utterly dark and still, its high brick walls cutting it off even from the lesser and more refined noises of the Mayfair street. The poor visibility prevented her from walking far and she leaned over for a closer sniff of a brilliant white rose.

"Exquisite, is it not, Miss Taylor?"

"Oh!" She jumped.

The voice came from the shadows on the path to her left. Roland crossed quickly and almost silently to her side, and she could feel his hot breath on her cheek. "My gardener bred that rose especially for me, but I haven't named it yet. Nothing I could think of seemed to fit its . . . perfect loveliness." He smiled. Lavinia was having difficulty not drawing back from his sour breath. "Until now. I think I shall call it . . . Lavinia. What do you think of that?"

"I think it a transparent attempt at flattery, Mr. Roland. Surely you can think of a better name than that. Your mother's, perhaps?" *Assuming you ever had a mother.* "After all, you do not even know me. Perhaps I am not the sort of person for whom such a delightful bloom should be christened." She smiled hoping to take the sting out of her words.

Roland smiled back, equally as falsely. "Miss Taylor, I might have offered this compliment to a dozen other women, all of whom would have leapt at the opportunity to be so immortalized. Why is it that you decline the favor?"

Lavinia began to back away from him. She did not know if she would be any safer from him inside the house, but there at least she could see where she was going; she could not see out here and if she had to run, could easily find herself tangled in a mass of thorns. Nevertheless, she felt she had to take some action. "I decline your offer, Mr. Roland, because I am not yet ready to be immortalized. Perhaps in another thirty or forty years. But, I suspect that, by then, you will have found an infinite number of equally suitable names for your rose."

He watched her closely and all but licked his lips. She was not beautiful, but she was young and, he thought, as lovely as his rose, which already had its own perfectly good name.

"I am pleased that you like my garden, Miss Taylor, but you seem to have taken a chill. Shall we go inside?"

The footman entered almost as soon as Roland's hand fell from the bell rope. "Pour the wine, Carlton. Do sit down, Miss Taylor."

She took one of the glasses from the tray held out by Carlton and tasted the wine. It was very sweet.

"The wine meets with your approval, ma'am?"

She nodded.

Roland smiled and sipped daintily from his glass, then sat back in his chair, one ankle balanced on the other knee. He pressed his fingertips together and examined her boldly. "Well, Miss Taylor, we are alone for our private conversation, as I supposed you would wish it. Tell me how I may be of assistance to you."

She ignored his condescension. "I am come about my brother, Samuel, Mr. Roland. I understand that he was gambling at your tables and now owes you money."

"He does. And a very substantial sum it is, ma'am.

I have tried to give him the advice a loving uncle might. Oh you know the sort of thing—too much gambling can be a bad thing and that it is proper and wise, very wise indeed, to pay one's debts on time. But you know young men, Miss Taylor, they can be so carefree and . . . careless. I have been quite patient—even for a fond, old uncle—but the lad has shown no signs of honoring his obligation. Pity." From under hooded eyes, he watched Lavinia place her wineglass on the side table and clear her throat.

"Yes, I quite agree that a gentleman should honor his debts, and Samuel will do so."

"I am pleased to hear it, Miss Taylor."

"But he will repay only his own vowels and only the principal that was lost." She met his gaze unflinchingly. "That amount, I believe, is one thousand five hundred pounds."

"No, madam, the amount is four thousand pounds, as I am certain young Samuel has already told you, and that is the sum to be repaid to me." His voice was even and quiet, the voice of a man used to being heard and obeyed.

Lavinia knew he was aware she was afraid, as how could she not be, but she hoped that she did not give him the satisfaction of displaying her fear. She knew that meeting Roland on her own was not the wisest course of action, but she had been determined not to involve Samuel—for her brave brother had vowed he would thrash the man soundly when they went to pay him. And who else could she have brought with her? Margaret would hardly have been of much use, although she had wanted to come. Her real mistake had been in coming here, and she was furious with herself now for doing so. Even in his establishment in Jermyn Street, they might have been surrounded by people; surely he would not have tried to harm her there. But here she saw all too late that she was at his mercy. There was nothing to prevent his killing her, and it might be days before anyone even found her body. Still, she refused to back down.

"Fifteen hundred pounds, Mr. Roland, not a shilling more."

It seemed that a full ten minutes passed while he tapped a finger thoughtfully against his chin. Finally, he stretched out his legs and laid his interlaced fingers across his middle. "You did not hear me, Miss Taylor. I told you that I want the full four thousand quid. I did not bring you here to bargain." The truth was that he had done just that, but he was not ready to say so yet.

"No. There is no reason why Samuel should have to pay that much. You are being quite unfair and you know it." Lavinia rose in emphasis of her offer and began to walk toward the door to leave, or at least make a show of doing so until he relented and accepted her terms. Then she realized that she had no way of getting back to Grillon's without a carriage—she would have to walk Lord knew how far before she could hope to flag down a passing hackney. But he might not even let her get out of the drawing room before hurting her. She stopped in her tracks.

He gave a quiet, diabolical laugh. "Going somewhere, Miss Taylor?" She turned back to face him, her lips set in a thin, uncompromising line. "Oh do sit down or I shall get a crick in my neck looking all the way up at you, ma'am." She remained standing. "*Sit*, Miss Taylor, do." She did.

"Now, it is apparent that your hearing is in order, so I must assume you are being difficult. I am going to propose an alternative." Lavinia held her breath. "I am prepared to accept your offensive offer of fifteen hundred pounds in cash. The rest I will accept from you . . . personally." His eyes raked her possessively and she gasped.

"Wha . . ."

He held up a hand to forestall her reply. "No, do not give me your answer yet, Miss Taylor, I beg you." He smiled again. Somehow this all seemed worse when he smiled. "Do not be hasty. Think on my offer." He waited.

"I do not have to think about your *offer* at all, Mr. Roland. My answer is *no*. Now, I wish to leave here. *At once!*" She began to rush from the room, but his voice halted her again. "You cannot keep me here, my friends know that I am with you."

"Ah, but they do not know *where* we are, do they? And I might add, although it is certainly no concern of mine, dear lady, that any friend who let you come here alone is not worthy of the name." He rose and began to walk toward her.

"You may remain here with me tonight and for as long as I wish you to stay, or perhaps I shall let you go in the morning. I have not yet made up my mind. But if I do let you leave, do you really think that your precious brother can escape me, Miss Taylor? Do you believe that I would *allow* him to do so? I have, after all, a reputation to maintain."

Roland was a monster, but Lavinia believed that if she let him see just how terrified she was, her cause would be lost. Her mind raced for a way out; then she smiled back at him.

"Mr. Roland, you will do nothing to harm my brother." He raised his brows. "No, you will not hurt him," she repeated. "Because if you do, everyone will know just who the culprit is."

"Indeed?" he drawled.

She nodded her head smartly. "Yes. For there are many who know he is indebted to you and will, therefore, know that you—or one of your henchmen"—her lip curled in distaste—"is guilty. And for those who do not, I shall tell. That is, unless you intend to force me to remain here forever, or perhaps you plan to murder both of us?"

"Madam, did I say one word about forcing you to do anything? Why, I am shocked that you would think so." He ran a finger down her flushed cheek and leered. "No, not at all. You see, I expect you will remain here with me by choice."

"By choice! You are having fun with me, Mr. Roland! Why on earth should I choose to do such a disgusting thing?"

His eyes narrowed to slits, and he grasped her shoulder hard enough to make her gasp in pain. "Why to protect your brother."

"But I have just finished explaining to you that you would never get away . . ."

"Miss Taylor, there are many ways to hurt a man. A few broken bones, a cracked skull or . . . worse. But there are subtler methods. What about Anna? Have you considered her?"

For a moment, Lavinia thought he must have run mad. *Who in heaven's name is Anna?*

He saw her confusion. "Ah, he hasn't told you about her then, has he? Lovely girl, lovely. From a very good family, too. Can't think of the name just now, but it will come to me." He made a show of pondering this. "Comstock, that's it! Yes, Anna Comstock. Oh, did I mention, a baronet's niece. Hardly the royal family, but then that's a good thing, ain't it!" He laughed, spraying her amply with spittle. "Well, well. It appears that I can tell *you* a thing or two, Miss High and Mighty.

"And so, I ask you, shall I tell her and her papa how the young gentleman who's been courting her"—*courting her?* Lavinia thought—"has lost a small fortune at my tables and refused to pay me, *and* how his big sister gave herself to me to get him off the hook? Well, shall I?"

"You are a fiend, Mr. Roland. . . ."

"Oh come now, my dear, you'll have to be nicer to me than that." He leaned over to kiss her.

A deafening noise split the quiet of the room, as the door burst open to deliver Templeton, Grover, and Samuel. Before Roland had time to react, Templeton had crossed the room ahead of his two companions, who were equally eager to dispatch the villain. He grabbed Roland's shoulder, tore him away from Lavinia, and planted him a facer that landed him on the floor in a heap, where he lay motionless and silent.

Samuel had detoured to Lavinia's side and now held her hand. "Good God, Templeton, is he dead? Did you kill him?" he asked. Lavinia's eyes were huge, and the color had rushed from her cheeks.

Grover knelt and roughly slapped Roland's face. The man moaned and opened his eyes. Grover hauled him to his feet. "No, Samuel, he'll be all right. Unfortunately." He turned to Templeton. "Shall I hit him again?" he asked as Roland, a wicked light in his eyes, showed signs of retaliation.

"Another time, Laurie." Templeton could not leave this work to anyone else, not even his best friend. He pulled back his arm and hit Roland harder than he had ever hit a man in his life, in or out of the boxing ring.

"Templeton!" Lavinia cried, as he drew back his arm again. "You'll kill him!"

He stopped and looked at her, as if suddenly recalling she was there. Blood was spattered on his neck cloth and his dark green silk waistcoat. Neville had been thrilled to dress his master for town that night.

"Lavinia!" He left Roland to his friend and drew her into his arms. "Lavinia, are you all right? Did this creature hurt you? I swear I *shall* kill him if he has." He looked into her face and she smiled up at him.

Eleven

Lavinia, Templeton, and Samuel dined the next evening at one of London's finer establishments, feasting on oysters and beef and drinking champagne. Lavinia noticed the bandages on Templeton's hands.

"Oh, Templeton, you hurt your hands when you hit that . . . that . . . awful man."

"Not just him, Lavinia. You should have seen what he did to the doorkeeper at Roland's hell in Jermyn Street. Leveled him, he did. And he was much bigger than Roland. Oh, you should have been there. I have never seen the like." Lavinia refrained from pointing out to her brother that he was not attending Oxford to make a study of such outlandish behavior.

Ordinarily, Templeton would have blushed at such compliments, but in this instance he wanted to be certain that Lavinia knew just how well he had taken care of matters without, of course, singing his own praises. Still, he thought he ought to keep up appearances. "Now, Samuel, I do not want you to upset your sister. She has been sufficiently distressed already. . . ."

Fortunately, Samuel was not to be deterred. "Not a bit of it, my lord. I've seen few men as handy with

their fives as you are. If it had not been for your
intervention, both of us would truly be in the suds
and well we know it." Lavinia acknowledged this
statement with a firm nod. "There you see? Besides,
I don't know if you are aware of it, but my sister is
no delicate flower, sir. She can hold her own with
the best of 'em. Right, Lavinia?"

She gave him a wry smile.

"Hardly a compliment, young man," Templeton
put in. "But I do know what you mean. Lavinia has
come to my rescue, you know, in Painswick. I was
merely returning the favor." He smiled into her
eyes and she grinned back at him.

"Yes, we do thank you, Templeton. If you had not
come, I do not know what I should have done."
She had told them of Roland's threats and she
shuddered again at the memory.

"I think, I *hope* that it may be a long time before
he torments anyone else," the marquess said.

"In any event, he will not be able to do so for
some time. It is going to take a while for him to
recover from that beating. I am still not certain,
however, that my not repaying him was the right
thing to do."

"Put it out of your mind, Samuel. So far as I am
concerned, that creature forfeited any right he had
to your money when he threatened your sister in
such a fashion." His face darkened at the memory.

"Lavinia, I want to say again how sorry I am that
I caused you all this trouble. Can you ever forgive
me?" Samuel asked contritely.

She tilted her head to one side and sipped her
champagne. "No," she said at length, "I cannot,
Samuel." His face fell. "Not until you tell me who
Anna is!"

He blushed. "I should have told you about her.

Indeed, I wanted to, it was only that the time did not seem right. I could just imagine your telling me that I'd no business thinking of marriage when, obviously, I was unable to manage my own business properly. And you would have been right. But, I need not tell you that I've learned my lesson, Lavinia."

"I should hope so."

"Oh, I promise you I have. And only wait until you meet Anna—Miss Comstock. She is an angel. So pretty and sweet. And smart. She says she wishes she could go to Oxford! To university, I mean!" he elucidated. Lavinia and Templeton exchanged glances. "You must meet her while you are in town. You will love her, too."

"I am certain that I shall, Samuel."

He soon took himself off to pay a call on his beloved, leaving his sister and Templeton to finish their champagne alone.

"Tell me, Templeton, was the doorman really so big?" she teased him.

He grinned. "As tall as a tree, with fists like small boulders."

"And you managed to overpower him and Roland without falling down once!" She could not resist.

"Astonishing what can be done when one puts one's mind to it." He paused. "I am sorry that I did not accompany you here in the first place, as you asked me to. You see, I . . ."

"There is no need to explain, Templeton. That is passed and I was hardly your responsibility, after all. Margaret told me that she had written to ask you to come and help me. What puzzles me is what possessed her to do so. I know that she was quite concerned. If she could have, she would have locked me in my room at Grillon's to prevent my going to meet Roland. Certainly there was no one here for her to turn to, but why on earth did she think to contact you?"

Templeton said that he was equally confused by the maid's action. "But the only important thing is that she did tell me you were in need of assistance. To say the truth, Lavinia, back in Painswick I had despaired of ever looking anything but the fool in your eyes."

"I wish I might say that I hardly noticed, but I fear I made things difficult for you."

"Well, do not chide yourself too strongly, my dear. I was not, after all, the most graceful of gentlemen. And if you had not noticed, Darnall was obliging enough to point out my, um, failings to anyone who might listen!"

"Yes," she agreed, "but only look at what happened to him!"

He laughed. "Indeed. Still, I am certain that I must have been the source of many a laugh for our friends. I suppose that I ought to thank Samuel for making such a mull of things, except that I would not have had you exposed to that scoundrel Roland for the world."

He covered her hands with his. "Lavinia, will you consider marrying me if I promise not to fall down or wreck our carriage or spill food on you—well at least not too often? I love you to distraction, my darling, and I have for such a long time. Will you be my wife, Lavinia?"

She returned his smile. "I would not have asked you to come to London with me if I had not believed you the most upright of men, despite all signs to the contrary, Templeton. And I never wanted to marry a paragon, anyway. I shall be honored to marry you."

* * *

Grillon's Hotel, London

> *Dear Mrs. Beatrice and Mrs. Waters:*
> *We have been successful! I must say that I had the most terrible fright of my life when Miss Taylor took it into her head to go off on her own and confront that disgusting Mr. Roland (the man young Mr. Taylor owed the money to), but thank the good Lord that the marquess finally came along and put everything to rights. Until he arrived, I was that worried, I don't mind telling you.*
> *We do not return to Painswick until the day after tomorrow, as Miss Taylor has decided to stay and order a few of her bride clothes here, even though she will give the bulk of her custom to Mrs. Kindle, as is only right. Lord Templeton will follow the next day, as he has some business to attend to before he comes home— and that is what I heard him call it—home! Well, I daresay you are on tenterhooks to hear all about it. They are to be wed! The marquess was all that a gentleman ought to be and he rescued Miss Taylor from that horrible creature. . . .*

It was lovely to return to Painswick, and Lavinia paid a call on Mrs. Caton to tell her the good news of her engagement to Templeton. Mrs. Caton hugged her and laughed that she, too, was to be wed, to Albert Breverton. Lavinia was hardly surprised, but most pleased nonetheless. The two ladies walked to Mrs. Kindle's Bazaar, Lavinia to look at patterns for bride clothes, Mrs. Caton for a fitting for hers, and to continue their chat about their wedding plans.

They had to wait until the modiste finished assisting a customer who had a demanding and condescending manner and very specific tastes. She looked at the display of lace and ribbons with a barely concealed sneer and asked again and again if Mrs. Kindle did not have higher quality stock—better gloves, finer fabrics, more up-to-date patterns.

Lavinia, having just visited the shops of some of London's finest ladies' costumers, was aware that Mrs. Kindle had no cause to be ashamed of her goods, and more than once was on the verge of saying so to this strange woman. The dressmaker was the most patient of women and merely smiled and displayed more and more of her stock to try to please her customer. At length, Lavinia could stand no more, and she spoke in a stage whisper.

"Oh, Mrs. Caton, did I mention that I visited Madame LeClerc's on my recent trip to London?" Madame LeClerc, who was actually no more French than Mrs. Kindle, was well-known as the most au courant modiste in London.

"Did you indeed? And are her things as nice as I have heard?" Mrs. Caton caught on immediately and played along.

Lavinia nodded. "Yes, *quite* lovely. And I was most pleased to see that her shop is no finer than this one, nor are her gowns and other fripperies any better. I am happy to report that Mrs. Kindle is just as talented a modiste as any you might find in London!"

Mrs. Kindle gave Lavinia a look of thanks, but her customer merely looked over her shoulder and raised her brow to see what sort of bucolic creature would have made such a statement. She was surprised to see a young, handsome, and very well-

dressed lady who stared back at her with an equally
haughty look in her eye.

"You are very kind to say so, Miss Taylor," Mrs.
Kindle said.

"Not kind at all, Mrs. Kindle. Just truthful. Your
things are indeed just as good as those I saw in the
metropolis and, I must say, a good deal less expensive into the bargain!" Lavinia turned full face to
the quarrelsome customer and smiled, hoping to
smooth her feathers. She held out her hand. "I am
Miss Lavinia Taylor. I live near here at Greenbriar
Lodge. And this is my friend and neighbor, Mrs.
Dorothea Caton." All three ladies nodded their respects. "Are you visiting here in Painswick?"

Althea recognized Lavinia's name immediately,
having heard Templeton's servants sing its praises
to the high heavens for one reason or another since
she had arrived. This would have been enough to
turn her against Lavinia, but she also had learned
that Templeton had gone to London on her account.

She extended a limp hand. "Ah, yes, Miss Taylor.
I believe I have heard of you."

Something in her eyes disturbed Mrs. Caton, who
decided it was best for her and Lavinia to get on
with their errand.

"Oh, Mrs. Kindle, did you know, Miss Taylor and
Lord Templeton are to be married. She is come to
order some things for her wedding."

Althea fastened Mrs. Caton with a basilisk's stare
and said, as if Lavinia were not there, "Mrs. Caton,
I am Althea Hubbard. I am, um"—her voice was soft,
but triumphant—"staying at the Park. With Templeton. And I am here to buy some, ahem, lying-in
clothes." She made a show of putting her palms on
the circumference of her belly, although in her soft

green walking dress, her pregnancy did not look as advanced as it was. "You are quite certain that he plans to marry *you*, Miss Taylor. I should have thought that he had obligations . . . elsewhere." She smiled smugly. "But you are right about one thing. I was much too harsh a critic of Mrs. Kindle's wares. If you will, Mrs. Kindle, I should like to place an order for a number of things. Might I have a chair? My back does seem to ache these days."

Lavinia tossed an old slipper that Neptune had left on her bed and it bounced off the far wall and knocked over a vase of flowers. She did not flinch as it crashed to the floor and shattered, but did feel guilty enough to draw the startled dog to her and hug him fiercely.

"I am sorry, dear boy. It is only that I thought for a moment that I hate men. But it is really only Templeton that I hate; you are still a darling." He licked her face. Lucky for her she had found out just how duplicitous Templeton was before her heart became too engaged.

After Althea Hubbard's speech, she had not been able to remain in the shop and, even knowing that was what the woman had wanted, she had left. Mrs. Caton had not known what to say to her friend and contented herself by remarking only that Lord Templeton surely had a perfectly good explanation. Well, Lavinia decided, when she saw Templeton, she would tell him just what she thought of him—very little— and just how much she detested him—very much. It did not then occur to her that these feelings were contradictory. What had he expected to do? Did he think that he could wed her and keep Althea *and* their child? Even he could not be that arrogant, could he?

As it turned out, Templeton did not come back to Painswick alone. His guest was shown to a room where he might rest, the carriage ride having done nothing to improve his painful attack of gout, and the marquess was alone when Althea found him in his library.

"Ah, Althea, I am glad to see you." She raised a brow as if to question the veracity of this statement, but he pressed on, eager to tell her his news. "I have brought someone with me."

"Indeed?" She was bored and eager to share some news of her own.

"Silvester."

"What? Have you lost your mind, Templeton?"

Well, to be perfectly truthful, he had not expected her to be ecstatic at his announcement, but it seemed the only way he could get rid of her. "No, I have not, Althea. The man is your husband and, you tell me, the father of your child, so why shouldn't it be wonderful that he is here?" He ought to have said, "He has come to take you home," since that was what Hubbard intended to do.

She read his thoughts. "I am not going with him. I hate him."

"Well, you might have thought of that before. . . . Well, never mind. It occurred to me that, if he could be convinced he is the father of the child he might actually be pleased. After all, he has no heirs, so I thought I might have a go at him. I will not claim that it was easy. For one thing, he wanted to plant me a facer because of our affaire, but I soon disabused him of that notion. Eventually, he listened and now he is here."

"Where?" she asked guardedly.

"He is resting at the moment. You could go up to see him."

"Oh, God, Templeton, must I? I loathe the man."

"I know, Althea, but you must simply make the best of things, at least for now, just as he is willing to do."

Althea thought a moment and sighed, then rose to go upstairs. She turned and with a flash of her usual self, said with a sweet smile, "I understand that congratulations are in order for you and Miss Taylor. You might want to call on her, Templeton dear. I do believe she wants to talk to you." She left the room.

Confused, Templeton turned to find Mr. Pratt standing just outside the door. "Ahem, er, my lord, I could not help overhearing Mrs. Hubbard. If you will forgive my presumption, sir, I should heed what the lady said." He gave a little nod of emphasis. Templeton shut his eyes in dismay and headed quickly for Greenbriar Lodge.

He had known for certain that he was in the suds when she refused to let him kiss her. Now, Lavinia sat, arms folded, and stared at him. She had wanted to be cordial and nothing more, to make him believe that she did not care a bit that he had no intention of marrying her, but she had not been able to be so cool.

"Lavinia, I have just come back from London and I understand that you met Alth . . . Mrs. Hubbard." She did not respond. "I do not know what she told you, but I wish to assure you that it was, in all likelihood, untrue."

"Indeed? Do you mean to say that she is not pregnant?"

"She told you that?"

Lavinia nodded. "Are you saying that she is not?"

"Well no, she is, but . . ." He stopped and drew in his breath sharply. "You do not think that I am the child's father, Lavinia?"

"What was I to think, Templeton? She all but assured me that was the case, *and* that you would marry her. Or at the least that you would not be marrying *me*. And *that,* I can assure you, is true!"

"But I am not the father; her husband is!"

"How droll, sir. She is already married?" Templeton said that she was. "Well, I am aware that, in most cases, it is done in that fashion, Templeton," she said dryly. "But I am not a green girl, and I am also aware that some women and some men pay little heed to their marriage vows. I would not be such a creature. I should give and demand faithfulness, so it is just as well that we will not be marrying."

"*Not* . . . Please, Lavinia, you cannot be serious. I tell you I am not the father of Althea's child."

"Then you and she have never been . . . lovers?"

He paused and looked at her contritely. "I will not lie to you, Lavinia. We were at one time, but that was over before I came here. I swear it. I love you. Only you."

Lavinia wanted to believe him, but she recalled that Templeton had left Painswick for a few days, on business he had said. He might have gone to London at that time; couldn't he and Althea have conceived the child then? She shook her head, it was unlikely; that was simply not the man she had come to know and love. She peeked at him doubtfully.

"I swear it," he repeated.

"Then I suppose I must believe you, Templeton. And if that horrid woman insists on marrying you, I shall tell her how awfully clumsy you have become here in the country. Your bravery can be our secret, for something tells me she would never spend her days with such a man!" She kissed him.

"Thank goodness, Sarah. I thought they would never get together," said Irene Beatrice.

"Nor I, Irene." Sarah Waters looked around the table at all her friends. They were all enjoying a glass of champagne, Templeton's gift to help him celebrate his coming marriage to Lavinia.

"I said all along they needed a shove, didn't I, Galen?" Alfie Sharp said.

"Alfie, you're just a romantic old fool. Isn't he, Will?" asked Jim Lewis.

Neville was overjoyed. "And I will get to dress the marquess for his wedding. Surely he will want only the best for *that!*"

"Well, my friends, I think we can honestly say that Lord Templeton and Miss Taylor would not be marrying if it were not for our intervention. Here's to us! And here's to our staying right here at the Park!"

"Here, here!"

"Jerrold, wonderful news! Lavinia is going to marry that poor marquess after all!" She came in, heavy with child, waving her letter joyfully.

"The 'poor marquess,' how splendid, dear."

She put her head on his shoulder and smiled. "You do realize, darling, that this would not have

come about if I had not pushed her along in his
direction?"

"Oh, Samuel, it is so romantic. And you were so
clever to bring them together!" Anna exclaimed
and looked at him worshipfully. "To think that if
you had not asked her to visit you here in London
and not invited him at the same time, they might
never have gotten together!"

He tooled his carriage expertly through the heavy
late-afternoon Hyde Park traffic. "Well, Anna, she
is my sister after all, and it is my responsibility to
look after her. Bringing Lavinia and Templeton together was the least I could do. Here, Pindar, move
along, boy!"

About the Author

Jessie Watson lives in Wayland, Massachusetts. She can be reached in care of Zebra Books.